ALSO BY BRIAN DRAKE

BLOOD MIST

SAM RAVEN
BOOK TEN

BRIAN DRAKE

**ROUGH
EDGES
PRESS**

For Ari,
who suggested the title and set off on new adventures of her own.

BLOOD MIST

BLOODMIST

PROLOGUE

THE PAST

RAVEN'S LEGS DIDN'T WORK. THE TWO MEN WHO YANKED HIM from the airplane seat did so with hostile faces. They wanted to kill him, not trade him. And he wanted to kill them too. He'd almost succeeded. So had they.

The two dark-skinned jihadist fighters supported him on the walk/drag down the aisle to the exit. He managed the steps to the cracked tarmac only because he leaned on the rail. Stepping on solid ground and staying upright required strength he didn't have. His legs shook, and his body hurt; the result of eight months of torture. He reached out a hand and grabbed the rail once again. Gripping the rail hard, he looked around.

An abandoned airstrip. Where? He didn't know. Clouds hung in the blue sky; it was warm. Mountains in the distance. He might have been anywhere. The tarmac sprouted weeds through thin cracks, with tall grass on either side of the strip. Raven finally settled his eyes on a second jet waiting thirty yards ahead. The jet he'd board for home unless his escorts pulled a double cross.

The sun stung his eyes and he squinted against the glare. He'd dreamed of seeing the sun again while expecting to die in the dark.

His two escorts stood behind him. Neither produced a weapon. They said nothing to him.

Their attention was on the other jet too.

The door of the second jet opened, steps lowered, and four people exited. Two wore orange prisoner clothes. One wore a suit and tie. The other wore full combat gear and carried a stubby submachine gun with a long magazine.

Raven recognized the man in the suit. His boss, Martin Bennett. The chief of CIA Ground Branch had come to see him home. How nice.

But they were trading him for two of the enemy.

Raven's heart sank into his gut. It was too high a price. Why had they agreed?

The past twenty-four hours had been a whirlwind he was still attempting to process. They'd hauled Raven from his underground cell, hosed him off with cold water, stripped off the rags he wore, and provided fresh clothes. Nobody spoke to him, and he hadn't the power to ask questions. He was in a daze from endless torture, sleep deprivation, starvation—and more. When somebody lowered a hood over his head, he figured going to the firing squad in new clothes wasn't a bad deal. As the Land Rover bumped and jerked on the rough terrain, he dozed off. He was too tired to think about a line of soldiers shooting him to ribbons. When he awoke, they loaded him onto the plane. They weren't taking him to a firing squad after all.

And now he stood under an unknown sky on a deteriorating tarmac.

A shove from behind. Raven stumbled forward two steps

and looked over his shoulder. The angry faces of his escorts made him tighten; he expected them to raise a fist, or worse.

"Go," the bigger of the two snapped, which wasn't saying much. Raven stood taller than both. "Walk to the plane!"

Raven shuffled more than he walked. He tried to straighten his posture. *Stand tall, you're going home.* But going home to what? A screw up on a mission put him at the mercy of the enemy. And not for the first time—he'd been a captive before. Who were they trading for him? What did his return cost his country?

Raven winced and bent over a little. Too much effort for too little payoff. The two prisoners from the other plane were now coming his way. They were smiling, moving faster than him, and they passed with a jubilant shout. He looked back. They embraced Raven's former escorts and hurried aboard the jet. Raven faced forward. His energy departed. He moved slower. Seeing the enemy happy...

He stopped in front of the CIA gunner and the man in the suit. He didn't know the gunner. He knew the other man.

Raven said, in a weak voice, "Hello, Martin."

"You look like hell, Sam. Come on. Let's go home."

Raven allowed Martin Bennett to help him up the steps. The CIA knew how to make a jet comfortable. Bennett sat Raven in a large leather chair. The gunner closed the door and told the pilots they were ready to go. Raven let his body relax. Bennett returned with a bottle of water and told Raven to sip. A medic appeared behind Bennett, and the CIA boss stepped aside while the male medic kneeled beside Raven and began checking him out. Raven was only half-conscious of the jet taking off.

Much later, Raven tried talking again. The water and a little food helped. The medic pronounced him dehydrated with minor injuries. Raven wanted to laugh. The medic hadn't been on the receiving end of the "minor" injuries. The terrorists had beat him well, not breaking anything, but inflicting as much pain as possible. When he finally broke, and told them what they wanted to know, the beatings stopped. Raven wasn't sure which was worse, the beatings or the talking.

Bennett took the seat behind Raven. Raven rotated his chair to see his boss.

Martin Bennett was in charge of CIA's Ground Branch, the covert action side of the Special Activities Center focused on land-based missions. He'd been "on the road" a while, Raven realized. His suit wasn't ironed and creased the way he liked. The wrinkles corresponded with a long travel time. He needed a shave. But he appeared alert and ready to answer Raven's questions. If he wasn't, Raven wanted to start asking anyway.

"Who did you swap for me?"

"Sam, please. Let's ease into this—"

"I've been in a hole for eight months, Martin. I want to know how much I cost."

Bennett sighed. "Too much according to some."

"You should have left me there. I broke under torture. What I told them did more damage than you realize."

"We realized fast, Sam. We recalled and recovered who we could. Damage was minimal."

"I held out as long as I could, believe me."

"I know you did."

"Pardon me if I'm less than relieved."

"You're free," Bennett said, "because of the president's orders."

"The who?"

"You heard me. Remember you saved his son's life in Afghanistan? He didn't forget. He ordered this trade."

"Who was against it?" Raven asked.

"Enough people who think you've become a liability. This

isn't your first capture. Last time, you barely made it home too."

"Last time, I had help escaping. There were four of us. It was only *me* this time, and—"

"Sam. You've had some bad luck. You're also getting older."

"You're saying it's time for me to go."

"I told you we shouldn't talk about this right now, is what I said. It's too much right now."

"I'm a big boy, Martin." Raven took a deep breath. The Agency was showing him the door. At least they hadn't left him to die. But hadn't he suggested—his thoughts were wild, going one direction, then another. Out of control. And the brain fog related to his capture and whirlwind release made it hard to think. Bennett was right. They needed to wait before having this conversation. Well, too late. Raven noticed Bennett hadn't answered his original question. He asked again.

"Who did you trade for me?"

Bennett examined Raven's face. Raven stared back. The CIA chief finally nodded. "Two prisoners we weren't done with yet. The president demanded we make a deal, and those were the men the Islamic Union asked for."

"What's their connection to the organization?"

"Part of a sleeper cell the FBI rounded up."

The Islamic Union was an upstart group of jihadists who wanted to pick up where ISIS and al-Qaeda left off. The US government decided it would be best to shut down the Union before they grew too powerful; taking out their leader was Raven's assignment. Instead, they'd grabbed him; the Union leader had laughed in his face. Seeing the man's laughing face in his mind's eye made Raven want to punch a hole through the plane's fuselage.

Raven let out a curse. "They'll go back into circulation and kill more innocent people, Martin. I wasn't worth it."

"You can argue with the president, if you'd like."

Raven scoffed. "What's next?"

"Debrief at the Farm, as long as it takes, and then—"

"Toss me on my ass."

"I'm sorry, Sam."

"Maybe I can talk to the president about keeping my job."

Bennett didn't acknowledge the crack. He said, "You'll get a severance, you can keep your pension, and, of course, you can put the Company on your resume. But those who agree you cost too much don't want you around."

"Hell, you might be right," Raven said. "If I'm getting caught twice, I'm getting too old."

He wasn't yet thirty-five, he wanted to note. But Raven stopped talking.

Only the drone of the jet engines filled the silence between the two men.

Raven tried to focus his thinking. It was time for him to get out before he caught a bullet, or worse. But what the future held for him once he walked out of the CIA for the last time, he had no idea. He'd face the challenge head-on as had so many others.

RAVEN RECOGNIZED where the jet touched down. There was no way to mistake the visual clues of the open country in which he now found himself. Camp Peary was where the CIA had its training area known as the Farm, a sprawling camp property, its layout classified. Instructors taught raw recruits basic trade craft in a fake "city" located on the property. There was also housing for operatives who needed nursing back to health. Those in the housing units were the deep cover officers coming in from the cold, and those who'd been through the wringer. Like Raven. Experts would question him, interrogation style, to put his story together. He'd be poked and prodded by expert physicians too.

Raven wondered what he'd face under the questioning. He'd broken under torture. He'd exposed secrets to the enemy. Operatives in the field may have died because of him. He wanted to crawl into a hole and never come out. All he wanted was a solid answer from Bennett about how much damage he'd caused. He expected hostility, but wondered if he was overthinking.

Raven remained still in the leather seat as the jet came to a stop. A reception party waited—two security men with weapons. Two SUVs sat parked beside them. Bennett said one SUV was for him; Raven would travel in the other to his domicile for the next couple of months. Bennett said he expected Raven's recovery and debrief to take as much time as he'd spent in captivity. To Raven, it sounded like he was only trading one cell for another. At least this new cell would allow him to see the sun, for whatever it was worth. The leash would be short indeed. This wasn't his first time at the Farm for such debrief and recovery activities. But last time, he hadn't been alone.

Raven and Bennett said goodbye. The boss, with his silent security officer, climbed into the first SUV. The other two gunners guided Raven into the remaining vehicle for the drive to the Farm's rest home. He watched Bennett's vehicle kick up dust as it drove away. Bennett's goodbye had only been a handshake and a nod. A nod with little sympathy.

The Suburban entered a clearing surrounded by trees and hills. They were well away from the main activity at Camp Peary. A large house lay ahead, with barns and small structures spread around. Armed guards didn't hide their presence or automatic rifles. The shooters wore full camo and dark shades for added menace, or a stereotypical joke, depending on one's frame of mind. As he examined the guards, Raven wasn't thinking about jokes. He was pondering his future. A future without the CIA.

The two gunners in the SUV exited, and one came around to open his door. Raven stepped out and took a deep breath of fresh country air.

A woman emerged from the house and approached. She dismissed his escorts and smiled at him.

She had dark hair, tied back, and wore a black blazer and slacks with a white blouse. No ID tag on her lapel. She'd put on too much makeup, Raven noticed. It looked like she'd layered shellac over her face. She was hiding something she didn't like about herself, maybe a blemish on her skin, or a flaw she only saw in her mind's eye.

"I'm Connie," she said. "Welcome, Mr. Raven. Please follow me, we have a room waiting for you."

"And some new clothes?"

"Everything you need."

Raven couldn't wait to see for himself.

He followed Connie and her bouncing ponytail as they entered the house. She showed him around "the facility," as she referred to the place. Common areas contained comfortable furniture, TVs, and table games. There was also a small library.

The other "guests," Connie explained, were a mix of men and women, some of whom shared Raven's dead-eyed stare. Others did not. They looked healthier. He wondered why they were still at the rest home. Adjacent to the main house was the medical center. Connie explained they had a full staff of medical and psychological personnel. She told him he'd be spending some time with them for the first few days. A third building, separate from the main house, housed secure meetings rooms. She told Raven his debriefing sessions would take place within. Raven was beginning to glaze over. Connie noticed. She led him to an elevator, and they went up to the third floor. The elevator doors opened on a long hallway.

They walked down the hall. It looked like any other apartment complex Raven had seen. "We have you in a private room," she told him. "I made sure to get you a window."

She stopped at a door marked 305 and used a key to open the door. A physical key, Raven saw. Not an electronic lock.

"Key is yours, Mr. Raven. You're free to roam the grounds but do not go beyond the marked perimeter."

"Guards have orders to shoot?" Raven asked.

"It's the dogs you need to worry about. Everything you need is inside. Go see your new home for the near future."

In other words, until the CIA deemed him fit to return to normal society.

BED, bath, television. It was like a small hotel room. Connie gave him the key, told him when the cafeteria would serve the next meal, and left him alone. Raven turned on the light in the bathroom. It was small, but the shower stall looked big enough to accommodate his tall frame.

He immediately turned on the hot water and stripped. He had eight months of desert to wash away. He took a lot of time to do so under the hot and therapeutic spray. His body was a mass of scars, lumps, and poorly healed lacerations. He ignored them. Or at least tried. No amount of soap could wash the marks away, or the memories of how he received them. Leaving the bathroom wrapped in a towel, he finally checked the closet and dressed. Clothes, socks, underwear. Everything was in the correct size because the clothing came from his own home. But after eight months in the hole, he'd lost so much weight he doubted the clothes would fit. He hoped his time in rehab would help him regain his former weight. And now he wanted to know the status of his apartment. Had the CIA been paying his rent the entire time he'd been held captive?

Raven tossed the towel and stretched out on the bed with a sigh. Soft pillow top mattress. His body relaxed as if deflating. Tension and stress departed. He never thought he'd lie in a bed again. As soon as Raven climbed under the covers, he passed out.

NOBODY CAME to collect him the next day. Raven reported to the cafeteria for every meal, as well as in-between snacks. He inhaled the food. Nobody told him not to eat too much either. He found books to read in the library and brought several back to his room. He preferred the history books, especially war history, delving into the details of military campaigns. He tried the gym the next day, out of boredom more than anything. He lifted light weights, two-pounders, and walked at a slow pace on a treadmill. His body did not protest as much as he thought it would. Once his initial stiffness went away, he worked up a decent sweat. No sign of Connie either the first or second day. But other "facility" managers appeared here and there. Sometimes, they paused to watch him.

He didn't speak to any other "guests" nor they to him. He wasn't about to talk until required to do so. He had no idea what level of security the other guests held, and they didn't know his. There was still operational security to adhere to, rest home or not. And he was aware some of the "guests" might be plants sent to see if he was loose with his lips or not. Better to keep his mouth shut and ignore them.

Raven spent his third day undergoing a full medical check-up. MRI, blood work, eye exam, and many other tests with copious poking and prodding. Raven stopped wondering how long it would take after a while. It ended up taking all day.

A psychologist finally saw him on the fourth day.

"TELL ME WHAT HAPPENED, MR. RAVEN."

Raven sat in one of the meeting rooms across the table from the CIA psychologist, a man named Gargarin. Instead of a suit and tie, he wore a sweater over his shirt, and had a Mr. Rogers air with a full head of salt-and-pepper hair. He spoke with a soft voice, but loud enough so Raven didn't have to ask him to repeat the question.

"What do you mean?"

"The mission. Your capture. As you remember it, of course."

Raven shifted with irritation. His jeans didn't fit despite the tightening of his belt. He had no idea why it irritated him so much. Had to be a symptom of his captivity, knowing he was going to go through a long debriefing, and then get tossed on the street by the Agency to which he'd dedicated so many years.

"What kind of clearance do you have, Doctor?"

Dr. Gargarin laughed. "Good. Not everybody asks me. I've served this agency for thirty years, and my country longer than that. You can speak freely, Mr. Raven. I have all the security clearance required."

Raven gathered his thoughts for a moment. His silence surprised him. He'd done nothing but think about *what happened* and how he might have prevented the error. Now, he couldn't find the words to explain what took place.

"Take your time," Dr. Gargarin said.

After another moment, Raven finally spoke.

"I was working solo, tracking the Islamic Union through Northern Iraq. Had the plan to shoot their boss from a distance. I was following a group of them through a mountain pass when I found a shortcut—or what I assumed was a shortcut. Anyway, by taking it, we ran into each other. I don't know which of us were more surprised. I tried to get away. They outnumbered me. So I surrendered and wound up at their camp, where they dropped me into a pit for almost a year."

"Eight months."

"Yeah," Raven said. "Tortured me regularly. Beatings, mostly. Starvation. Noise. The whole bit. I held out as long as I could, Dr. Gargarin, I promise."

"Everybody breaks, Mr. Raven. It's why you're trained the way you are, to hold out as long as possible. But everybody cracks."

"What I told them—"

"Is of no concern at this moment."

"I need to know how many people died because of me."

"No, you don't," the doctor said. "And it's not an answer I can give you anyway."

"Why am I here then?"

"We need to talk about stuff. How are you feeling right now?"

"Like shit."

"Sleeping okay?"

Raven scoffed. "Like a rock."

"Nightmares?"

"Not yet.

"You impressed us with your early initiative," the doctor said, "by using the gym, finding the library. You haven't lost your appetite."

"I was bored. And hungry."

"Most of our guests stay in their rooms up to a week when they first get here."

"Uh-huh," Raven said.

"It's a good sign."

"If you say so."

"And your medical report came back as satisfactory."

"Doesn't sound too exciting," Raven said.

"You're in rough shape, but they weren't as harsh with you as we've seen with others."

"Because I *talked*, Dr. Gargarin. They eased off because I gave them usable information."

"We can't change what happened, Mr. Raven."

"You haven't asked if I feel guilty."

"It's obvious you do."

"Okay. How do I *not* feel guilty?"

"We'll work on that."

"Doctor—"

"Mr. Raven, listen. My job is to determine if you're strong enough to handle the questioning. You will be forced to recall and relive your experience."

"Do you think I'm ready?"

"Do you?"

"No," Raven said.

"Why?"

"Because while you want answers from me, I need answers from you, and nobody's giving them to me. I don't understand."

"Mr. Raven."

"*What*? I'm losing patience, Doctor."

Gargarin raised an eyebrow. "All right. Let me ask you this. If I told you the information you gave caused the deaths of three people, how would you feel?"

Raven began to shake. He moved his hands under the table so the doctor couldn't see them trembling.

"Awful," Raven said.

"And if I told you ten? Twenty?"

"What are you getting at?"

"What I'm *getting* at, Mr. Raven, is no matter what I tell you, no matter what Martin *Bennett* tells you, or anybody else tells you, it won't change anything. What can you do?"

Raven blinked a few times.

"Do you have an answer?"

"No," Raven said.

"What would change?"

"I don't know."

"What if I told you nobody died? What if I told you that as soon as the Agency knew you were a prisoner, they immediately made changes. They pulled people out, rearranged deployments, did everything possible to mitigate any potential losses when you *did* break under torture. What would you think then?"

"Did it happen?"

"I don't *know*," the doctor said. "Do you know Martin Bennett to be a liar?"

"No. He's a good man. He wouldn't—"

"What?"

"Lie to me."

"Then you have to take what he told you at face value. They changed the playbook before anything bad happened. You're feeling guilty. What you're feeling is normal. But you don't need to *mentally* torture yourself, especially after all you've been through. Do you understand?"

"I do."

"Do you feel you're up to official debriefing?"

Raven nodded.

"So do I," the doctor said.

"Great, Doctor. I can't wait."

Raven gave Gargarin a flat smile.

THE DEBRIEFING SESSIONS took up the next ninety days. The interrogators were thorough. They took Raven back through every minute of his mission against the Islamic Union.

Each morning started with an hour-long visit to a physical therapist, who put him through a variety of strength-building exercises. After the workouts, grueling or otherwise, Raven ate lunch, then went to one of the conference rooms for an afternoon of conversation. The Agency officials were trained to get deep, dark secrets out of those not used to spilling such, and Raven left nothing out. They helped him remember details using memory and recall tricks he'd never used before. For three months he dumped as much data as he remembered about his captivity—almost a day-to-day, hour-by-hour account. Bennett visited twice a month to let him know his information was helping to clean up the elusive terrorist group. One CIA task force, Bennett said, even sniped the group's boss, completing Raven's mission. There were a lot of happy bureaucrats on the Seventh Floor of CIA headquarters, but not enough to let Raven keep his job. They saw his data and the successful removal of the group's leader as a consolation for giving up the two Union captives. But the bad blood over the situation remained, and Bennett wasn't sure how to smooth it over. By the end of the ninety days, Raven had stopped caring. He was still mad but had come to accept his fate. Soon, he'd be a civilian again, and would need to figure out how to live life as such. He hadn't been a civilian in a long time. Prior to the CIA, he'd been an airborne Army officer. What did civilians do nowadays?

But Bennett did promise a going away party once Raven finished at the Farm.

It was something to look forward to, anyway.

———

MARTIN BENNETT ARRIVED to pick Raven up on his last day at the Farm. Raven looked much better than when he arrived but hadn't gained back all of the weight he lost. His clothes hung on him like heavy drapes. But he didn't look half dead any longer, there was brightness behind his eyes, and the aches and pains had gone. The scars? Still there, but he'd lived with scars so long, a few more wouldn't hurt. Raven tossed a suitcase and tote bag into the trunk of the Agency car and dropped into the passenger seat. Neither man looked happy. Bennett had brought with him Raven's dismissal papers. They'd spent almost an hour signing papers and going through the rules of secrecy Raven would have to live by.

"I'm sorry, Sam," Bennett had said, as he collected and stapled the papers together. Everything went back into his briefcase. "You were a good operative. Remember, you can't write a book, you can't talk to anybody about your work at CIA. You *can* say you worked here, and we will confirm any reference calls. You cannot talk about Stalker Team Charlie or anything else you did. There are counselors at your disposal to help you find a new line of work. Maybe go back to construction like you did before the military. Have you thought of that?"

"Stop talking, Marty," Raven said. He was trying very hard not to blame Bennett for the change in his situation. He kept reminding himself Bennett wasn't the man who made the decision. But Bennett was the man in front of him, and the man easiest to vent his frustration to. Getting angry at

Bennett wouldn't do any good, so Raven kept his mouth shut instead.

"On the bright side," Bennett said, ignoring Raven's request, "we have people waiting for us at the tavern. Shall we go? You all packed?"

Bennett was talking a lot. Raven knew why. Bennett knew he was angry, and hoped by talking too much Raven wouldn't have a chance to talk back. Raven had no intention of talking. If his now-former boss wanted to spin his wheels and verbally vomit the rest of the night, it was his choice. After a couple of drinks, Raven might have a different opinion.

And the Agency *had* kept his apartment up to date. They'd paid his rent and utilities, so he had a place to go when the party was over.

Bennett drove the Agency car to the airstrip, where a jet waited for them. Bennett said they could get a head start with their drinking. He'd asked for a couple of bottles of gin and plenty of tonic. Raven started to come around. At least the boss remembered his favorite drink. They wouldn't have *much* of a head start; it wasn't a long flight.

RAVEN SMILED as he entered the bar.

The Golden Lime Tavern. He'd never been a regular patron, but appreciated the dimly lit interior and hardwood motif. A noisy crowd filled the place. Raven looked at a group of people around a pool table. They were looking back at him and smiling.

Raven moved forward and shook hands with and hugged the three men playing pool. Victor Matson, Carlos Vega, and Billy Anzell—his teammates from Stalker Team Charlie. The combat specialists, the gunners, the shoot-and-looters—

they'd been three of the best, and Raven was proud to have served with them. They'd succeeded together, failed together, and everything in between. Their bond was strong.

Stalker Team Charlie was Raven's old unit, tasked with tracking terrorists throughout the world. They'd done well, until a fateful mission in Afghanistan, resulting in the capture of all of them. The three men were already tipsy, as was Raven. They raised their voices to compete with the rest of the crowd and the blaring jukebox. Martin Bennett hung back with a grin, watching.

A lone woman stayed on the edge of the jovial reunion. She was Mara Cole, another former member of STC. She'd been their sniper and analysis expert. She'd preferred the ambush to the straight-ahead attack; outthinking the enemy was her skill, and she'd employed it well. Her glassy green eyes examined Raven as he broke away to approach her. They had once been on-again, off-again lovers, their relationship always rocky. Mara was the one who flipped the on and off switch; each time, Raven didn't argue. After escaping Afghanistan, their intimacy ceased to exist. She'd told him they were over for good and quit the CIA. It surprised him she'd made the effort to show up, and he looked at her only as a friend now. Her drunken state was odd. Not like Mara at all.

She held a glass of red wine, almost empty, which she placed on the pool table to hug him. She expressed shock and surprise at his thin frame and staggered as she stepped away. Her eyes darted for her wine before stepping away from the table again. Mara was as tall as him, and her eye-catching outfit made Raven look more than once. Hip-hugging jeans highlighted her curves, and the knotted flannel shirt showed off her belly. For someone cooped up as long as Raven, she might as well have been nude. He had to remember they weren't a couple any longer. She wore her long curly hair over her shoulders, a look he'd always preferred.

Matson called a shot, shoved his cue stick forward, and the clack of balls took Raven's attention off Mara's belly and back to her eyes.

"Aren't you playing?" he asked her.

She leaned toward him. "Those aren't the kind of balls I like to play with." She laughed.

Raven reacted with a start, cleared his throat, and looked for Bennett as if the boss were a life raft. The pool game continued with neither Matson, Vega, nor Anzell noticing the exchange.

Bennett grabbed Raven's arm. "Let's get a round for everybody."

Raven nodded. The crew shouted out what they were drinking in response to Bennett's query. He and Raven headed for the bar.

"You look pale," Bennett pointed out.

"What's going on with Mara? She's drunk and made the dirtiest joke I've ever heard her say. It's not like her."

"She hasn't been doing too good since she quit. Really hitting the booze. Afghanistan messed her up."

"No kidding. Messed us all up. And now I got a double dose of messed up."

They found the game still in progress when they returned. Mara watched, but it appeared keeping her balance was her only focus. She wobbled in place very subtlety, but Raven noticed. Against his better judgment, he handed her a fresh glass of red wine. She downed what remained in the glass she held before taking it from him.

Carlos Vega, at the pool table, leaned over the green velvet and called a shot. He drew back his cue stick, thrust forward, and sent the cue ball into the red six. The six rolled

toward the corner pocket but caromed off the edge to rico-
chet into another ball. Carlos cursed and stepped back.

Billy Anzell lined up the next shot. "Six ball, side pocket."
He leaned in and smacked the ball into motion with the tip
of his cue. He also missed.

"Too many beers, Billy!" Mara shouted.

"Usually improves my aim!"

Victor Matson handed Raven a cue. "Try it, Sam. You're
the only one sober."

Raven took the cue and moved to the other side of the
table where Carlos and Billy stood.

"I don't plan on being sober for long," Raven announced.
He turned to the wall behind him and set his beer on a tall
table.

Raven hoped nobody noticed his trembling hands. Why
did he feel anxious? He was among friends. Raven didn't like
their eyes on him, he decided. It was a shock seeing pals he'd
shared hell with; he'd wished they'd been with him in Iraq.
Perhaps the mission wouldn't have gone sour if they'd been
there.

And Mara...

You've been through a lot. Take it slow.

He lined up the shot. Mara moved around the table to his
right. He briefly zeroed on her belly button like a cat on a
laser dot. Back to the pool table.

Mara yelled, "Make the shot, Sam, or this is going down
my throat!"

He glanced at her. She held his beer. Her empty wineglass
sat on the table.

Damn, girl.

She needed help. And dammit if Raven didn't want to try.

She'd refuse, he knew. Despite their off-and-on history,
they knew each other well. Too well.

Raven drew back the cue and let it fly forward with more

force than he thought he'd muster. The white ball smacked into the red six, and finally, with a solid *thunk*, the red six dropped into the side pocket.

Raven straightened with a satisfied smile. His former teammates whooped and high-fived him. Bennett watched with amusement. Raven reached for his beer. Mara moved her hand away, then began to lose her balance. She swayed backward with a laugh. Billy grabbed her. Raven snatched his drink from her hand. The three guys and Mara laughed, but Raven didn't think it was funny.

LATER, they found a table in a corner and sat close. Everybody had a fresh drink, except Mara. She'd finally decided enough was enough and sipped ice water with a wedge of lemon. Her eyes remained glassy, and she seemed sleepy. But she kept up with the conversation, listening more than talking, and Raven wondered how much listening she was actually doing.

"Won't be the same without you, Sam," Carlos said.

"What will you do now?" Billy asked.

"Take it easy for a few weeks," Raven told them. "Got a nice exit package." He grinned at Bennett, who only raised his glass in acknowledgment.

"Still..." Victor Matson said, trailing off, but then speaking up again. "It's a raw deal and they're making a mistake."

Bennett said nothing.

"Wasn't my decision," Raven said.

Bennett spoke up. "And before you start giving me the stink eye, remember I'm only the messenger. The one who carried out—"

Mara jumped in. "The execution," she said. "There's more

than one reason I got out, boys. Go and do likewise." She drank some water and scowled. Raven wondered if she wished for something stronger.

Raven said, "It will be a tough adjustment." He felt something touch his leg under the table. He fought the urge to look. The something brushed up the side of his leg and pulled back. He glanced at Mara. She grinned at him.

"Can't expect to snap out of old habits right away," Victor said.

"It might be nice," Carlos added, "and maybe easier, if you went and whacked those two guys they traded for you. Even the score a little."

"Not my call," Raven said with a side glance at Bennett.

Bennett said, "Another round?"

Mara was still looking at Raven, eyes glassy but focused. She licked her lower lip.

"I think it's time to call it a night," Raven told him.

RAVEN HAD Mara half out of her flannel shirt before he kicked her apartment door closed.

She'd offered him a ride. He'd had enough to drink to say yes, with visions of her licking her lips in his mind. He'd grabbed his luggage from Bennett's car and tossed it into hers.

The door shut, he threw the locks, and shoved her against the wall. He only had the knot of her top undone; there were still four buttons to tangle with. They kissed hard, breathing hard, hands roaming for buttons and zippers. Her breath and lips tasted like wine. They pulled apart for a moment. Raven felt like an animal unleashed. Mara's eyes begged him for more. To make it real. He scooped her up in his arms and carried her to the bedroom. He remembered how to get there. Tossing her on the bed, her wind-chime laughter filled the room as she bounced. Raven straddled her and Mara lifted her arms over her head as he undid the last buttons and then she helped him remove the top.

Her breasts flattened within the red bra as she lay on her back, and Raven plunged his face into the deep cleavage created by the twin cups. The soft mounds and her hot skin made him relax, his entire body releasing the tension of the last twelve months. She moaned as his lips pressed against her bare skin from cleavage to neck, tilting her head back to give him more room. He paused as she worked awkwardly to loosen his belt. The buckle fell free and his pants were so loose they were easy to shed. Raven quickly climbed out of the rest of his clothes, but not fast enough for Mara.

"Hurry," she urged, getting out of her own jeans, and tossing her bra on the floor. The only garment remaining were her matching satin panties, and she raised her bottom for Raven to slide them down her long legs and onto the floor with the rest. He tried not to feel uncomfortable in his ultra-thin state, but she didn't seem to mind, and with the lights off, it almost didn't matter. Only the light from the hallway provided any illumination, a soft glow within the room.

She reached between his legs as he leaned over her again. Her warm hands found him. "Now *these* are the balls I remember…"

When she guided him to the wet tunnel between her thighs, it was like they'd never been apart, their bodies moving together as they clutched at one another as if each were a lifeboat cast from a sinking ship, two people desperate for safety amid crashing waves and a darkness deeper than any they'd experienced before. She held on tightly, digging fingernails into his back, her hot breath brushing his ear, urging him not to stop. When they twitched and shuddered with climaxes much sooner than they wanted, they remained entwined, but as Mara caught her breath and Raven eased to her side, she began to shake with choked sobs.

She clutched at him once again. "I thought you were gone."

He wiped tears from her face. "Me too."

She finally settled down, and they spoke no more, which was fine for Raven. He didn't know what else to say. He wasn't sure there'd be another night like this, much less a morning after. The nature of their relationship always seemed like balancing on a tightrope above a pit of starving sharks, each with its mouth open, razor-sharp teeth bared, and ready to devour whatever came within range. Why he'd tolerated her as long as he had, he couldn't answer. But he wondered if he did so because there wasn't anybody else. He wondered if she ever thought the same thing.

For now, it was best not to think. He wanted to stay on the lifeboat a little longer.

SHE MADE breakfast the next morning but asked him to keep the noise down. The bongo drums in her head were all the noise she could handle. He noticed she didn't try to ease the hangover with a morning drink. A good sign? He hoped so.

After showering, Raven dug into his shoulder bag for clothes. He stopped when he discovered a thick envelope on top of his clothes. He opened the envelope. Two pictures—photos of the terrorists traded for him, he'd never forget their faces. A stack of US dollars held together with a blank band—high denominations.

A note:

Bad guys need R+R too. Ka'Ana Resort, San Ignacio, Belize. One week—the 12th thru 18th. Borba is in the area. Good luck.

Martin Bennett's signature was scrawled at the bottom. Raven tried not to feel too smug. Bennett, the chess master, the man who moved the pieces around to checkmate the bad guys, had struck again.

Raven dressed and thought about the note. He realized he'd never been to Belize. It was time to rectify the error. He checked the date on his watch—the tenth. Two days before the two jihadists arrived. It would be nice to arrange a reception for them.

RAVEN STEERED his rental along the two-lane George Price Highway on the lookout for the Ka'Ana Resort.

The region once known as British Honduras, and now Belize, impressed him. He liked warm climates, within reason, of course. The Middle East didn't count. And the City of Ignacio fit the bill. His knee-length shorts and Tommy Bahama shirt were perfect for the current season. Warm air dusted with sea breeze filled the car through the rolled-down windows.

Plush green jungle left and right, blue sky above. No wonder the Islamic Union operators wanted to R&R here. It was the total opposite of what they were used to in the desert. He might have chosen Belize himself. It beat the hell out of the rehab farm.

The trip had been costly, using up most of the stash Bennett had provided. He still had plenty of working capital to see him through, with access to his own account should he need more funds. And he'd need more money. He'd entered Belize without weapons, after all. Can't kill bad guys without weapons. Luckily, the CIA's man in the Caribbean region, a sharp chap named Ricky Borba, had access to guns to solve Raven's problem.

San Ignacio sported some of the better tourist stops in Belize. Mayan ruins, caves, and the like. People from all over the world visited to put their feet where ancient civilizations once walked. As a history buff, the attractions appealed to Raven as well. Especially Mayan military history. He was sure there were plenty of weapons left behind to study, but not this trip. The only sights he planned to see were gun sights. There'd be another time, another visit, when he wasn't preoccupied with killing terrorists.

The circular wooden sign announcing the Ka'Ana Resort at Mile 60 ¼ appeared on the left side of the road. Almost there.

Raven slowed and made the turn, pulling into a packed parking lot. He found a spot for the rental at the far end of one aisle. He'd have a bit of walking to do, but no matter. More time to enjoy the fresh tropical air.

Raven began sweating as he walked, the Tommy Bahama clinging to his back and shoulders. The chill of the lobby was a welcome relief.

The wheels of his suitcase made a racket across the stone floor. He stopped at the reception desk, waiting for another couple checking in to clear the way. He stepped up to the desk.

"Checking in, sir?"

The petite woman behind the desk was Chinese, one of the many mixes of races making up Belize's population. Her long black hair resembled fine silk. She looked at Raven with big brown eyes.

"Jim Birch," he said. He was using an old cover name. He

had his ID, credit card, and passport ready, all bearing the Birch moniker. She checked him in with quiet efficiency and handed back the items. Last, she gave him a key card and a map, and circled the location of his shared cabin with a black marker.

"If you get lost or wander along the way," she said, "ask any of our attendants and they will help you."

"Thanks. I wander off a lot."

Another walk. This time along one of the many concrete paths crisscrossing the Ka'Ana grounds.

The layout surprised and intrigued him. If somebody wanted a private vacation, or to have a minimum of people around, Ka'Ana was the place to go. Large and small cottages filled the inner campus and outer perimeter. The larger private villas belonged on the outer edge, set deeper in the surrounding jungle. Much of the inner area had been cleared, replaced with wide-open areas of grass, but lush vegetation surrounded every cabin, a privacy screen from prying eyes.

Each cabin had a private or shared pool, and activity outside the guest buildings was very small. Raven passed others on the path as they came and went. Overall, he had a feeling of solitude. The planners had designed the environment to help people relax in peace. There was none of the riotous activity or screaming children found at other resorts.

Raven arrived at his shared cabin. White walls and wood accents outside, along with the expected pool. There were five rooms in the dwelling. Four other adults, two men and two women, lounged in the pool enjoying champagne and conversation. Raven's room was on the upper level in the corner. The other guests greeted him as he approached. He tried not to look at the women. Both had dark hair, fine figures, and wore red and blue bikinis, respectively. The one who spoke to Raven wore the red bikini, and the fabric worked hard to keep her from bulging out of it.

"Get your swimsuit and join us!" she called.

Raven promised to do so as soon as he unpacked.

Up a short flight of outside steps, and he reached his door. The key card snapped the locks open and he went inside.

More white walls with rich wood accents greeted him, as did the small bedroom and bathroom. An adjacent sitting area contained a padded wicker chair and table, but no television. Who needed a television when there was a hammock hung between two walls? And a big window showing the mass of jungle beyond the glass?

Raven whistled. He set his rolling suitcase beside the door and secured the lock. The hammock held his attention, and he eyed it eagerly. He wished he was there for vacation instead of a hit. But what the heck, all work and no rest and all that...

He sank into the netted hammock with a satisfied sigh. The hammock moved gently from side to side. Raven's eyes fluttered; he dozed off. He was feeling better, stronger, every day. But sleeping was becoming a problem. As he improved, the nightmares Dr. Gargarin asked about began to take place.

Visions of darkness split by flickering candlelight. Angry faces yelling. The slapping of open palms against flesh. Screams—*his* screams. Sobs. A feeling of dread. The vivid flashbacks woke him up and left him in a daze of depression for most of the day. He didn't sleep for long. One such flashback forced him awake with a start. He'd heard the sound of a rattling chain echoing through the dream. He clutched at his belly. The Islamic Union interrogators had whipped him with a metal chain. Chained to a rock wall, Raven couldn't dodge the blows. They'd struck at his back, belly, and sides. The rough metal ripped his skin open like a child tearing into a Christmas present. The puckered flesh all over his body testified and left lasting proof of each ordeal. The uncompromising agony finally made him crack.

And that's when he spilled his guts. Answered every question. A moment's hesitation made one of the interrogators bang the chain against the rock wall of the cave.

Raven swallowed, but his throat was dry. Laughter from outside. The party continued in the pool. He rolled out of the hammock and stumbled into the bathroom. Cupping his hand under the faucet, he swallowed a mouthful of water. He remained leaning against the counter with his head down. He didn't want to look at his reflection in the mirror.

Dr. Gargarin had not told him what to do once the nightmares started.

He needed to strike back. *Hard.*

He needed to recapture some of what they'd taken away.

The rest of it he'd have to find a way to live with.

HIS TARGETS WEREN'T hard to find.

Raven sat in the bar after lunch lingering over a gin and tonic. He'd been there for a day already, and he watched the lobby from the restaurant. When his two targets checked in, he saw them. They paid no attention to him or anybody else. The Chinese lady handed them their key cards and wished them a pleasant stay.

Raven occupied a corner table and admired the repeated white wall and wood accent motif. Thick crossbeams supported the V-shaped ceiling. He sat with his back to the wall. Nobody could come up behind him, they had to approach from the front. It wasn't long before his targets visited the restaurant and took a center table in the dining room. The two men questioned their waitress about the ingredients of various dishes. They needed to find something their diet allowed, and the waitress accommodated them. Raven examined them further but didn't look too hard. He didn't want them to see him observing.

He ran through their names in his mind.

Kaalim el-Tawil filled out in the middle and styled his thick black hair with oil. His hair was stuck in a slicked-back wave.

Rashad Mina was shorter and leaner, with a hungry look in his eyes. He was hyper vigilant, casting furtive glances around the room every few seconds.

Raven would have to kill Mina first. He'd be the fighter. El-Tawil made bombs, and spent most of his time sitting, hence his extra weight. He was good with a pistol but lacked close combat skills. Raven hoped the CIA's assessments were spot on. They usually were. Except when they weren't.

Raven ordered another gin and tonic. He kept the two Islamic Union fighters in his periphery as he found other people in the restaurant to watch too.

The two bartenders stayed busy hustling drinks. Waitresses moved between the bar and kitchen delivering drinks and food. Guests filled the room with chatter. El-Tawil and Mina made their selections and took their time eating. Raven lingered over a third drink. The two terrorists looked vibrant, rested, and bright-eyed. Raven wondered if they had nightmares too. He doubted the CIA subjected them to the same trauma as their people had him. He wondered if they'd been waterboarded. Probably not. The liberal pansies in the CIA's legal section had put an end to the practice, but it still took place when other methods failed. Raven hadn't cared if waterboarding worked or not; he'd enjoyed nearly drowning mass murders to make them talk. And they always talked. And most of the time, they told the truth.

When the two men finished their lunch and departed, Raven left money on his table and followed them. He used the lush foliage and other guests as cover. The pair crossed the resort to the far edge of the property. They had one of the private two-bedroom villas. Lots of glass. An indoor pool. Dense foliage around the exterior to help shield it from passersby.

Raven continued his walk once they disappeared inside. He left the perimeter edge and started up a hill, pushing through the overgrowth. The heat of the day beat down.

He crested the hill and followed the down slope until he heard cars on the roadway. At the bottom of the hill, he peeked through the leaves and found the Price Highway. Off the road was a clear patch of dirt. Plenty of space to put a car for a short period of time, once it was dark.

Raven started getting ideas.

RAVEN MET the CIA's local man at a bar in downtown San Ignacio.

Raven had a mug of beer in front of him, in a corner with his back to the wall same as in the afternoon. If anybody came near him, he wanted to see them. It was an old habit, but an urgent one now since he was on his own, without official Agency support.

When his contact arrived, the man stood in the doorway a moment scanning the bar. Raven made no move to wave him over. The center-piece bar and the patrons encircling it blocked him from view. The contact entered and started checking faces. Once he spotted Raven, he smiled and made for his table. Raven used a foot to push out a chair for him.

"Sam."

"Ricky, how are you?"

Ricky Borba sat down. He carried a wrapped box and placed it on his lap. Borba was assigned to the Caribbean

Station and worked undercover as a smuggler in several unfriendly circles. Martin Bennett asked Borba to assist Raven using his unofficial connections. It was the best way to keep the assassinations quiet, and Borba had agreed. Raven knew the other man well, and they had a long history. They'd worked together several times when Stalker Team Charlie visited the Caribbean.

Borba had tanned skin and a wiry body and wore a tank top under a loose button-up shirt, currently unbuttoned. Borba knew how to fly anything with wings, and was good with a boat, too.

"What's this I hear," Borba began, "of the boss showing you the door?"

"It's true."

"Then what do you call your visit to my neck of the woods? One where the boss told me to extend any help you requested but keep it quiet."

"Private matter," Raven said. He updated Borba on his capture, the prisoner swap, his dismissal.

When he finished, Borba only shook his head. A waitress arrived and this time he ordered a beer.

"Big mistake," Borba said when the waitress left. "They'll regret it."

"I doubt it. Did you bring what I need?"

Borba slid the box across the table. "You can owe me."

"I'll pay you now."

"To do this right, it's costing two grand. You got it?"

"Half now?"

"You can owe me," he said again. "Don't worry about it."

Raven pulled the box closer to him but made no attempt to open the lid. "What make and model?"

"Beretta 92FS. Box of ammo and two mags."

"Is it hot?"

"It's clean. Old stock. Unfired."

"Did you include—"

"Yes, the silencer is there, too."

"Suppressor, Ricky."

"Bullshit. The inventor's *original* patent called it a *silencer*, so fuck them Delta wannabes and those phony 82nd Navy PJ Rangers who prowl the internet looking for somebody to correct." He smacked the table for emphasis. His drink arrived. He thanked the waitress and Raven told her to put it on his tab.

"You're so easy to rile up," Raven told him.

"Wanna know what gets me riled up lately?" He leaned forward.

Raven and Borba spent the next hour talking shop, sports, and future plans. Borba pointed out, should he desire an extended stay in the Caribbean region, there would be plenty of work. On the dark side, of course, but Borba knew people who'd appreciate Raven's skill set. Raven declined the offer. The only thing on his mind was payback.

As the conversation finally ended, Borba said, "Don't tell me what you're doing. But I gotta know. You're in, you got a piece, and you're going to do your thing. But how are you getting out?"

Raven grinned. "I was hoping I could prevail upon a pilot to get me out of the country. Stamp my passport, all that."

"How many pilots do you know?"

"Only you."

"You're going to owe me your firstborn."

"Will you do it? I can't get out of here without help, not after I make use of this Italian steel you brought me."

"Yeah, I'll do it. Buy me another drink and let's work this out. When and where."

They talked into the night.

RAVEN SLIPPED on loose soil and landed face first.

He'd left his rental in the cutout off George Prince and reversed his path over the hill climbed on his initial recon. Coming back the opposite way, in the dark, was proving difficult, Raven decided, as he spit dirt and bits of dried leaves out of his mouth. He rolled onto his back to catch his breath and felt for the Beretta 92FS on his belt. The gun remained secure, the suppressor attached to the end of the barrel. *I don't care what the patent said, Ricky.* Raven rose to one knee. His face hurt. Raven hoped the slip and fall would be the only complication for the night, because he had no idea what to expect once he entered the villa.

Through the trees at the bottom of the slope, the glare of interior lights broke through. The Islamic Union terrorists were inside, for sure, Raven had no doubt. What they had in terms of weapons, if anything, was what he didn't know. Did jihadists travel with hardware on vacation? A few more days' surveillance would help him get more answers, but the longer he waited, the bigger the chance of missing his opportunity, the bigger the chance of making a mistake and revealing his intentions. He wanted to strike while they were cozy and comfortable and unsuspecting.

But, as he waited on the slope, the warm night breeze rustling the trees, he wondered if a delay was worthwhile. The slip and fall could be a warning from the ghosts of battles past. His timing wasn't right. *No.* He was losing confidence out of fear. This was his first piece of action since his captivity and release. He had the jitters, is all. He was fit, felt sharp, and there was no reason to abort. Raven eased to his feet and started down the slope again, trying to "read" the ground before each step. He quickly gave up. He didn't hurry, but with only moon and starlight to guide him, which wasn't much in terms of illumination, he reached the bottom of the slope and entered the tree line without further incident.

He kneeled beside a tree trunk, placing his weight against the trunk for cover and to avoid another slip. The ground still sloped, and now he had better light thanks to the glow of the interior from the villa. There were too many other tree trunks and a tangle of branches and leaves to see inside. He needed to get closer.

Raven wore head-to-toe black, with his face smeared with black makeup to further conceal his silhouette as he moved. The brightness inside would affect the ability of his targets to see outside, too—if they bothered to try. Raven hoped they were busy watching television or doing something other than behaving as if they were on high alert. He wondered why they didn't have a bodyguard or two to handle security. Then Raven remembered Bennett told him the Islamic Union had suffered more than one loss since his debrief. They couldn't spare the extra men, so—

Wait.

Raven's train of thought stopped. If they couldn't spare guards, then how could Mina and el-Tawil afford to leave the reservation at all?

Unless their presence in Belize was a prelude to—

Retaliation for the CIA's attacks?

El-Tawil was a bomb expert.

Raven's resolve strengthened. He had to find the answer. If he was wrong, it didn't matter. If he found evidence of a planned attack, he needed to get the information back to Bennett as fast as possible.

Raven took out the Beretta. He stayed low as he worked down the slope, presently sliding onto his belly to crawl to where dirt finally met concrete. He'd reached the path leading around the villa from the back. The concrete strip extended around to the front. If he followed it to his right, he'd end up at the rear patio doors. But now he faced a new problem. The villa, like the other cottages, had more glass than solid wall on the lower level. Lots and lots of window glass. Well, there were ways to deal with it. Raven found a rock and held it in his left hand. He threw it as hard as he could. *Thud*. The glass didn't break, but it made a racket. And soon Raven spotted Rashad Mina, the skinny one, coming to investigate. Mina's face showed alarm.

Raven extended the Beretta. Ain't no plate glass existed to stop a bullet. The pistol's front and rear sights were taller than normal to accommodate the suppressor. He had a perfect sight picture. Raven fired once, twice, a third time. The first bullet punched a hole in the glass. The second followed the first and smacked into Mina's nose, boring a hole through the middle portion of his head. The hollow-point stopped before exiting his skull. He fell. The third bullet flew over Mina's falling body and went deeper into the villa's interior. Raven broke right, followed the walking path, and shot the lock on the patio doors. He slipped inside a small dining area. The concerned shouts of Kaalim el-Tawil, the fat one, the bomb maker, filled the villa. He kept asking Mina what the problem was.

Raven stepped left into a brighter room, furniture and cabinetry to contend with as he advanced. El-Tawil continued yelling, until he stopped mid-sentence. He finally realized Mina wasn't going to answer. Raven dropped into a squat at a corner and held the 92FS pistol at the ready. El-Tawil would come around soon. He'd see Mina's body. The skinny jihadist lay on the carpet a few feet away. The blood leaking out of him turned the white carpet red.

Raven's heart raced. Sweat trickled down the side of his face. He was in black against a white wall in a brightly-lighted room—laughable. But one target was down and only one remained. He breathed hard and his legs began cramping. El-Tawil was taking too long. Raven left the corner and—

El-Tawil opened fire from behind the rail of the stairs, poking the muzzle of a short submachine gun through the vertical bars. But the narrow space between them didn't allow him to shift his aim as Raven dived over a couch for cover. The salvo ripped at the walls around him. Raven fired four times, then scrambled under a table. El-Tawil jumped back as two of the 9mm rounds splintered a pair of vertical bars, but none of the hastily fired shots struck him. The other two left holes in the wall behind him. The echo of his unsuppressed SMG hung in the room; Raven's ears rang. As the chunky Islamic Union bomb maker raced down the rest of the stairs, Raven decided his original guess at the man's lack of combat skill was wrong.

El-Tawil reached the ground floor and ran into the entryway. He stopped at the corner. Raven fired twice. His rounds punched through the sheetrock but didn't score a hit. Raven advanced, staying low, working around the furniture. He shifted to the right as he neared the corner, exposing himself a piece at a time as he took in the length of the entryway. Had el-Tawil run out the door? Then Raven saw him. He lay flat on the floor with his SMG probing ahead and his eyes sighting down the front and rear sights.

Raven tucked and rolled. The SMG spit flame. Not fast enough. The shots went wild, impacting the nearby décor. Then the SMG went silent. El-Tawil was out of ammo. Raven took his chance as el-Tawil hurried to reload. Laying on his side, Raven fired his pistol. *Bull's eye.* El-Tawil's face registered shock, then nothing as his body went limp and the half-inserted magazine fell from his grasp. Raven put two more rounds in his body, making sure, before he slapped a fresh mag into the 92FS and ran up the stairs. El-Tawil had come from there; presumably, so had Mina. If the pair had any documents or maps to show they were planning an attack, the material would be upstairs.

But his time was limited. The gunfire would have woken many. The numbers ticking to zero in his head began ticking faster. He had to hurry...

———————

WITH A BACKPACK over both shoulders now, full of papers and a map and a small tablet computer, Raven ran up the slope, down the other side, and climbed behind the wheel of his rental. Still no sign of authorities. He was out of time, though. Borba was waiting at a secluded field with an airplane, and Raven didn't want to keep him waiting. As he drove away, he remembered tonight would be the last time he killed to protect his country. But he'd made it despite his own doubts. He'd evened the score.

Borba waited aboard a single-prop Cessna 182. Raven drove over the open field's rough terrain and stopped near the plane. All of his luggage was in the back, all collected by Borba in advance. Raven's bill under the Birch name was also squared away. He was leaving nothing behind to trace back to him.

Raven joined Borba in the plane and pulled on a headset with an attached microphone. Borba wore a similar set and began the start-up procedure. He had the engine going by the time Raven pulled the passenger door shut and secured the lock. The noise of the Cessna's engine filled the cabin. Even with the ear covers of the headset, Raven heard the loud drone.

"Any trouble?" Borba asked. "What's in the bag?"

"They were planning something," Raven answered. "They were on a recon trip, not a vacation."

"Wow." Borba eased the throttle forward and the Cessna began a bumpy acceleration toward the line of trees a hundred yards away. When he reached takeoff speed, he eased back the controls and the Cessna climbed into the dark sky, the trees below resembling a thick carpet, a place Raven didn't want to suddenly find himself if the plane fell from the sky. Luckily, it continued climbing.

Borba keyed the radio and advised any nearby aircraft of their altitude and position. No response. They may have been the only small craft in the air in the middle of the night. But Borba kept the radio tuned to the local traffic frequency in case they weren't.

"What will you do now?" he asked Raven.

"Something better than this," Raven said. "Something heavy on peace and quiet."

"Good luck." Borba finally leveled off. "We'll be in the US in a few hours. Just remember, Sam, this line of work—you can walk away, but somehow it always finds you again."

Raven had no idea how true those words would be over the next two years.

But for now, he only wanted to enjoy the rest of the trip home.

"What's the in-flight movie?" Raven asked.

Borba only laughed.

Raven smiled too.

1

THE PRESENT

THE GUILLOTINE WAITED FOR HIM.

He was the last survivor, but wouldn't hold the distinction for much longer.

Zaven "Darbo" Darbinian leaned against the steel bars of his cell. In the center of the camp, thirty yards from him, stood the frame of the guillotine. The executioner was in the process of sharpening the blade by hand. He'd already tested the twenty-pound hunk of steel on watermelons and found it too dull. The camp commander ordered it sharpened. He wasn't a cruel man, he told Darbo; he'd make the process of lopping off the Armenian mercenary's head as quick as possible. Then he laughed. Darbo suspected he enjoyed the verbal torture more than physical. Quick or not, it was little consolation. Dead was dead.

Darbo hated to die in the jungle. The one he found himself in particularly stank. The odd odor permeated the camp. It was a government camp run by the ruling dictator Darbo had helped try to overthrow.

A man named Juan Santos, "General" Santos, ruled the South American nation of San Remo with an iron fist. A group of rebels, spurred by the oppressive regime's cruelty, formed an opposition army. They hired foreign mercenaries, Darbo among them, for help. Not only to fight, but to train the rebel troops so they had a chance to survive the battle.

But informers within the rebel units tipped off the government forces. The resulting raids left most of Darbo's clients dead, and Darbo in a cell.

Nobody talked about efficient murder when Darbo's rebel friends faced the blade. The camp commander was probably cutting him a break because he wasn't native to the country.

San Remo would have to wait for another generation of rebels to rise and, hopefully, defeat "General" Santos. Darbo wished he'd be around to see it happen.

What kind of thinking is that? Enough moping around, Darbo decided. *At least you're not dying in bed. The cause was just. Raven would have been proud.*

He let out a breath and turned from the bars to sit against the rough concrete wall. Raven. Yeah. It was the kind of job he'd have taken. If only Darbo had thought to reach out to his old pal when the contract came through. When they worked together in the past, it was always the other way around, Raven calling *him*. He'd alerted Roger Justice, another member of Raven's "Raiders," as they called themselves, to what was going on in San Remo, but Justice had been unable to lend a hand.

He knew the camp backward and forward.

All he needed was a chance to break away.

If he could get out of the cage...

San Remo was hot—no matter where one was in the country, the heat crushed like a vise. It was worse in the cell, where even with the bars, where the air seemed not to circulate. Darbo sweated constantly, but the camp captain was "generous" and supplied fresh water. Darbo closed his eyes and tried to block out the sounds around him. Men shouting. Engines rumbling and fading as vehicles came and went. Gunfire in the distance—troops practicing. Darbo had to acknowledge "General" Santos knew how to train an army. They may have been conscripts, but Santos turned them into hardened combat machines.

Darbo opened his eyes as footsteps crunched the ground outside the bars. He looked up. The camp captain, Ramos, grinned at him. He wasn't immune to the heat. Sweat soaked the bandanna around his forehead. His neck and face glistened with wetness.

Darbo frowned. Ramos held two bottles of beer.

"Did I wake you, Senor Darbinian?"

"Only resting my eyes."

The captain laughed. He was clean-shaven with bushy eyebrows. One of his front teeth was missing, but it didn't stop him from smiling.

"Trying to blot out of the sight of that massive blade, yes? I'm so sorry it must end this way. My orders are very strict. But if you had been fighting on our side—" He shrugged.

"What do you want, Captain Ramos?"

"You're going to die soon. I thought you deserved a final *cerveza*. We don't do last meals here." Ramos pushed one of the bottles through a gap in the bars.

Darbo hesitated. The cap remained on the bottle. Condensation dotted the glass.

"If I wanted to poison you, why is the executioner working so hard? Take the beer."

Darbo took the bottle and twisted off the cap. Ramos offered to clink bottles; Darbo did so.

"I'd toast to your health, but—" He shrugged again.

Darbo stood to better look at the other man. If these

visits and "conversations" were his idea of torture, he had a good thing going. Darbo wanted to scream. They drank instead. The frosted bottle felt good in his hand and the cold beer tasted amazing.

"You are a real soldier," Ramos said. "I hate to see you go. The rebels? They were very brave, and I hated to dispose of them. We may be on opposite sides, but it doesn't mean we can't share respect."

"Sure," Darbo said. *What a load of crap.*

"Later today, I will bring you paper and something to write with. You may write letters to your family, or whoever, about your fate. You have my word I will send them."

"Sure," Darbo said again. He swallowed more beer.

"You don't believe me?"

"No," said Darbo.

"I understand. Yes, I am the enemy. But soldiers do things for each other. We don't have to be monsters. Besides, when it's my time—"

"You want the favor returned."

Ramos looked sad. "You hate me."

"No, but I do want to kill you."

"Yes, I murdered your allies, the rebels. The woman especially—"

"Don't talk about her," Darbo said.

"Ah, I do understand. Soldiers understand each other. And I do regret everything. If only—"

"What?"

"The rebels hadn't tried to kill my general," Ramos said. "He cannot forgive what happened. He must teach a lesson."

Drabo drank another mouthful of beer. He examined the bottle. The glass was thick and heavy.

Ramos laughed. "A good weapon, yes? I won't let you keep it."

"I know."

"It's a shame my country has so much strife. It's a beautiful place. Except for the awful heat."

Commotion at the guillotine. Darbo and Ramos turned their attention toward the executioner. He was barking orders at his two assistants to raise the blade. The men worked a rope and pulley system to do so; the blade shined at the top. The executioner placed another watermelon in the neck notch. He made a gesture. The two men let go of their ropes. The blade descended in a flash and split the watermelon in two with a sharp pop. Both halves dropped into a basket at the front and back of the base. The executioner turned to Ramos and gave a thumbs up.

Ramos finished his bottle, waited for Darbo to do the same, and Darbo pushed the bottle through the bars. Ramos grinned again. The blank space in his teeth looked funny.

"Your fate awaits you, Senor Darbinian."

"We'll see," Darbo told him. *I need a miracle for sure...*

2

RAVEN HATED THE JUNGLE, AND SAN REMO'S WAS THICK.

He moved through the thickness. Leaves green and brown surrounded him; tangled tree branches with sharp leaves scratched at his exposed skin. Thick tree roots bundled like snakes caused tripping hazards. And it was hot. The jungle had a stench he couldn't quite identify, couldn't determine where it came from, and he hated it. But Darbo needed help, and Raven wasn't about to turn away.

Raven's CIA days were only a memory now. He'd attempted to forge a quiet civilian life after his dismissal, and it seemed as if he'd achieved a peaceful existence. Then fate dealt a cruel blow with sudden tragedy, and vengeance became his new mission. The only link to his past was the sterling silver locket around his neck. He never talked about what was inside, but it motivated his war without end. He pursued the world's predators, those who created victims and heartache, to deliver justice one bullet at a time.

Like now.

He was rigged for war. Black combat fatigues, black face paint, black cap on his head. Body armor and assorted weapons and grenades. Everything one required to fight a small war. According to the intel Roger Justice had brought to him, they'd indeed be facing an army ready for war. Captain Ramos wasn't a pushover. Neither was General Santos.

Darbo was the priority. Santos and Ramos? He didn't rule out a return to help San Remo secure the freedom so far denied its citizens. Raven was taking a detour from another project to rescue Darbo. He needed to get back on track as soon as his friend was free.

The other two black-clad fighters with Raven carried similar equipment. Roger Justice and Lia Kenisova bore an extra item with their personal arsenal, a pair of heavy machine guns. The chattering of the two lead weapons would be the signal for the rest of the force. They weren't the only ones assaulting the camp. Darbo had a lot of friends. Roger Justice called as many as he could, and they all agreed they couldn't let their friend face his end in the middle of Central America.

Roger kept pace with Raven, while Lia stayed at the rear and moved at a slower pace. She was watching their back, front, sides, her eyes scanning every direction. What she couldn't see, she might hear. There was always a clue to a predator close by. So far, they'd been lucky. The only problems were the natural obstacles they had to deal with.

Then they heard the shooting.

Raven held up an arm. Roger stopped, held up his left arm, and Lia stopped. Carefully, one after the other, Roger and Lia moved up on either side of Raven. They had no electronic communication between them—for the moment. They wanted radio silence in case the enemy was scanning for foreign radio signals. Roger didn't know what, if any, high-tech gear Ramos had at the camp; they weren't taking chances.

Raven, Roger, and Lia looked for the source of the shooting. It was a steady stream of fire, a pause, another stream. Then, single shots. Silence. A man started speaking with a raised voice.

"Training," Lia said. "This isn't a fight."

"Yeah," Raven said. "And if we keep going in this direction, we're liable to bump into them."

Roger produced his paper map, unfolded it, and spread it out on the ground. Raven had to hold a thick leaf out of the way to make room. Roger said if they marched to the right for about two miles, they'd clear the training area.

"It'll take us further from the camp for a bit, but we can make up the time," he added.

"And have them at our backs when the shooting starts?" Lia said. "I say we get closer and take them out."

"And let the main camp know there's an attack force coming?" Roger said. "We need to avoid them."

"We're running out of time," Raven said, "and the other teams are moving into position. We only have till sunset. We'll go around. We'll have to hurry and set up a surprise for when these shooters come our way. Copy?"

Roger and Lia agreed, though Raven saw the woman frowning. She always frowned. She was Russian and carried an air of perpetual annoyance. But Raven knew she'd follow orders. She was also a good soldier. When she wasn't working as a merc, helping Raven in his war without end, she was a rescue and recovery specialist.

Roger Justice, an American like Raven, was a freelance black ops veteran with an appropriate surname. He never said much about his personal life, and Raven never asked. Roger knew from Darbo himself that there was action in San Remo, and when news of the failed coup reached him, he went into spy mode to sort the details. He learned the fate of the rebels and the coming fate of Darbo and assembled the rescue team.

"Which way, Roger?" Raven asked.

Roger put away his map and gestured to the right. Raven took the lead, and the march continued. But Raven had a problem. He had no idea how to surprise the returning troops once the main battle started. He'd have to get creative, and fast.

CAPTAIN CHRISTOPHER RAMOS designed his camp from scratch. He had efficiency of movement, defensibility, and security in mind when he drew the design. General Santos approved it, and Ramos supervised the work crew. He was far from the city and out in the middle of the jungle because he didn't like urban environments, especially where there was so much poverty. He'd never tell anybody, but Ramos understood why the rebels wanted to fight.

He held the two empty beer bottles in his left hand as he walked away from the brig. Ramos hoped there weren't more prisoners coming after the Armenian mercenary. He grew wary of up-close murder. It was one thing to shoot a man from a distance with a rifle. You didn't see the result. But when ordered by the general to execute rebels? Distance wasn't an option. Even with a firing squad, you were close. Close enough to watch formerly vibrant bodies turn limp and lifeless. Close enough to see the shock in wide-open eyes at the moment the bullet switched off the living organism. Ramos wasn't a man who thrived on violence. He was in a violent line of work, but there were lines he didn't like to cross. But in this case, he had to, otherwise General Santos might ask if he was feeling sympathetic. Then *he'd* end up in front of a firing squad, or under the guillotine.

He glanced up. Crews had cleared a patch of ground two miles wide to accommodate the camp. It was a hot day, but the sky was clear—except for a few scattered clouds here and there, hardly noticeable with the bright blue. Guard towers stood at the four corners of the camp, three troops within each, with a mounted machine gun covering a left-to-right pattern. Concertina wire—with sharp razor blades instead of barbs—with electronic alarms buried beneath encircled the perimeter inside the outer wall. Ramos hadn't specified a generator to power the camp in his design. Generators were vulnerable to attack; he had a row of solar panels on the east side of the camp, which powered everything they needed. Generators only worked as a back-up system. Anyone getting through the concertina wire couldn't avoid the buried sensors. Before an attack force reached the center of the camp, Ramos and his men would be well aware of the problem.

And Ramos didn't want any more problems. He'd dealt with enough for a while. The coup was over. It was time to get back to the everyday business of San Remo, and for Ramos, "everyday business" meant running the camp efficiently and keeping his troops sharp. Because another problem would arise, someday.

3

RAVEN, ROGER, AND LIA REACHED THEIR LAUNCH POINT fifteen minutes later than planned. They took their position on the southern side on a patch of flat ground, surrounded by plenty of coverage. A portion of the camp's southern wall lay ahead, concertina wire beyond. Anybody getting over the wall had to face the wire right away, and Raven figured the wire held more surprises than razor blades.

They couldn't see the guard towers through the roof of trees, but the towers weren't their targets. Raven wasn't worried about the towers. Once the shooting started, the squad on the east side would take out the solar panels and back-up generators. Snipers would take out the guards in the towers. Raven and Roger and Lia then planned to punch a hole in the wall, head for the brig, and grab Darbo.

The detour put them fifteen minutes behind schedule. The sun was almost behind them. Raven had broken radio silence long enough to tell the attack force of the delay. The other two squads were already in position, waiting for Roger and Lia to fire their machine guns.

Raven lay prone between the pair. They were on a slight

rise giving them a decent view into the camp. Through a pair of binoculars, he watched the concrete building where they held Darbo. There were no guards, but a lot of back-and-forth activity. Not all of the personnel carried rifles. Some packed only sidearms. It was the busyness at the guillotine—a freaking *guillotine*—where Raven focused his attention the most.

"Looks like they're planning to cut his head off," Raven reported.

Lia said, "Will anything fall out?"

"Always gotta be smart, don't you?"

She laughed. The heavy barrel of her machine gun rested on a bipod; a container full of ammunition locked under the receiver. A belt of .308 ammo extended from the container into the weapon's firing mechanism. Roger lay behind an identical weapon. It was the MK48 machine gun favored by US special forces as well as India's commando units and the Czech Republic's 601st Special Forces Group.

Roger said, "We're ready, boss."

Raven turned his scan to the right, the east side, and examined the solar panels.

"Open fire," he said. "Target the asshole at the guillotine."

Gonna wish I had earplugs...

Raven flinched as the pair of MK48s began hammering their messengers of destruction. The rain of bullets fell on the camp without mercy, angry hornets searching for targets. Raven watched the executioner through his binoculars. Lia focused her fire on him. The wood of the guillotine frame began to splinter with hits, the executioner turning to run. Her next line of slugs stitched him from butt to neck. He flopped onto the ground and didn't move. His assistants hid behind the guillotine frame, but it wasn't very good protection from the swarm of .308 NATO boattails. The hard-nosed slugs punched through the frame and

BLOOD MIST | 53

into their bodies. Raven sensed the wet slaps of the impacts.

He panned right. The solar panels. A large section of the eastern wall exploded in a blast of orange fire. A shower of concrete chunks fell from the sky, smashing into the panels, destroying many of them. Metal beams supported the panels, and the beams buckled. The crash of metal and solar cells joined the cacophony of gunfire. A follow-up shot from a shoulder-fired rocket launcher did the rest. The high-explosive projectile, trailing flame and smoke, hit the ground in the center of the panel farm. The explosion created a giant crater which swallowed some of the panels and knocked down the rest. The camp now had no electricity. Alarms, radios, any electronic countermeasure—gone.

Roger and Lia took a moment to change ammo boxes. Locking fresh belts into place, they looked to Raven.

"Let's go!" Raven shouted. He had his own weapon at the ready, a US M4 with a thirty-round magazine locked in place.

Radio silence no longer mattered. As they rose and started running down the rise, the voices of the other squad leaders filled their wireless ear units. Both secondary teams were meeting heavy resistance. The snipers had taken out the guards in the towers. Raven advised of the incoming practice squad from the west. As they reached the wall, the sounds of fighting intensified. Automatic weapons blazed; grenade explosions thumped; men yelled when hit, or screamed to communicate. Raven hoped Darbo was keeping his head down; or maybe he was watching from his cell with a big grin.

Raven reached the wall. Roger and Lia turned their backs as they scanned for threats.

Raven applied a C4 charge, and the trio ran for cover. The blast opened a gap in the wall wide enough for the three of them to go through side-by-side. Raven went through first. He fired at stray targets running across his field of vision—they were fifteen yards away, focused elsewhere, and Raven's popping M4 took them down before they knew he was there. Roger and Lia followed. Raven grabbed a satchel from his back, activated the timer on the C4 charge inside, and tossed it into the wire. They ran back to the wall to distance themselves from the explosion. The charge detonated, breaking the wire into pieces, clearing a narrow path. Pieces of wire and chunks of dirt flew at them. Raven charged ahead. Roger and Lia opened fire behind him. He had the brig in sight and ran hard.

DARBO FELT THE GROUND SHAKE. He sat up, then flattened again. Bullets were flying. Things were going boom. He saw the flame and smoke. The camp was under attack.

The guillotine. A swarm of machine gun fire attacked the structure and the executioner fell, shot in the back, landing face first in the dirt. His assistants died next. Darbo smiled. He'd have preferred the executioner to suffer a bit before dying. But watching his prone body twitch was rewarding enough. Smoke from the eastern side indicated somebody destroyed the solar panels. The camp's power supply was gone. Unless Captain Ramos had battery-operated radios, he'd have no way to call for help.

Whoever was on the other side of the wall knew what they were doing.

But *who* was on the other side? Rebels the government missed?

Or...

Captain Ramos stood at the entrance of his living quarters. He had a large shed converted into living space, complete with a small porch. Painted green to match the Quonset huts used for barracks by the rest of the troops, it wasn't safe for him any longer. Smoke from the solar farm drifted through the camp. The smoke was thick and gray, with enough density to sting eyes and choke throats. Ramos ran back inside. His Kalashnikov and a bandoleer of magazines hung on a wall near the sink. He first strapped the mags around his waist, then grabbed the weapon. A loaded mag hung from the receiver. He snapped a cartridge into the chamber and ran out into the fight.

The air crackled with tension, continuous gunfire, and acrid smoke. The once serene outpost, with a dedicated crew of disciplined soldiers in the service of General Santos, was now a death trap. If the solar panels were gone, the enemy destroyed the back-up generators, too. Without power, they had no way to work the radios. Without the radios, they had no way to call home base and request reinforcements. This fight depended on him and his men. *Nobody else.* Automatic weapons fire continued to pop as he looked for targets. At the same time, he shouted for his men to rally stray soldiers to his lead. Presently, three troops focused on him and ran into line. They crossed an open area to the row of parked transport trucks. The big tires of the trucks provided cover from the melee.

Panic clawed at the edges of his consciousness. He suppressed it with the stern discipline of a seasoned leader. His men couldn't see the doubt. He trained them *not* to doubt. But the unexpected attack—

Enough!

He faced his men.

"We need to gather as many as we can to this point and make a defensive line," Ramos said. "Make them come to us."

"They came from the east!" said one.

"I saw an explosion on the south end," said another.

Stray bullets smacked into the truck and shattered a window. Ramos winced as bits of glass rained on him. Conventional tactics weren't going to work. The enemy was everywhere.

"All right, we fight. No prisoners!"

Ramos left the truck and opened fire on the enemy. It was obvious they were the opposition, because they wore black, even over their faces. His men wore camouflage green. The thick smoke made it tough to distinguish though. Perhaps the enemy was counting on the hesitation. No. Ramos shouldered his AKM and let the rounds rip. Two black-clad gunmen collapsed; a third pivoted to return fire as he ran for cover. A man beside Ramos cried out. Ramos fired twice, but the black-clad gunner reached cover behind a stack of empty oil drums.

Ramos grimaced; he clenched his jaw. He wasn't going to let the man live.

"On me!" he shouted. He didn't look behind him. He started moving fast toward the barrels. More bullets zipped around him. He heard men yelling as they tried to coordinate. The voices had no accents, then again, if they did, the chaos of combat prevented him from identifying his own people. More gunfire and the voices stopped. His men had answered the question for him.

He fired into the oil barrels. The metal sprouted holes as the 7.62x39mm slugs ripped through. As one toppled over, he saw the body of the man he wanted to kill. But he didn't see the man for long. A string of the 7.62 death bringers tore off the bottom of his face and punctured his neck. He flopped back and didn't move.

Ramos crouched behind the remaining pile, taking potshots at any target he saw. The smoke made it tough. He slapped a new magazine into the AKM. This was madness! Had the army not rounded up all the rebels? And what was the purpose—

His heart pounded in his chest as he exchanged fire with unseen assailants. Their shots smacked into the barrels, but none found him. Worse, his shots didn't connect. The smoke blocked his vision. But the gunfire from the enemy ceased too, or at least wasn't directed his way any longer.

One of his men dropped beside him.

"Another group is coming from the western side!" he shouted. Ramos turned to ask a question but stopped before any words left him.

A shot drilled a hole in the soldier's head. His body fell back. Ramos screamed and returned fire but saw nobody to shoot at. *Madness!* He had to—

Wait! Only one thing made the camp valuable to an attack.

The prisoner.

Ramos looked around. He was alone. The others were either dead or scattered elsewhere. No matter. He could fight alone. He left the oil barrels and ran for the brig where the Armenian mercenary waited in vain for his rescuers.

4

Raven coughed as they ran through the thick smoke, but he did not stop. His friend was in danger. Until they had Darbo out and free, he had no time to complain about present conditions.

Raven, Roger, and Lia sprinted across the compound. The brig sat on a visible foundation, gray, pock-marked, walls on three sides. The bars of the cells faced the guillotine, no doubt to mentally torture anybody inside awaiting execution.

"Status!" Raven shouted as he ran.

Reports came in quick succession over the earpiece, as the other two teams reported the enemy forces were losing numbers fast. The attack force on the west side of the camp reported they'd neutralized the trainee soldiers—no more threat from them existed. They'd not been prepared to handle targets shooting back at them.

But there wasn't time to celebrate.

As they approached the brig, a trio of enemy troops cut through the smoke. They stopped short, opening fire. Raven and Roger and Lia dropped and rolled. Roger's MK48 chugged. Raven fired from prone. The enemy troops jerked with hits and fell. Raven looked back—Lia was firing on a distant position, pinning down a group of soldiers. Raven plucked a grenade and tossed. The men screamed and ran as the grenade landed near them. When the explosion came, they were too far for the shrapnel to hurt them, but they were also running away.

"Lia, on me!" Raven shouted. He continued his approach.

Gunfire continued to rain through the camp. Bullets whizzed past them. Lia pivoted to check their backside. A trooper was trying to outflank them. She triggered her MK48 and watched the soldier's head vanish in a spray of brain and bone. Raven told them both to provide cover fire while he grabbed Darbo.

Approaching with caution, ready to fire the M4 at the first sign of a threat, Raven shouted Darbo's name.

"Here!"

Raven ran to the cell in the middle.

Darbo grabbed the cell bars and seemed to throw his body through them. He let out a whoop and a laugh. Raven told him to get back and shot the lock with a single round from his M4. The cell door swung inward as Darbo pulled it open and stayed at Raven's back as they returned to Roger and Lia. Darbo only stopped long enough to grab a rifle from one of the dead government soldiers.

He smiled at Lia. "Nice machine gun," he said.

She winked. "Mine's bigger than yours."

"Isn't that always the case?"

Raven snapped, "We gotta go!"

Roger shouted, "Get down!"

RAVEN DIVED FOR LIA. Roger swung his machine gun toward a man in uniform running at them, but Darbo told him to hold his fire. Raven landed on top of Lia and her machine gun and kept her pinned as he turned to watch Darbo and the incoming threat.

Captain Ramos's boots thudded on the hard ground. His lips were pulled back in a snarl, his eyes fixed on Darbo.

Darbo, with a swift motion, positioned himself in front of Raven, Lia, and Roger, and raised his rifle. Ramos skidded to a stop and fired from the hip. Darbo didn't blink as the bullet whizzed beside his left ear. He fired once. The crack of his rifle echoed.

Ramos staggered as Darbo's shot smashed his right shoulder. Ramos put his left hand over the hole, blood seeping between his fingers. He tried to lift the AKM, but the effort, mixed with pain, was too much. The muzzle dropped. Ramos screamed, as much from pain as rage. And then Darbo reached him in three easy strides and shoved him onto the ground.

The camp captain landed hard, Darbo wrenching the AKM away, twisting Ramos's right hand in the process. Another scream. Darbo clamped a boot on Ramos's chest and pressed down. He aimed for the camp captain's left eye.

"You might not be a cruel man, Captain," Darbo said, "but I am."

Darbo fired a second round. There wasn't need for another. He stepped away from the corpse with, now, only half a face, and hurried back to his friends.

"You got a way out of here?" he asked Raven. Lia and Roger covered their flanks with the big machine guns, but the fighting was fading. The other team leaders radioed the fight was almost over. Raven ordered a withdrawal. They had what they wanted.

He urged Darbo and the others forward, back to where he'd blown a hole in the south wall.

"I got a way," he told Darbo, "and you got a lot of friends, you know?"

"Yeah," Darbo said. It was all he could manage as he kept pace. But Raven saw the smile on his face. And the relief. He'd come close to getting his head chopped off, and then his friends showed up. Darbo didn't have to say anything. Raven knew how he felt. They'd have plenty of time to talk later.

THE TRIO of helicopters flew across the Peruvian border well after midnight, each machine containing the mercenaries who'd pulled Darbo out of San Remo. Not all survived—the third chopper carried six casualties, all of whom had died fighting. Raven, in the first chopper, where he and his compatriots sat in quiet contemplation, wanted to have a short service for the dead after they buried the bodies. He hated to leave their remains in the middle of nowhere, but they'd all understood the risks. The mission had been unofficial and unsanctioned. Raven promised to get their bodies out of the war zone, but then they'd be buried somewhere in Peru. He promised to keep proper coordinates in case any of their families wanted the remains recovered. And he'd collect their remains himself should their families ask.

They had a landing and staging area picked out far from prying eyes, so there was no need to rush, but Raven didn't want his small army in Peru any longer than necessary. A bunch of armed men and equipment stood out no matter where they sought concealment. If any CIA satellites happened to pass over looking at Peruvian drug sites, for example, the US might drop a line to the Peruvian military...

Raven didn't want to think about it. They'd take care of business and scoot. There'd be no conflict with Peru.

The sleek black helicopters touched down one-by-one in a grassy field. It wasn't a large open area, but very overgrown, and surrounded by thick forest. Each chopper dropped into the clearing to land, unload, and take off again. It was the end of the pilots' responsibilities; they were on their own, as were the rest of the crew, Raven and his friends included. Everybody had made their own exit plans. Vehicles hidden in the surrounding trees would get everybody away. The mercenaries, faces smeared with dirt and sweat, still carrying what remained of their assault gear, spread out into the forest. They had a campsite already secured. Raven and Darbo and a few others helped unload the six dead mercs from the third chopper. Another crew began digging their graves. Darbo found a spare shovel to help. Raven didn't stop him. But Darbo's work kept getting interrupted by his pals coming over to say hello, and him stopping to thank them. As Raven noted, Darbo had a lot of friends, but Raven wasn't sure he truly realized how many had come to his aid.

Later, after the burials, every man—and Lia—tired, but not ready for sleep, sat around fires at the temporary camp. The temperature had dropped, and the heat of the fires was nice. The flames produced a lot of smoke though. There was no way to avoid it drifting around them. A few coughed when the smoke hit them; the rest ignored it. One complained the campfires would make his clothes smelly. Another told him he was already smelly. They had no way to clean up, after all, except with sponges and hot water warmed over fires. Even Raven was looking forward to getting into a real shower in the next twenty-four hours.

Raven, Darbo, Roger, and Lia sat around one such blaze, Raven using a stick to adjust the wood so it caught pieces at the bottom not yet burning. The fire popped and snapped;

Raven was watchful of sparks. The warm glow lit the small area where they sat but left the outer portion of the camp in deep darkness. The conversations around them remained at low tones. Some slowly broke away to climb into sleeping bags.

Darbo finally broke the silence. "When are we going back?"

Raven shook his head. "I had to leave another matter to come here," he said, "and need to get back to it. The Spanish Syndicate—know of it?"

Darbo looked confused.

Roger and Lia said they hadn't heard the name before. Darbo started to speak but stopped. Raven noticed. He didn't ask Darbo to complete his thought. Instead, he continued.

"Drug cartel. Huge. Very violent. They're trying to expand into the Balkans. I need to stop them," Raven said.

"Need help?" Lia said. She looked sleepy.

Darbo said, "Wait."

"Yes, Darbo?" Raven said.

"I was hoping, you know, that we'd go back to San Remo."

"Finish what you started?"

"Yeah."

"With whom?" Raven said.

"Well, us, and—"

"There is nobody else, Darbo," Raven said. "Any surviving rebels have gone into hiding. It may be years before they come out again."

"But, Sam—"

Lia jumped in. "Who was she, Darbo?"

"Why do you think there was a woman involved? They paid me for the job. I should finish it."

"Don't you dare," Roger Justice said, "go back and get caught again or killed after what we just went through for you."

"No, not that," Darbo said. "I won't do that."

"Why so eager, Darbo?" Raven said.

"There *was* somebody. She...died. They put her in the guillotine."

Raven softened his voice. "I'm sorry. I really am. But we have to give the rebels time to regroup. There's nothing for us to do there right now. We'll go back when it's time. I promise. I'll keep an eye on things. When the time is right, we'll go."

Determination filled Darbo's eyes as he nodded. "Okay. I trust you. And if you need me on this other thing, I'll be there."

Roger and Lia said the same.

"No," Raven told them. "I need to do this one alone. We'll get out of Peru, you all go get some R&R; especially *you*, Darbo, and go back to your normal business."

"What's special about this syndicate, Raven?" Lia asked.

"There are some rumors I'm checking out," he told her, "about a new member of the cartel. It's a rumor I don't want to be true. At all."

"What's the rumor?" she pressed.

Raven shook his head and stabbed into the fire with the stick again. A burst of sparks, more cracks, and pops. The fire blazed.

"Not now, Lia. We should try and get some sleep. I want to be out of here before the sun comes up."

5

THE OPULENT PENTHOUSE WAS DIMLY LIT, AND IT SUITED ALEX Riba fine. Secret meetings were supposed to be held in darkened rooms full of cigar smoke. Well, they had to forego the cigars—he didn't mind them outside, but inside? Nuh-uh. He'd converted the top floor of the penthouse into his meeting room. It was too big a room for the large oval conference table by the window, a window so wide it took up space where a wall would have been. There was no other furniture other than the chairs around the table. Only the steel frame of the building suggested more than rubber strips holding the glass in place. He could have filled the room with more, but what was the use? He liked the sparsity. The rest of the penthouse had all the comforts required. He liked how the outside lights of Madrid offset the dim inside; no matter what, they had enough light.

Riba finished his climb up the spiral staircase from the second floor and crossed the open floor with a confident stride. He wore a pressed Saville Row suit, matching the men who sat around the oval table, all of whom were talking quietly. One noticed him and shushed the others. They stopped talking. A slinky hostess in a too-tight, short party dress waited near the head of the table, Riba's seat. She was there to see to the needs of the others until the meeting began. The low-cut dress, her narrow waist, and flaring hips might as well have been non-existent. The men around the table were too preoccupied with the topic of the meeting to be looking at the eye candy.

Riba stopped at his chair and dismissed the woman. Her name was Alecia and she walked away on tapping heels. Nobody watched her go. Riba frowned. He could always count on at least three to watch her leave. But all eyes were on him. The chatter had ceased. They were waiting for him to speak. He noticed none of them had asked for any refreshment. Alecia had wasted her time, standing around for nothing.

"All right, let's begin," he said, "as it seems you're all waiting for the latest. We have a lot to cover, and time is short."

He glanced at the speaker phone in front of him. A light flashed. The phone was connected.

Riba said, "Are you listening, Martin?"

"Hear you loud and clear," came the deep-voiced reply from the triangular speaker.

Riba addressed the men around the table.

"Our merger talks with Vasko Popadic failed, and we must exercise our back-up option. We will destroy his organization and infrastructure, and if he doesn't turn over what we want when we're finished, we'll kill him and take over."

His men looked nervous. Somebody cleared his throat.

"I know it's expensive, scary, and uncharted territory for us," Riba said. "But if our cartel is going to survive, we need Popadic's resources. We need his connections into Eastern Europe."

His men only listened. Riba wanted to smack some life into them. They were all older, successful, men of status and means, and the idea of a little shooting made their knees knock.

"You've all forgotten how we got where we are," Riba told them. "Am I the only one who remembers? Is that why I'm in charge, and you work for me? Because I'm the only one willing to spill blood to get what we need to survive?"

A man at the other end of the table spoke up.

"We are with you. We support this effort."

"You better," Riba answered. He looked at the speakerphone as if it was one of his men instead of a new recruit on the other end of the scrambled line. "What's the status of the mercenary team, Martin?"

"They are in place, scouting targets. I gave them orders to contact me before the first mission began. Then we'll watch the results."

"Make sure they understand what's at stake, and the consequences of failure."

"They already know, Alex."

"I'm just saying—"

"Did you bring me aboard to get results, or not?"

Riba flinched. Martin Bennett wasn't *one of them*. He was an outsider trying to work his way into the organization. He'd impressed Riba so far, had not misrepresented himself at their first meeting, but he had a mouth on him, an attitude. If it had been anybody else, Riba would have killed him.

He told him so.

"Martin, I've killed men for talking to me this way."

"Answer me."

"Martin—"

"Did you, or did you not?"

"I did. Now listen—"

"The Balkan Pipeline will be yours, Alex, just like I showed you. Kill me later if you aren't happy."

Riba took a deep breath. He scanned the faces of the men watching him. Nobody was smiling, nor were they behaving as if they enjoyed watching the boss get taken down a notch. Riba decided to carry on. There was nothing he could do to Bennett from the penthouse.

"Martin, stay on the line. The rest of you, are there any questions?"

Head shakes, murmurs of "No," and somebody said, "We got it, boss."

Riba dismissed the crew.

His men left the table quietly, heading for the spiral staircase where Alecia would meet them. She'd escort them to the exit, and the elevator to the ground floor.

"Martin?"

"What is it, Alex?"

"Do not talk to me like that again."

"You need to ditch the movie gangster attitude, Alex. This is real life. If you can't take pushbacks from somebody as smart as you, perhaps we shouldn't be in business together. Do you want to part ways?"

Riba shut his eyes. He bit his tongue, but he wanted to start yelling. But Martin had a point, and Riba knew it. Riba also knew Martin was well aware the cartel didn't have the money or the resources to mount an attack. Riba had to work with an outside force to hit the Serbians. The goal was bigger than any petty arguments.

"Our alliance will continue," he said, "but your men better deliver, Martin."

"Or—"

"You know what."

"Get a glass of wine, Alex. Leave the rest of this to me. Your part will come up very quickly."

Riba smashed a finger on the disconnect button with more force than intended, but he enjoyed the silence in place of Bennett's voice.

6

RAFAEL SALAZAR'S FAVORITE BAR IN THE LAS LETRAS DISTRICT of Madrid was a small backstreet joint favored by locals instead of tourists. The occasional tourist did show up, though, and they were certainly welcome. The owner was not in the business of turning away somebody's money. For Salazar, it offered a quiet place to have a drink after a long day and enjoy some of the best *tapas* in the city. The dish in front of him at his private corner table was a thick slice of cheesy octopus toast. Circular bits of octopus were glued to the toasted bread via three layers of exotic cheeses.

His cocktail of choice for the evening was a rum and ginger ale mixture in a tall highball glass. His table offered a view of the bar and the large TV screen on the adjoining wall. The futbol game only occupied moments of his attention; his mind was elsewhere.

Salazar was one of the men who'd attended Alex Riba's penthouse meeting. He had concerns about the expansion into the Balkans. He knew the Spanish Syndicate was having cash flow problems and facing strong competition from rivals outside of Spain. . The Colombians, the Mexicans, the

European cartels; the conflict often led to shooting. Riba seemed to think fighting the Serbians for access to their smuggling routes was easier than fighting the others. Salazar wasn't sure. But he was in no position to argue with the boss. If the scheme worked, they'd all prosper; if not, they'd all be dead within six months. If the Serbians won, they'd dish out revenge with twice the firepower Riba employed.

Salazar chewed his octopus toast and drank his cocktail and watched the players on TV kick and pass score goals.. The muted conversation blended into noise; he didn't bother with it. After a long day he finally felt relaxed and ready to tackle more tasks the next day. Running his portion of the Riba empire demanded many, many hours each week. There were no days off. Salazar took a break when he could and hoped his phone didn't blow up in an emergency.

Salazar was tall, with long legs and a trim build. He'd once been a track star, but a knee injury during a race late in his college career racked up medical debt and forced him to find a way to make a lot of money fast. He turned to drug peddling, found he liked the lifestyle, and worked his way up into the Riba organization to finally control drug sales on the north side of Madrid. Now he had college-aged men and women working for him. Someday, he knew, one of them would take over, but hopefully after he bowed out gracefully and retired to a villa in the hills. He didn't want to be replaced because of a bullet in the back of the head.

There were more than a few women in the place; he caught them glancing at him, but only the curious type, with their "who is that guy sitting by himself?" expressions of interest. He didn't return their attention. He wasn't in the mood. And the women found other interests. The bar's décor offered much more to look at. Spanish posters of international movies, including popular US and UK titles. A large plastic Elvis in one corner. The King had his mouth open and was supposed to be singing into a microphone, but the owner, in a fit of inspiration, replaced the microphone with a rubber hot dog. It was the owner's private joke.

Salazar finished the toast and washed it down with another sip of his cocktail. He allowed himself a comfortable sigh. He hadn't expected to relax after the meeting but wound up surprised. He even smiled to himself. Everything was going to be fine. The Balkan operation wasn't cheap, but he'd make up his share of the contribution fast enough.

When the door swung open and a big American entered, the good feelings Salazar briefly enjoyed vanished. He instead felt a chill up his neck.

This man was different than anybody else in the bar.

Rafael Salazar didn't know how he knew, but the American wasn't a tourist. He was a hunter.

And once the American's eyes passed over where he sat, and zeroed on him for a brief moment, Salazar knew he was the prey.

———

RAVEN FOUND a seat at the bar and scanned the patrons. He spotted Salazar right away, at his corner table. The drug runner sat with his back to the wall, facing the door. He saw Raven looking at him and blanched. Raven turned away. Salazer didn't know him, but he'd know the look was more than a casual glance. He'd know he was a target. Raven didn't care if he knew. A running man was a scared man, a man who made mistakes. But Raven needed Salazar alive. He was one of Alex Riba's inner circle, and Raven wanted to squeeze him for every ounce of information inside his head.

Salazar may have been alone in the bar, but he had help a phone call away. If Raven didn't play his cards right, he'd soon have more than Salazar to face.

After Raven and his Raiders made their exit from Peru, Roger, Lia, and Darbo went their separate ways. With Darbo free, Raven was back on the mission he'd set aside, and Alex Riba and the Spanish Syndicate were the next targets of his war without end. Raven began his campaign against the Riba cartel because of an anonymous tip. The tip told him about a new member of the syndicate. Allegedly, a former CIA officer Raven once called a friend now had Riba's ear; if the rumor was true, Raven wanted to know why.

The bartender finally came over. He had a slight build and boney chin. He asked Raven what he'd like.

"Gin and tonic," Raven told him. It wasn't one of the fancy cocktails he was used to preparing, or what the bar special-ized in, but he quickly filled a glass and set it in front of Raven on a coaster. Raven grinned. He picked up the glass, turned in Salazar's direction, and raised the drink in his direction. Salazar's eyes burned back at him.

SALAZAR LIKED to think nothing scared him, but the way the American raised his glass gave him doubts. He needed to get out, and the only way out was the back door. No way did Salazar want to walk past the American to the front door.

He started to reach for his wallet. Then he stopped. He wasn't done with his drink, and the worst thing he could do was show fear. And why should he give the American any satisfaction? The man wanted him spooked. His brazen behavior was a psy-op, a trick; there were other ways to handle this. He didn't need to run like a frightened rabbit. He reached for his drink again, and this time took a sip in defi-ance. Then he grabbed his cell phone from the inside pocket of his jacket.

He speed-dialed the top name in his contact list, a man named Hugo Colina, one of his more trusted compatriots.

"What is it?" Colina answered. He sounded out of breath.

"Did I interrupt something?" Salazar kept his voice low. The bar's light music helped. He watched the American, but the American wasn't looking at him. He had his attention on the TV above the bar.

Colina laughed. "I'd say."

"Get your pants on. I have a problem." Salazar quickly explained. "Get as many men as you can and come help me. I'll stay put until you arrive."

"Got it." Colina was all business now. "I have three men available."

"Hurry. I don't know what this man is going to do."

"We'll be there before you know it."

Salazar ended the call. Despite the nervous tension in his body screaming for him to run, he enjoyed playing the American's game very much.

HUGO COLINA SHOVED the dark-haired woman away from him and rolled out of bed.

"Hey!" she protested.

He grinned at her as she pulled the sheet up to cover her body. She'd had no such inclinations earlier.

"Duty calls."

"You promised me all night."

"I hate making promises I can't keep," he said, pulling on his boxers and grabbing his pants from the floor. "But the boss needs me."

"You're always running to save him," the woman said. "Tell him to go to hell."

He zipped his pants and leaned over to kiss her. "You

first, babe," he added, then found his shirt. He tied his shoes, skipping socks, and found his clip-on holster on the dresser and jacket on the back of a chair. With a final wink, he left the woman, and her smoldering expression, behind. Duty called indeed.

He left her door unlocked and hurried down the hall to the stairs. He never took elevators. As he descended, he made a call. He reached one of the three troops on stand-by for such emergencies, who agreed to call the other two, and meet him at the bar.

Colina found his car on the curb and jumped behind the wheel. He was breathing hard, excited energy flowing through him. The prospect of action was better than sex. But he'd never say so to his girlfriend.

RAVEN WATCHED Salazar's reflection in the mirror behind the bar. Liquor shelves covered most of the reflective glass, but he still had a decent view of the Spanish Syndicate henchman. He smiled. *Yes, call for back-up. It's not going to help you, my friend.*

Now they were at an impasse with each other. Raven could leave and wait in ambush, but he had to guess which exit Salazar might use. If it were Raven, he'd use the back; he figured Salazar was of the same opinion. It made sense. The back door opened into an alley. You could either go to the street or wind through connecting alleys to other points of exit. If Salazar hoped to shake Raven's target lock, the back door was the only way to go. The next problem Raven faced was figuring out which path Salazar would take. It was almost guaranteed he'd pick the wrong way and lose Salazar's trail. He could have told his men to come and get him at the easiest exit point, or one further away. Raven had to sit and drink slowly and stay with Salazar as soon as he moved.

Raven's information on Rafael Salazar indicated he didn't carry a gun. He left the carrying of weapons to his men. All Raven cared about was making sure the gun battle didn't take place where civilians might get hurt. He worked by two rules: one, no roots. Nothing to tie him down. Two: no gunfights in public. He was in the business of protecting and saving people from violence, not creating more victims. The ghosts of battles past demanded he take precautions as long as possible, but if the enemy ever forced his hand, he also had to fire true.

Raven drank more of his gin and tonic and wondered how much longer he had to wait. He wanted to get the show started.

Unlike Salazar, he carried a weapon. The Nighthawk Custom Talon .45 autoloader rode under his left arm, spare ammunition magazines under his right, and a HK submachine gun in his car. He hoped not to need the SMG or the car. If he could handle the problem with his pistol, he wouldn't have to get the heavy artillery.

And then it began.

Salazar dropped money on the table and scooted out of the booth. Raven turned his head to watch. Salazar showed him his back as he headed down the hall to the restrooms and the rear exit beyond.

Raven slid off his barstool and followed.

7

SALAZAR GLANCED BEHIND HIM AS HE HURRIED DOWN THE hall. Yeah, he was going faster than he intended, but Colina and the three gunners were waiting, and he wanted out of there fast. The American was following, as predicted, and moved with a confident stride. Salazar went by the restrooms and turned left, where the rear exit, marked for emergency use by a yellow and black sign, waited for him. The back hallway wasn't dressed up at all; brick walls, concrete floor; a chill throughout. Salazar pushed open the emergency exit and ignored the low-key alarm that started going *beep beep*. When his shoes scraped on the concrete outside, and he saw the street at the mouth of the alley to his left, relief flooded over him. There was Colina in the car as promised.

"Salazar!"

The American.

Closing fast.

Salazar no longer cared about how he looked. He broke into a run.

THE DOOR SLAMMED SHUT before Raven reached it, and the alarm didn't stop. Now the bartender was telling, running Raven's way. When he saw the .45 in Raven's hand, his voice cracked. Instead of shouting, "Stop!" the word came out "Eeeek!" Raven grabbed the door handle with his left hand, dropped low, and eased the door open. Salazar was running toward a car at the mouth of the alley, and almost there. A man looking out the passenger window shouted and swung a gun Raven's way. Raven slammed the door. Two rounds hammered into the metal. Raven opened the door again and somersaulted into the alley. Two more rounds smacked the brick wall behind him as he stopped on his belly. Raven watched the white Mercedes speed away.

Raven cursed. Witnesses on the sidewalk gawked or screamed and ran away. Drivers screeched tires with sudden braking to avoid the speeding Mercedes. Raven jumped to his feet and ran. He didn't hide his gun, and more people ran away upon seeing the tall, and armed, American. He ran across the street. He'd parked his rental on the other side of the road but facing the opposite direction than the Mercedes had gone. He jumped behind the wheel and started the motor. Spinning away in a screeching U-turn, cutting off both directions of traffic, Raven corrected and began his pursuit. Horns blared around him. He hoped it wasn't too late to catch the other car.

Flaring brake lights two blocks ahead suggested he wasn't.

Raven weaved around the slower traffic, in and out of lanes, slamming the horn in warning. Salazar and his men would hear the horn, but so what? They knew Raven was after them. But what if they opened fire in the middle of a traffic jam?

They wouldn't, Raven decided. Not even Salazar was dumb enough to take the chance. He'd be in enough trouble if caught. Killing civilians was an extra charge he didn't need.

Still a gamble, Raven thought. *What's another charge on top of what he'd already face?*

As he reached the cluster of cars, he spotted the problem.

A truck sat diagonally between lanes, partially blocking the Mercedes, which looked as if it had tried to pass as the truck made its move. Horns honked. The drivers of the truck and Mercedes yelled at each other through open windows. Then Salazar leaned out the passenger side window and fired a gun into the air. The yelling stopped. The truck driver hit the gas, sideswiped part of the Mercedes's front bumper, and scraped another car parked curbside in his haste to get away. The crunch of metal sounded flat in the crowded street. The Mercedes followed. Raven had to wait until there was enough room between cars to move and stayed on the Mercedes. If Salazar and his men only wanted to get away from the jam up, they might not look for Raven right away.

The Mercedes screeched tires turning left. Raven turned the wheel to follow, and the cars sped through a roundabout heading northeast. They were on a short stretch heading for the M30 motorway. Structures became less dense, replaced by thick forest with buildings hidden within the growth. Less traffic too. It was a good spot for a fight. If they reached the M30, Raven might lose them.

Raven yanked the tote bag on the passenger seat to his lap. He pulled on the zipper with one hand and reached inside for the Heckler & Koch MP5K submachine gun. The compact 9mm SMG delivered its death blasts at 900 rounds per minutes. All he had to do was get close enough to shoot out a tire, and the hardball cartridges stacked within the thirty-round magazine were more than capable of putting the Mercedes out of action.

He pressed the throttle and the engine surged. They knew he was on their back now; the Mercedes pulled away. Raven kept pace and hit the window switch in the door. The driver's window whispered down and cold air rushed inside. Raven stuck the HK out the window and pulled the trigger. The three-round burst stitched holes in the trunk. Way off. He had to aim on instinct—but, really, he was guessing. If he aimed a little higher, he might shoot out the back window.

Why not?

Raven raised the muzzle and fired again, but as he squeezed, the car hit a bump. His burst went wide—over the roof of the Mercedes. He compensated and fired a third burst. The back window only cracked. One shot struck the glass, while the other two sparked off the side pillar. One of Salazar's gunmen leaned out the driver's side back window. He returned fire with a pistol. Raven ducked, pulling the HK back inside. The return fire turned his windscreen into a mass of spider cracks. Raven dropped back. The Mercedes pulled away. Raven slammed the snout of the HK into the glass to make a hole. More wind, and bits of glass this time, rushed in and hammered in his face. But Raven was still in the fight. With only a few kilometers to go before they reached the M30, he had to hustle.

Raven pressed the accelerator. He ran smack into more return fire but kept his head low. Bullets slapped at the car. They were going for his tires, too. He made it tough by swerving left to right. But the movement did him no favors, either—he couldn't shoot back and expect to hit anything. When the gunman retreated back into the car to reload, Raven struck. Holding steady, he extended the HK out the window and fired again and again. His first burst kicked up sparks on the road. The next struck the rear fender and tire on the passenger side. The tire exploded with pieces of rubber flying at Raven's broken windshield. Raven held the car still and fired once more. Bye-bye back window. The glass caved and showered pieces on the gunmen in the rear seat.

The Mercedes swerved and the exposed rear rim ground into the blacktop. The driver lost control. The car veered right, crashing through a metal barrier, and tumbling off the road. Raven aimed his car for the shoulder and stopped. Pausing to reload the HK, he stuffed two spare mags inside his jacket, and then exited. He ran to the wreck.

The Mercedes lay on its roof at a downward angle. Tree branches stabbed at the underside, and despite the still-running engine, Raven heard the men inside screaming. They were stuck, desperate to escape. Raven hosed the driver's side with a long burst. The yelling stopped. He left the road and went down the dirt slope to the passenger side. The gunner in the back pleaded with him for help. Raven shot him in the face. He stopped at the front passenger door to look at Salazar but cursed instead.

Salazar was still in his seat, held in place by the seat belt, but the blood running down his face, his wide eyes, and the odd kink to his neck told Raven all he needed to know. The impact had broken the drug runner's neck. There'd be no Q&A with Rafael Salazar now.

Raven hurried up the slope to return to his rental. He tossed the HK inside and dropped behind the wheel. Out of there—pedal to the floor. He could get away clean by reaching the M30. After that...

He caught his breath and settled down. Then he gave the wheel a frustrated smack. So much for his bright ideas. Plans didn't always work out, as he knew all too well, but this failure meant a further delay.

He needed to ditch the shot-up rental and regroup. One

82 | BRIAN DRAKE

dead end didn't mean the end of the trail. He'd only have to start from zero. Again. Next time, there couldn't be any mistakes.

8

ON FOOT THROUGH ANOTHER PUBLIC AREA, RAVEN DUCKED into an alley and dialed a number on his cell. A man named Oscar Morey answered on the other end without delay.

"Success?" Morey asked.

"The lead didn't pan out," Raven said.

"Did you kill him?"

"Not on purpose, I promise."

Oscar laughed. "All right. Not to worry. We've got another one. It's a woman named Abby Fox."

"Who is she?"

"Information broker. She's not affiliated with the cartel, but she knows the things I don't."

"Oscar, I never thought I'd hear you admit you don't know everything."

"First time for everything," Oscar said.

Oscar Morey hadn't always been on the side of the angels. He was an underworld character, well known in Europe, but one who managed never to spend a day in jail. With ears to the ground in many areas, and contacts all over the world, there wasn't anything he didn't know, or could learn, if given enough time.

Years earlier, when a much younger Raven was in Paris to kill a man responsible for several murders, Morey had intercepted him with a warning. *Stay out of our business. You don't want this kind of trouble.* Raven explained why his target had to die and drew Morey to his side. Some crimes were too heinous for even Morey to tolerate, and he allowed Raven to finish his mission.

When Raven finally confronted the killer, he made him kneel before shooting him in the head.

The next time their paths crossed, Raven saved one of Morey's daughters from certain death. The underworld legend then pledged his support. From there, the bond between them grew stronger. Raven was smart enough to know when fortune handed him a talisman. In this case, it was a crusty old bastard named Oscar Morey.

"She'll want money," Oscar said.

"I got money. Where is she?"

"Madrid."

"Awfully convenient," Raven said.

"Play your cards right, and she may lead you to the belly of the beast."

But hopefully not with a gun at my back. It was hard not to be paranoid. Raven didn't express the thought, however. He stuck to business. Oscar's leads were solid. The old man wouldn't knowingly send Raven into a trap. "When and where?" he asked.

Oscar told him.

———

THE NEXT DAY, before noon. In the busy heart of Madrid, Raven sat in a loud café, waiting for Abby Fox. He had a picture of her so he'd recognize when she arrived, but he hoped the photo wasn't outdated. She was a blonde in the photo. If she'd changed her hair to red or black or miscellaneous, he'd have to rely on her recognizing him, which gave her the advantage. Raven at least wanted an even playing field.

He took a deep breath and drank more of his tea. He was treating this new mission with a greater sense of importance than any other. He couldn't. He had to think of it like any other—except this time, there might be an old friend mixed up with the bad guys. He was anxious to learn the truth, which was making him anxious overall. *You know better*, he thought. *Maintain discipline. Now is not the time to get stupid.*

But when the old friend was Martin Bennett...

It wasn't an idea Raven could rationally consider. He and Bennett had been through too much for Raven to put a gun to friend's head.

A lot of years had passed since the last time the two said goodbye, and Raven had never expected to see Bennett again. When he learned Bennett had retired from the CIA, Raven silently wished him luck in whatever he decided to do next. He'd expected Bennett would take up fishing or another benign hobby. Getting mixed up with the Spanish Syndicate? No. It didn't compute.

He couldn't stop fidgeting where he sat. Raven had to concentrate on remaining still.

This one might be too personal...

The bell above the door broke Raven from his spiraling thoughts.

Abby Fox was still a blonde.

She paused in the doorway a moment, looking around, then proceeded to the counter. Raven stayed in his seat. She ordered coffee and waited. Presently she turned from the counter, cup in hand, and approached his table. Raven made eye contact with her, and a smile pulled at the corners of his mouth but didn't form. She wasn't smiling. She didn't look friendly at all. She wore jeans ripped at the knees, a blouse tied at her belly, but open to reveal the tight tank top beneath. Her large handbag could have concealed a machine gun for its weight, and she wore her hair tied back with stray strands rebelling to fall alongside her face.

She pulled out the chair opposite him, sat, and placed her bag on the floor. Raven waited. She slouched against the backrest. She was playing the familiarity card. They were supposed to be longtime acquaintances or lovers. He remained upright and made no moves, keeping both hands on the table. But his jacket was open too, so he had quick access to the Nighthawk Custom .45 should she pull a machine gun from the handbag.

"You're Raven?"

She spoke with an American accent.

"Sure."

"Who told you about me?"

"About whom? You're a stranger who took a chair not offered to her."

"I'm Abby Fox."

"What does that mean to me?"

"I can go if you want."

"What's Oscar's last name?"

"Morey."

"All right. I'm Raven."

"Good."

"Should we have worked out one of those silly secret agent codes?"

"Watch your mouth," she said.

"It's too loud in here, Abby. Also, be careful with your coffee. The table wobbles a little."

"Don't they always? We can land a man on the moon, but we can't make straight table legs."

"Fair point," Raven said.

"Okay, listen up. My fee is eight thousand. And we aren't talking here."

"Eight thousand for what?"

"In advance."

"Eight thousand for *what*?" Raven repeated. He hoped his face didn't register the annoyance he felt.

"Details on the Spanish Syndicate."

"I want details on where *Alex Riba* is currently living," Raven said. "I know all about the syndicate. If I wanted to blow up his distribution and kill off his smugglers, I'd never have time to sleep. I want the top man, Abby. If you can't deliver, get lost."

"Eight thousand US," she said.

"You better know what he had for breakfast this morning if I'm giving you eight grand," Raven said. "All I know about you came from Oscar. You've never crossed my radar before. I have no idea if you're legit or not."

"How do I convince you?"

"Show me something. Show me what I'm paying for."

Abby Fox swallowed a mouthful of coffee and lifted her handbag onto her lap. After rummaging through the contents, she pulled out a small tablet computer. She pressed a button on the side and the screen lit up.

"I have everything else at home," she said, passing him the tablet. Raven examined the display. It showed a house on a hillside slope, supported by thick beams, with the surrounding forest almost enveloping the building. The front showed a wide deck and a lot of glass behind the rail.

"This could be anybody's house," Raven said. "You find dozens of places like this in Beverly Hills."

"Quit talking and scroll."

Raven raised an eyebrow at her. She sipped her coffee. He looked at the tablet and swiped his finger across the screen.

Details inside the house. Other pictures included Alex Riba himself, dressed comfortably, or in a bathrobe. He always had an alcoholic drink in hand.

"You got inside?" Raven asked her. "Impressive."

"Not me. The contacts I cultivated. I can find out what he had for breakfast this morning, Raven. With a phone call."

"Uh-huh." He handed back the tablet. "All right. I need to see the rest. At home, you said? You got a flat near here?"

"We can walk."

"Let's go."

She walked fast. Raven kept up. They joined the flow of foot traffic on the vibrant street, the sun bright, the day warm. Madrid had a rhythm to it, Raven thought. From the traffic to the sidewalk vendors to the hustle and bustle similar to any other city—it felt like home despite being far away from home. It didn't take long for Raven to feel comfortable no matter where he went, because so much of the world was the same. The only differences were cultural. Everybody's concerns about day-to-day living were identical. It made him wonder why wars began so easily.

"How far?" Raven asked. They crossed a street with a crowd of others.

"Another two blocks."

"How long have you been in Madrid?"

"Been working here about six months."

"You're American?"

"You noticed!"

"You're West Coast, aren't you? California?"

"Oregon."

They passed a row of shops with large window displays. Then one of the shops exploded, a thundering blast of fire and glass, the fireball spreading from one side of the street to the other.

The blast shook the ground and knocked Raven down.

He didn't see where Abby fell.

and viewed the rubble, pushing from one side of the street to the other.

Another shook the ground and knocked Raven down.

Bodies here were ripped...

9

RAVEN STUMBLED THROUGH THE SMOKE-FILLED ALLEY, TRYING to find an outlet away from the choking cloud filling the street. The ground beneath him trembled, tilted—he was dizzy and disoriented, breathing hard, the pounding heartbeat in his chest filling his senses. He tripped, falling to hands and knees, uttering a cry of pain which turned into a heavy coughing fit. He lay flat, resting his left cheek on the rough concrete. Screams filled the air, audible now after the shock of the explosions faded. Screams of pain and fright and desperation. The ringing in his ears muffled the sounds, but they were the stuff of nightmares, and all too familiar to Raven in his war without end. He jerked with his own frightened response. Where was Abby? He didn't see her fall, and she wasn't near him now...

Raven pushed himself to his feet, turned, and staggered back into the smoke and the street where carnage waited. He viewed everything through a blur. He leaned against the left corner of the alley. Rubble and debris filled the road, along with the blasted hulks of cars wrecked by the explosion. And bodies. Many bodies. The horrible scent of burning bodies filled his nostrils. Raven scanned the chaos, and tried to see the mangled corpses clearly, but nothing indicated Abby lay among the dead. Nothing indicated Abby was anywhere near him.

He yelled her name. "Abby! Abby!" Then he doubled over as another coughing fit seized him. This time his legs buckled, and he fell again. He wasn't conscious of any pain or damage to himself, but his blurred vision didn't help. Part of his mind screamed for him to get up. Get up, help the wounded. *Get up!* But he wasn't Superman. This time, *he* needed help. And as the wailing sirens of emergency responders reached his numbed ears, he relaxed. Help was on the way. A medic would find him once they took care of those who needed more help than he. Raven told himself he was fine. Other needed attention more. Others…

He passed out.

WHEN RAVEN WOKE UP, the pain began running through his body.

Where am I?

Hospital.

Hospital bed. It's cold. No, I'm cold. Whole body hurts. Head to toe. Sore. I've been put through a meat grinder.

Raven slowly began moving his arms up and down his chest, pressing, feeling. *Hospital gown. Arms hooked to IV. Drowsy. But I can see.* No bandages on his chest. There were scrapes on his skin—elbows and hands. From falling. He touched his face. Sore spots. *Bruises, probably.* He lifted the sheet and glanced at the exposed portions of his legs, below the knees. His knees were skinned, too. Cuts and bruises. *No major damage, you lucky SOB.* His injuries came from hitting the ground and crawling around, trying to find Abby Fox.

But as minor as he thought they were, he sure couldn't move without hurting. He had to wait for a doctor to find out the real extent of what happened to him.

Machines beeped near him. Heart monitors. He looked around. There were others lined up along either wall, nobody shielded by drapes. They were stuffed into the room out of necessity. They were all victims. Waiting. Lying in a daze. Somebody groaned, but Raven didn't try to look. Victims deserved their dignity and privacy. He deserved his too. If he had to let out a noise, he didn't want any eyes on him, either.

He felt around his neck for the sterling silver locket he wore on a chain. His neck was bare. He wanted to panic, but he'd learned long ago, when in a hospital, to take a breath, and examine his surroundings. He'd been in several throughout his life, some in cities like Madrid, others in less friendly environments. He looked to the left side of the bed, where hospitals often placed a nightstand or table for the patient's personal items. There it was, next to his wallet and cell phone. But his gun was missing. He smiled a little. He would have liked to have seen the expressions of the paramedics when they realized he was armed and had no identification showing he was legally allowed to carry a handgun. If they'd run his prints for an ID, they knew he was American, they knew his name, and somewhere at the local police station a red alert sounded. He'd have a lot to explain when the cops finally came around to speak with him.

But none of what passed through his mind was as important as what *he* wanted to know. *Who set off the bomb? Why?*

It was another interruption on his quest against the Spanish Syndicate. It was like they were protected— protected by the forces of darkness if he wanted to be outlandish about it. But arguing was tough. It sure seemed like they had something to watch out for them. Protecting them from Raven's claws.

He took a deep breath and turned his eyes to the ceiling. He didn't know how long he had to wait, but he was used to waiting. In the meantime, he'd lay in bed and hurt. He was one of the lucky ones. Many others weren't as fortunate. He wondered what the death toll was.

You think too much.

Lay still and be quiet.

What happened to Abby?

He shifted, reaching out to the nightstand. He didn't want to lay there alone. Raven grabbed his locket and stifled a response to the aches and pains resulting from moving his head. He donned the chain and let the locket rest on his chest. His conscience was inside the locket. The reason for his fight. The ghosts of battles past who guided him through the war without end. The locket comforted him. He could never explain why, but the locket had power, even if only he understood what it really meant.

RAVEN'S MIND continued to swirl with confusion, with questions, and nobody offered answers. The nurses who came to check on the group only told them to shush, not talk, to rest and wait for the doctor. They claimed to know nothing about what happened, they were only concerned with the well-being of their patients. Raven let them check him over and give him pain meds. They asked where it hurt, if he was feeling dizzy or nauseous, the usual questions. Then they departed as efficiently as they arrived. When a doctor came through for his own checks, the response was equally as cold and uninformative.

Finally, Raven grabbed his cell phone. Then all the questions came at him because the other patients wanted to know what he knew when he discovered it.

Raven unlocked his screen, the brightness making him wince. He turned the screen's brightness down. His battery was running low. There wouldn't be a lot of time. With a sense of urgency, he navigated to a news ap. The answers he found might lead to more questions, but he'd never learn the truth without looking.

The screen displayed a series of grim headlines, worse pictures, and details of the aftermath of the explosion. Bombing—confirmed. Not an accident. Not a gas line. A *bombing*. Set off on purpose. Basque terrorists? The government wasn't sure. They said it was unlikely. The death toll? Forty-five dead, at least thirty more wounded. Between the blast itself and the residual damage, the bomb destroyed half the block. The city was dealing with grief and chaos in equal amounts, and nobody knew why.

A list of names. Raven wanted a list of names of the dead. He couldn't find one. Still no idea if Abby survived or perished. If he had survived, she *may* have.

Raven related the details to his hospital mates. Their raised voices of alarm ultimately brought a nurse in, who zeroed on Raven's bed like a heat seeking missile and snatched the cell phone from his hand.

"No phones, sir. We need everybody to stay calm and focused."

"Then why did you leave it here?"

"We apologize for the oversight."

She turned on a heel and marched out. Raven didn't get a chance to ask when he'd get the phone back. He traded glances with his fellow patients. They all looked confused, still carrying the shock of the event with them. Raven's shoulders sank. More victims. Always more victims. No matter how many he tried to save, the tide never turned.

10

THE POLICE FINALLY ASKED TO SEE RAVEN ON THE THIRD DAY.

He'd been expecting it, especially if they'd identified him. A nurse brought him a wheelchair and told him he had a visitor. Raven managed to get out of bed, slowly, with pain, ignoring the rear-end exposure the loose hospital gown didn't prevent, and dropped into the chair. The nurse wheeled him along the white-tiled hallway. It smelled of antiseptic solution. The smell annoyed him.

The nurse brought him into a private room where a man in a suit sat on the edge of a bed, waiting. Dark-skinned, bushy mustache and eyebrows, full head of hair. He watched Raven curiously until the nurse departed, and she told him he had ten minutes, per the doctor's instructions. He was not to excite the patient. The man, in a deep voice, told her the patient was probably already excited enough.

The nurse shut the door.

"Mr. Raven."

"Good morning."

"Afternoon, actually."

"I have no sense of time," Raven said.

"On purpose. No television, radio, all that, right?"

"They don't want us knowing anything, apparently."

"Better for your health, as fragile as you are. Except you, right, Mr. Raven?"

"Get to the point."

The man chuckled.

"I am Detective Marc Valverde, Madrid Police." He showed Raven his badge and identification. "The government is in the process of taking over the case, but before they do, I wanted to see you personally. You see, when we discovered your name, alarms went off. We have questions, and you're going to answer them, Mr. Raven. Why are you in Madrid?"

"Personal business."

"We have no record of your entry. We searched your hotel room. You are registered under another name. Your passport is in another name as well. Posing as somebody else to avoid detection is a serious matter, Mr. Raven. For all we know, you came here under false pretenses to commit a crime in *my* city."

Raven remained silent. His fingerprints would have revealed his true identity, while the alias created a cloud of suspicion. They weren't talking to him because of who he was, or his background; they were talking to him because they thought he was responsible for the bombing. *He was a suspect*.

"Why should I tell you what you already know, Detective?" Raven said.

"Indeed! You used an alias, not only to enter the country, but to register at your hotel. Only your fingerprints told the truth, and now I want the real truth. Why are you here, and what did you have to do with the bombing?"

"Nothing."

"You were there."

"Detective, if you know who I am, then you know my reputation. Right?"

"I know violence follows you. I know Interpol has a thick file on you. Some can't decide if you're a good guy or a bad guy. Is the bombing related to your activity? Speak up! Or we'll *make* you cooperate."

Raven smiled. "Even with the shape I'm in, I doubt you could *make* me do anything, Detective."

"You're getting on my nerves, *Mr.* Raven."

"Being hostile with me isn't going to help you. The truth is, I want to know who's behind this as much as you do. And no, I do not believe it's related to anything I'm doing. I'm in Madrid on another matter. I'm here trying to find a lead to the boss of the Spanish Syndicate."

Raven stopped talking. Admitting his task in Madrid was a calculated risk. If Valverde was on the take, working for the Spanish Syndicate, he'd report back; Raven would have hitmen on his back before the sun went down. If Valverde was an honest cop and believed the "good guy" reports in the Interpol file, he might offer assistance. Maybe. He seemed like a strait-laced cop to Raven. But the detective was stepping out of bounds by talking to him when the government's investigation was about to push the locals aside.

"The Spanish Syndicate," Valverde said, as if spitting. "Alex Riba? You're after him?"

"If you've read the Interpol file—"

"Yes, yes, I know. I know what the report says. You're chasing a drug pusher. Okay. You were in the wrong place at the wrong time, is that it?"

"Just out for a walk."

"Ten miles from your hotel?"

"I tried out a restaurant near here. Somebody recommended it."

"Which one?"

"My head is scrambled. I can't remember."

"Sure," the detective said. Raven noticed he wasn't taking notes. It didn't matter. The interrogation continued, the tension growing thicker as Valverde asked more questions, aggressively so, clashing with Raven's stoic expression and simple answers. Raven didn't tell him the whole story. He didn't mention Abby Fox's name. It wasn't until a doctor entered, informing Valverde that his ten minutes had passed, that the cop finally relented.

"I'll be back," Valverde said. He pushed past the doctor to exit.

"I've heard that before," Raven called after him.

He was grinning when the nurse returned to take him back to his bed. But he knew, eventually, he'd have to officially ask if Abby Fox was among the dead.

Or not.

AT CIA HEADQUARTERS IN VIRGINIA, an urgent meeting gathered to discuss the bombing in Madrid. The CIA had more than the usual interest in what happened.

Clark Wilson arrived last. Wilson served as a Senior Staff Operations Officer for the CIA's Special Activities Center. His boss, DDO Christopher Fisher, put him in charge of the Madrid investigation. The other staffers around the conference table hushed their chatter to give him their attention. Some turned from viewing the large monitor on one wall, which featured live footage of the disaster. It was a loop of collected news footage from stations and networks around the globe.

Among the usual talking heads of reporters, there were closeups of the chaos. The damage, the dead, the walking wounded being tended to by medical personnel. The gaping charred hole now serving as the only representation of the bombed store continued to smolder, trickles of smoke still lingering around the edges.

Witnesses who'd been spared harm spoke on camera, but the muted audio didn't give Wilson any clue as to their statements. Wouldn't have mattered anyway. He didn't trust eyewitnesses because ten different people could see the same event and give ten different descriptions. The facts would sort themselves out shortly, and then he'd have a clear picture of what took place. What they needed to determine was the who, and the why.

"What the hell happened over there?" Wilson said, watching the video as he pulled out a chair. It wasn't his nature to begin a meeting with such language, but he knew what the bombing meant. The blast sent a good number of headquarters personnel into a state of shock, confusion, and concern.

"What do we know?" he asked the table.

The room filled with tension. Wilson knew better than to push too hard. Everybody was extra sensitive, and yelling wasn't going to do any good. The newest member of Wilson's staff, a man named Victor Harris, opened the conversation. He was the youngest member of the staff, but Wilson had found him eager to serve, if a little too quick to talk. If the kid lacked anything from his extensive Harvard legal education, it was thinking before he spoke, but Wilson didn't stop him. He was once again going to see the kid's motor mouth in action.

Harris said, "Somebody blew up a CIA surveillance site."

Wilson stared at Harris and called on a reserve of patience.

"Victor, a lot of us in this room know somebody who died in that blast, so watch your mouth."

"My apologies." The younger man's face remained stern.

It was an automatic response. Wilson wondered if he was really sorry or not.

"Any survivors?"

A middle-aged woman on Wilson's right had notes in front of her but didn't have to consult to answer the question.

"Nobody," the woman said.

"Did they recover the bodies yet?"

"They will soon," she said. "Once they find the basement, they'll know it was more than a typical antique store."

"And they'll find our equipment, too," Wilson said.

"Do we have a liaison with CNI?" the woman asked.

The CNI was Spain's foreign and domestic intelligence agency, combining the tasks of the US FBI and CIA into one government department. The *Centro Nacional de Inteligencia* kept its office in Madrid. They'd be on the scene quickly, taking over for the local police.

"You're looking at him," Wilson said. "I'll be heading over there by the end of the day. When they find out we were hiding a surveillance team smack in the middle of Madrid, they're not going to be happy. So, who did this? How was our team discovered?"

Wilson turned to the man on his left for the answer. Paul Heinrich was his personal assistant, an expert analyst and confidant. He was a little older than Harris, but knew how not to voice every thought in his head.

"No chatter from the usual suspects," Heinrich said. "Basque Separatists, the al-Qaeda remnant; nothing, from nobody, at all. This came out of nowhere, Clark."

"I don't buy it," Wilson said. "The team in Madrid were working on a lot of stuff. One of their targets must have done this."

Victor Harris said, "What about—" He stopped.

Wilson frowned. He'd never seen the young man hesitate before.

"What? Finish your through, Victor."

"Somebody we saw on camera," Harris said. "One of the CCTV cameras. Somebody in our files—" Harris checked his notes. "A man named Sam Raven. Used to be one of ours."

"I know who Sam Raven is, Victor. Get that footage on the screen."

It was Heinrich who went to work. Using a wireless keyboard, he rotated his chair to face the monitor, cleared the news footage, and typed a command to call up the CCT video. A static black-and-white shot filled the screen, the camera facing the antique store from across an intersection. Wilson tried not to look at the storefront. He was watching the people on the sidewalk. He spotted Sam Raven right away. He told Heinrich to freeze the frame. Leaving the table, Wilson stepped closer to the monitor.

Wilson and Raven had been friends for decades. Wilson had also once been a dedicated field officer before marriage and children made him take a desk job. He tried to stay in fighting shape, but the hazards of desk work contributed to him going soft in the middle no matter how hard he exercised. And as he examined the footage, he had no doubt. The man on the sidewalk was Raven, and there was a young woman beside him. They were talking. Walking casually. Wilson told Heinrich to run the video. The conversation between Raven and the woman continued as they walked, oblivious, paying no attention to the antique store. The woman broke away from Raven before the blast. Then the storefront exploded. Raven went down. The woman ran into an alley.

If Raven survived, he was hurt. He'd be in a Madrid hospital, and soon CNI would have their hooks in him, if they hadn't already. Wilson's pulse began to race. Had he survived? Or was Raven among the dead? And who was the woman with him? What brought him to Madrid?

"Rewind it and run it again, Paul," Wilson said.

This time, Wilson looked at the antique store. Nobody entered, nobody exited. It was just there, like any other storefront. People passed by on the sidewalk. Then the brightness of the initial blast filled the screen. When the brightness faded, smoke, debris, and scattered prostrate bodies filled the street and sidewalk on both sides. Cars flung into the buildings opposite the antique store created more damage and casualties. Wilson let out a slow breath. How did the bomb get into the shop? How was it not found once it had been placed?

"All right, listen up," Wilson said. "I want a rundown of what the Madrid team was doing. Access their reports and compile *everything*. Go back six months—to start. I want to know if Sam Raven survived. He may be irrelevant. We don't know yet. Everything has to be checked. Any questions?"

He looked at the people around the table. They finished scribbling notes and looked at him.

"Get to work," Wilson said, "right now."

Chairs scraped the tiled floor as his staffers departed, but Wilson remained where he was, watching the footage.

What were you doing there, Sam?

And he hoped his friend was still alive.

11

CELL PHONES WEREN'T ALLOWED INSIDE CIA HEADQUARTERS. Even spooks knew they can be hacked and used to listen to conversations, even transmit video without a user's knowledge. Bring a phone into the building, you risk getting fired. Victor Harris had to wait until he had a chance to leave the campus to use his cell phone. He drove out of the main gate and turned onto the freeway, finally pulling over after traveling ten miles.

It was a long-distance call, connecting to a point somewhere in the Caribbean. Harris sat on the roadside shoulder, watching cars go by, waiting for a pick-up on the other end. After four rings, a male voice answered. But not the man Harris wanted to talk to.

"What is it?"

"Put Bennett on; it's urgent."

"Wait."

Harris waited and tried to stop fidgeting. He didn't want to be nervous, but while the bomb had gone off as planned, it might have killed somebody important to the counterplan. If Sam Raven was dead, they might as well pack up and quit.

"Harris?"

Victor Harris stopped fidgeting and jerked in his seat at the sound of Martin Bennett's voice.

"What's urgent, Harris?"

"The bomb might have killed Raven," Harris said, then detailed the meeting Clark Wilson had called. "If he's dead—"

"Raven is alive," Bennett said. "He's hurt and in the hospital. We have people watching. CNI is going to take him into custody as soon as he's discharged, but once he gets free of them—we'll intervene if we have to—he's going to start putting the pieces together. He'll go exactly where we want him."

Harris felt a wave of relief. "Everybody is going apeshit, Marty. What do we have, six CIA dead? Plus, the civilians? Was there no way to warn them?"

Bennett's silence lasted longer than Harris would have expected. It lasted longer than Harris wanted. When Bennett spoke again, he lacked the authority his voice usually carried.

"If we'd have warned them, the entire mission would be at risk now. They didn't die in vain, Harris. I promise."

Harris said nothing.

"Victor?" Bennett didn't usually use his first name. "It's the spy business. Remember, we're trying to protect many more lives. The casualties we suffered today will pale in comparison to what will happen if we fail."

As if that explains anything. But Harris kept the response to himself. "I need to get back." He hoped his disgust wasn't obvious. He didn't like the bitter taste in his mouth. His stomach didn't feel right, either.

"Keep me posted."

"Yes, sir."

"We're counting on you."

"I know."

Harris hung up, put his cell back in the glove box, and rejoined the flow of traffic. Bile burned his stomach. He'd joined the CIA to serve his country, protect its people. He came from a long line of servicemen; in one way or another, the Harris family had been in military or government work for generations. Nobody had ever said the spy business wouldn't be dirty, but Harris was in the middle of an operation dirtier and riskier than any legend whispered in the hallways or written about in books. He wanted to be a hero, but, right now, he felt like a villain.

But as long as Raven remained alive, they still had a chance to win.

———————

THE HOSPITAL finally released Raven three days later. But he was still without answers. Worse, his gun wasn't with the rest of his personal items when the hospital discharged him. The cops had it, obviously. He wondered when he'd see them again. He *should* be under arrest.

Three men barred his access to the elevator. One showed him identification from CNI, Spain's intelligence service. "Mr. Raven?" the man in the middle said. His associates stood behind him. The man was as tall as Raven, looking trim in his business suit.

"Yes."

"CNI. You'll come with us."

Raven didn't resist or argue. The quiet elevator ride led to a quiet car ride, and to the underground garage of CNI headquarters. Presently, they locked Raven in an interrogation room. They'd confiscated his stuff and patted him down for hidden weapons. The pat down didn't take his still-healing injuries into account, and he winced several times. But the

CNI men didn't care. They left him to sit in the silent room and stare at the walls. They'd even taken his watch, so he had no idea how long he sat. But it was a significant amount of time.

When the trim CNI man returned, he was alone. He sat opposite Raven on the metal table. He didn't have any pen or paper for notes. The lines on the man's face were premature. He was too young for them. But The Job had put them there.

"Mr. Raven."

"Yes."

"You're here illegally, under an assumed name; you were found with a weapon, which is a serious violation by itself; and a man with your background in the vicinity of a terrorist incident has caused us great concern."

"Sure."

"Are you going to cooperate, or do we need to make this difficult?"

"I know nothing. I'm here on another matter entirely."

The CNI man folded his arms and looked mad. "Why is it you think you can freely violate sovereign territory, ignore our laws, and do as you wish? I've read your file. I know your reputation. You act like you own the world."

"The *file* you mention really only—"

"What? Tells half the story? I wish you were a wanted man, Mr. Raven, I really do."

"There's a reason I'm not, Mr.—"

The CNI man didn't give his name. "At best, you're looking at being charged with false entry. Worse case, we throw the book at you for setting off a bomb. Get it?"

Now Raven folded his arms. "Do I get a phone call?"

The CNI man smiled with bitterness. He left the chair and then left the room. Raven sat alone once again.

"They aren't going to simply hand him over."

Clark Wilson nodded. The Madrid CIA station chief, Tony Wolfe, wasn't wrong.

"We're going to have to give them everything, I think," Wilson said, "at least as I've been able to put it together."

"It may not help," Wolfe said. "The CNI guys are tough nuts. I'm surprised the Spanish government hasn't filed an official protest with the White House."

The two men rode in the back of an embassy car on the way to CNI headquarters. So far, the CNI only admitted to having Raven in custody, and because of his frequent collaboration with the CIA, they figured Agency representatives should be brought into the conversation. The CIA was within its rights to say they had no *current* association with Sam Raven, but Raven had pulled the CIA's butt out of so many fires in the past, they figured they owed him in return. If Raven didn't have friends in high places, he'd have been left to rot. And if the Spanish government was mad enough, he *would* rot. Just because.

Wilson knew there was more to the story, more to Raven being in Madrid at the time of the bombing. From what he'd learned of the surveillance team's efforts, and what he suspected Sam was up to, the events might even be tied together. Raven didn't realize the connection yet.

A junior CNI officer met Wilson and Wolfe in the lobby and escorted them to the office of the director, a man named Javier Bandara. Gray-haired, moving a little slow, Bandara shook their hands and introduced them to a trim man in a suit. Agent Antonio Ronaldo. Bandara explained Ronaldo had spoken with Raven and advised him on the issues facing him. Bandara wanted to know if the CIA had sent Raven, officially, or unofficially.

Wilson did the talking. Wolfe was there to make sure the

conversation didn't go off the rails and cause a diplomatic problem.

"Sam Raven is not working for us," Wilson said, "and hasn't been an official employee for some time. If you've read his file and spoken with him, you know he follows his own agenda."

"Does his agenda have anything to do with the operation you've been hiding from us, Mr. Wilson?"

"Mr. Raven and I haven't spoken," Wilson said. "I don't know why he's here. I'm hoping to find out."

"Why did you set up this CIA team without telling us?"

Wilson cleared his throat. His boss had given him permission to explain *almost* the entire story.

"And don't lie to me, Mr. Wilson," Bandara said.

Agent Ronaldo, standing beside his boss, watched Wilson with fiery eyes.

"The Spanish Syndicate," Wilson said.

"You were conducting a counter-narcotic investigation?"

"Yes and no."

Bandara sighed. "I'm used to double-talk, Mr. Wilson; I'm hoping we can avoid the cliché this time."

"Yes, we were investigating the syndicate's drug activities. No, we weren't specifically interested in how Alex Riba distributes cocaine and heroin. We wanted to know if the syndicate has a connection to any terrorist groups, specifically jihadist cells operating within Europe. There have been rumors—"

"Did they find such a connection?"

"According to the reports they filed, they were getting close to finding answers when the explosion took place."

"You think the syndicate blew up the building?" Bandara said.

"It looks probable," Wilson said. "My team discovered a connection, they got too close, and Riba needed to take them out. Problem is, he either didn't consider we have their reports, or he didn't care."

"But you don't know for certain what your team found? The reports are incomplete," Bandara said.

"Yes," Wilson admitted.

"We know Riba," the CNI boss continued. "Well, we know *much* about him. If he's going to risk killing those people, he'll have a good reason. Perhaps your theory is correct. We'll be filing an official protest, of course. But at the same time, we need to decide where we go from here."

"What do you have in mind, sir?" Wilson said.

"I suppose it depends on how your boss wants to proceed. Will the investigation continue, or has this bombing set you back?"

"It hurts," Wilson said, "in more ways than one. Whatever data the team collected after their last report is lost."

"A shame," Bandara said. "The loss of life is also regrettable. Be advised this does not give you permission to come into my country and shoot our citizens, whether they're criminals or not. We also will not condone any drone strikes on Riba or his property. Do you understand me?"

"Loud and clear, sir," Wilson said.

Finally, Agent Ronaldo spoke. "If anybody deals with Alex Riba, it will be us."

"Of course," Wilson said.

Bandara spoke again. "You said you haven't seen Mr. Raven?"

"We haven't talked in several months," Wilson said.

"We have him downstairs. I'll allow you ten minutes."

"I was hoping—"

Bandara raised an eyebrow.

Wilson continued. "I was hoping we could make a deal to take Raven with us."

"No," Bandara said. "Agent Ronaldo will show you to the

interrogation room. We'll be moving him to a proper holding cell as soon as you leave. He's facing several charges he needs to answer for."

"All right," Wilson said. The defeat was absolute. He wasn't going to get anywhere with the CNI.

Raven was on his own.

12

The door shut behind Wilson.

Raven looked up. He wanted to smile at the sight of his old friend but found nothing to smile about. He said, "I'm up a shit creek, aren't I?"

"Understatement," Wilson said. He approached the table and sat opposite Raven. "They are *p-i-s-s-e-d*. You really ruffled feathers, this time."

"Why are you here, Clark?"

"We only have ten minutes, so I'll be quick." Wilson explained the antique shop was a CIA front covering a surveillance team investigating the Spanish Syndicate.

Now Raven let out a short laugh.

"What?" Wilson said.

"I'm after Riba, too."

"Really?"

"My own reasons."

"Aren't they always? Did you have any idea—"

"None. I was in the wrong place at the wrong time."

"Who's the woman?"

Raven frowned.

"We saw you on the CCTV footage. You were talking with her prior to the blast."

"Yeah," Raven said. "An informant. Abby Fox. She had the inside straight into Riba's private hideaway. I think she died in the explosion."

"I'll see if I can find what happened to her," Wilson said. "The CCTV footage shows her running into an alley actually, but we don't know what happened after. A lot of bodies haven't been identified yet."

"She ran?"

"Yeah."

Raven's mind raced with the possibility of linking up with her again, but it would have to wait. He had more pressing issues to deal with.

"What about me?" he asked.

"Good luck."

Raven shook his head. "I'm going to have a hell of a time explaining this, Clark."

"You've gotten away with it for so many years, it's ironic something like this puts you in the crosshairs."

"And while I'm dealing with the Spanish government, Alex Riba is out there running unchecked, unchallenged, and now even the CIA doesn't know what he's doing."

THE CUFFS SNAPPED CLOSED behind Raven's back. His shoulders immediately registered the discomfort of having his wrists locked.

Two CNI agents, under the watchful eyes of Bandara and Ronaldo, loaded Raven into the back of a government sedan. They took the front seats. Raven looked at Bandara and Ronaldo, and they looked back. None of the three showed any emotion to each other. They offered only indifference.

The driver put the car in gear and departed CNI headquarters.

Raven sat forward. He was going to be booked and charged. He'd need to bring in his own lawyer. He didn't want to leave his defense to Spain's version of a public defender. He needed someone who could also engage in backroom negotiations in an attempt to get him released and cleared. There was something the Spanish government wanted; something Raven could help with, or even provide. He had to find out what it was. Perhaps a trade would sort everything out. Unless they wanted to make an example out of him to punish the United States. It was an odd punishment, of course. Raven ultimately meant nothing to the US, though he meant a lot to a number of *people* in the US. Maybe they'd find a way to help. There was always a way out. He only had to find the key.

The drive across town was uneventful.

Until a van ignored a red light, screeched to a halt in the middle of an intersection, and blocked the CNI car from going forward.

It took Raven a moment to catch what was happening. The sudden braking by the driver startled him, ripping his mind from his strategic thoughts. The van doors opened, and three men with covered faces jumped out. They wore zipped black jackets, black slacks, and black shoes—their face coverings matched as well. But it wasn't their attire that caught so much of Raven's attention, and the attention of the CNI men up front. It was the shotguns and submachine guns they clutched and pointed at the CNI men. It was their command to get out of the car or die.

One gunman stood in front of the car, aiming through the windshield. The other two approaching either side, pointing their weapons at the CNI man. The agents put up their hands and complied, exiting the car. Both were shoved to the hot pavement and ordered to stay. The man at the front of the car came around to Raven's side, opened the door, and hauled Raven out. He shouted at him to get into the van. Raven, still confused, complied, and jumped into the van to get on his knees, then sat against one wall. The driver, with his face turned away, seemed familiar. His bushy eyebrows stood out the most.

The three gunmen hustled back, shutting the van door, and the driver pressed the gas. The lurch of forward movement tossed Raven onto his side. With his hands cuffed, he had trouble getting up. One of the gunmen helped. He set aside his weapon and used a key on the cuffs. They fell free with a clatter on the van's floor.

"You're a lucky man, Mr. Raven," the driver called. He turned his head. Bushy mustache. Detective Marc Valverde. "I told you, didn't I? *I'll be back?*"

"This wasn't the return I expected," Raven told him.

The van drove on.

VALVERDE PULLED off the road outside the city. He stopped the van on the side of the road where a wooded area began. Raven noticed another car parked there, too, a compact Honda.

"Let's get out and talk," Valverde said.

Raven joined him outside. The fresh air felt good after the stuffiness inside the van.

Valverde said, "We don't speak of this ever again."

"I'm not sure whether I should say thank you or not," Raven told him.

"This Spanish Syndicate. That man Riba. He will not go quietly. I know people he's murdered. My friends too." He gestured to the masked men watching them. "CNI thinks they can throw their weight around and tell us what to do. Well, guess what? Now *we're* calling the shots. And our best shot is *you* getting to finish what you started."

"I'm listening."

"Riba will fight, but he's already hurting. For money, mostly. Competition is cutting into his business, costing men and material; the rivalry has done more to weaken him than two decades' worth of law enforcement effort. Now, he's almost bankrupt. Nobody will cry when Riba takes his last gulp of air."

"Is this all the help I'm going to get?"

"Yes. Except—"

Valverde called to one of his men, who went back into the van an emerged with a black briefcase. He brought the case to Valverde, who handed it to Raven.

"You're going to need this."

Raven took the case and placed it on the trunk of the Honda. Popping the locks, he raised the lid. His Nighthawk Custom Talon and shoulder harness with spare magazines lay inside.

"Use it well," Valverde said, "and don't miss. You won't have more than one opportunity."

Raven closed the case. "And the car?"

"Key is in the ignition. Don't keep it for long."

"I appreciate this, Detective," Raven said.

"I'll catch hell if anybody finds out. The CNI will be looking for you too. See you're hard to find, okay?"

Raven promised he would be.

13

IN THE NO MAN'S LAND OF THE BALKANS, THERE WAS ALWAYS A target on your back.

The words of advice remained fixed in Louis Perry's mind as he led his team through the rough, overgrown terrain. They'd been spoken by a friend who warned Perry not to accept the mission into the Balkans, and added he'd be walking into a lion's den. There weren't four-legged threats to worry about; it was the two-legged variety one had to watch for. The drug traffic through the Balkans was big business for the clans involved. While they might cooperate with each other, now and then, when it served all to do so, bitter rivalries existed between the groups. Sudden violence was a day-to-day reality. The clans also watched for people who didn't belong in the area, who might be attempting to get a toehold on the drug business, access to the infamous "Balkan Pipeline" into Europe. Perry and his merc buddies for sure didn't belong, but they had a job to do. The fact they might get killed at random, by somebody other than their primary target, didn't bother them. Went with the job. Mercenaries aren't like other soldiers. What could scare off the average infantryman only motivated a merc more.

Under moonlight, as they were now, moving was easier. Perry and his team took advantage. They traveled slowly down a rocky slope into a quiet valley. Falling in the dark was dangerous, too. The rocky slope had plenty of sharp points along the ground, most concealed by green vegetation. The valley was a perfect bowl shaped by jagged mountain peaks on the outer edge. It was a lousy place to get killed. But the target was less than two hundred yards away. Perry planned a quick in-and-out hit. Problem was, the only way out was the way they came in. Climbing those jagged mountains wasn't an option. If they messed up, any bad guys who survived the attack would dog their trail all the way out.

When Perry accepted the mission from Martin Bennett, he was told failure of any kind meant disaster for a bigger operation, so they had to do it right.

The crew continued their downward trek, one step at a time, using the natural concealment to their advantage. They were too far out to worry about patrols, but they listened and watched just the same. When Perry, on point, finally raised his right hand, they dropped low and lined up on a ridge overlooking the target. It was a drug lab hidden in the valley, a drug lab belonging to Vasko Popadic's clan. As one of the bigger Balkan drug traffickers, Popadic had pissed off Perry's client; therefore, he had to go. But Martin Bennett wanted Popadic to *hurt* first, and the only way to make him hurt was to wreck what he'd spent so much of his life building.

"All right, eyes sharp," Perry said as his men joined him. The team had impressive credentials. All four were British, former SAS men who'd gone into business for themselves. They'd fought in some of the toughest places around the world, from the Middle East to the depths of Africa and all points in between.

Finn Bell, a wiry and agile man was, at twenty-nine, the youngest on the team. He crouched to Perry's right under big leaves connected to a tree a few feet behind him. He checked the digital map on his mini tablet. "Trail is supposed to continue, but it looks overgrown from here."

Luke Richards, next to Finn, a towering presence with a shaved head, didn't miss the opportunity to tease the younger man. "You scared or something?"

"Stop it," Perry said. Finn and Luke liked to pick on each other. "The trail as-is will be fine. Getting through here after the fight is the bigger concern."

Luke adjusted the strap holding his automatic rifle on his shoulder. "Let's make it count. I'm itching to kill some drug dealers."

Luke Richards was the only member of the team with a personal grudge against the targets. He'd even offered to take the job free of charge, but Martin Bennett refused to allow him to do so. Luke had a cousin who died from a heroin overdose in his teens; since Popadic trafficked in, mostly, heroin, Luke Richards wanted to help put the clan leader out of business. He only wished their mission involved killing Popadic.

Perry kept his eyes on the compound not far away. He told his men to fan out and watch for any patrols. They were close enough now there could be plenty of Popadic troops about. Perry noticed Kit Jordan, the strong silent one, faced their right flank right away. Luke and Finn covered rear and left. Perry wanted to watch the drug lab a little longer before making his move.

He selected a pair of night vision binoculars from the pouch on his left hip and held them to his eyes. The outer perimeter was marked by barbed wire fencing. Intel said it wasn't electrified, but Perry didn't plan on taking the chance. If his plan worked, they wouldn't get close enough to find out. It was the square metal structures he wanted to know more about. Low light glowed inside each one, the light visible through small windows lining the walls. Processing crews would be at work. Where were the guards? Intel suggested there'd be a heavy presence of armed troops—the other reason for his plan. The troops weren't well-trained, reportedly, as Popadic used his experienced fighters elsewhere. He liked putting rookies in the labs to gain experience. Popadic believed the harsh environment he placed his drug labs in was enough of a deterrence. No attacking force would dare venture through the hostile terrain simply to blow up his labs. Perry agreed; getting there sucked, big time. But if he and his team had been motivated enough to tackle the terrain, anybody could. Unless the rival gangs were too lazy. Perry thought there was a Slav joke in there somewhere but couldn't think of any perpetually lazy Slavs to make it work.

Finally, he spotted the sentries. A pair made rounds at each structure to check on things; then they crossed to the far side of the compound, the north side, which Perry couldn't see from his current position. Probably had a barracks there, some form of lodging, where their transportation might also sit.

Perry lowered the binoculars. It would be nice to be a little higher, have a bit more elevation, to see such portions of the lab as the north side. But the ridge was the best highest place to work from, offering the best shot at the actual laboratories. Bennett didn't simply want dead gunmen. Popadic's processing power had to be knocked out.

Perry whispered for Kit, the strong silent one, to leave the right flank and rejoin him. Kit moved so quietly Perry wondered if he broke even one blade of grass.

"Yeah, boss," Kit Jordan said. He was the quiet one, which meant he never argued with orders. He was the typical show up on time, get the job done type of fighter, and Perry wished he had ten more like him. Perry and Kit were the same age but had never served in the same SAS regiment despite being deployed to the same regions over their careers.

"You launch your rockets from here," Perry said. "Building on the right."

"Got it."

Kit carried the same weapons as his teammates. Not only was he armed with a Galil 5.56mm automatic rifle and Glock 9mm pistol, but two LAW rocket launchers were slung across his back. He set the Galil down long enough to remove the rocket launchers and place them on the ground before him. As he did so, Perry called Luke and Finn. The two mercs rejoined, and silently they began their descent along the overgrown trail to the next attack point.

14

AT THE NEXT RIDGE, MAYBE TWENTY YARDS BELOW THE FIRST, Perry ordered Like to set up and prepare to launch his rockets. Perry and Finn continued down the slope.

The jagged rock at their feet, with the overgrown vegetation masking dangerous steps, remained a challenge. Perry remained in the lead, slowly testing each step he made, Finn following his exact movement to duplicate the step to make sure he didn't slip and fall. It was a good strategy until Finn missed his mark. With a startled grunt, he slipped, landed hard on his rear, and fell to the left off the trail. The missile tubes across his back clattered; his rifle buttstock hit the ground; coupled with his grunt, the noises echoed. Perry rushed to his aid.

Perry brushed aside a hanging limb stabbing at his head. Finn's face was twisted in pain, but he bit off any further exclamation.

"It's okay," Finn said.

"Nothing broken?"

"Me or my gear?"

"Both."

"Just hurts like hell. Help me up."

Perry braced himself to lift Finn to his feet, the fallen merc getting his legs under him and rising. He leaned against Perry a moment to catch his breath, then shook him off. They continued their descent, stopping at a cluster of tall, thorny bushes to examine the area. Perry wanted to know if Finn's fall attracted unwanted attention.

They'd stopped at the right time. A bright spotlight flashed on in the middle of the drug compound, the beam slowly shining up the hill, probing the rocky and overgrown area for signs of intruders.

Perry kept his head low behind the bushes. Finn did as well. Perry hoped Luke and Kit were doing the same.

"What's that noise?" Finn said.

"It's—"

"Oh, shit."

"A chopper. Make yourself small."

The whipping rotor blades grew louder in the bowl of the valley. The chopper lifted off from the north end of the drug compound, and Perry cursed. Their intel didn't mention a helicopter; nor had the satellite photos shown one parked. *The usual snafu and now it might get us all killed...*

He wished he could communicate with Luke and Kit, but they'd gone without coms to avoid detection.

The spotlight continued to roam, but it never stopped on anything for long. Perry felt confident the light operators couldn't see them, but the light was probably of more use in directing the chopper pilot where to go. The noise of the helicopter engine was much louder now, the flying machine looming large in the valley confines as it approached the hill-side. The spotlight in the compound switched off. A light below the chopper cockpit replaced it, and the closer distance made the chopper's light much brighter in comparison. Perry covered his eyes. The brightness penetrated the thorny bushes he'd crawled into. He felt the thorns biting through his combat fatigues.

"This is gonna be close," Finn hissed. There was no reason to keep their voices down any longer. The chopper noise drowned them out. The rotor wash also whipped the trees and their long branches to and fro, places breaking off to land near the two mercs. If the drug compound commanders were sending troops up the hill along with the chopper, Perry realized they'd never hear them coming with all the noise.

The chopper hovered above the hillside, shining its own light into the foliage, but Perry wondered how much they really saw. There were too many places to hide, dark crevices the spotlight couldn't illuminate. What were they hoping to see?

When the chopper rotated on its axis, so the starboard side faced the sloping hill, Perry sucked in a gulp of air. A man sat behind a mounted machine gun, and he opened fire. Flame flashed from the muzzle and the hammering of the full-auto salvo joined the chopper's engine noise. The bullets didn't land near Perry and Finn, but elsewhere; maybe where Luke and Kit were hiding. Perry was about to yell for Finn to use his rockets when a flash of flame from Luke's position told him he wasn't the only one thinking it was time to switch to Plan B.

The LAW rocket fired by Luke struck the chopper cabin. The explosion ignited immediately, a ball of fire filling the cabin, blowing the chopper into large and small flaming pieces. The chunks fell to the ground like fiery meteors. The wreckage tumbled down the hillside to the foot of the valley, the lingering trail of fire eating at the foliage and spreading fast.

"Go!" Perry shouted, unslinging his own rocket launchers from his back. Finn did the same. As they extended the tubes for firing, Luke triggered his second rocket into the compound. As they'd planned, he hit one of the metal buildings, and the resulting explosion added more fire and flame to the mix. Smoke from the burning chopper and hillside drifted their way. Perry tried to ignore it, but his eyes stung from contact. Kit fired his rockets, one after the other, at his targets; as the flames from another building reached the sky, Perry and Finn had their LAW launchers shouldered. They sighted their targets and let the first two go. Perry coughed from the smoke. The backblast from the rockets lingered too. More smoke to contend with. But it wasn't time to run, yet. He and Finn discarded their first tubes, shouldering the seconds. They didn't bother to aim. They fired into the inferno. Dropping the tubes where the first set fell, they rushed back up the hill.

The flaming hillside actually worked in their favor, the light from the fire helping them see where they stepped, while at the same time sending a million shadows into a spirited dance all around them. Perry found Luke at the second ridge, in one piece, no holes in him he wasn't born with.

"What made you shoot?" Perry asked as they continued their ascent.

"Came damn close," Luke said. "They shot a branch off a tree that bonked me on the shoulder."

"Let's get Kit," Perry said. He wiped his eyes, the smoke less now, but the flames still uncomfortably close. The blaze was going to spread until it burned itself out. Luckily, it would stay in the valley, and the drug lab would be swallowed by the unstoppable fire. *How appropriate*, Perry thought. There'd be no chance of recovering anything of value because the flames wouldn't stop until there was no more fuel to burn. There'd be a no riding to the rescue for any of Popadic's force. Maybe nature would then have a chance to reclaim the valley for its own and erase the black mark of the drug trade that flourished in the no-man's-land of the Balkans.

Perry, Finn, and Luke climbed a few more feet, then stopped at the first ridge. Kit rose from hiding, and started moving a few feet ahead of them, effectively taking the lead from Perry.

"You guys all right?" Kit said.

"Only some boo-boos," Perry said.

A secondary explosion shook the ground. The mercenaries stopped to look at the flaming compound. The blast knocked down the skeletal remains of three of the metal buildings; they spotted a few burning trucks as well.

"If they had any real troops here—" Luke began.

"They'll choke to death before they burn," Perry said. "Come on. Forget them. Fall back to the camp. We have more of the same on the agenda for tomorrow."

Perry re-took the lead, and his men followed behind him.

15

IT WAS ALWAYS GOING TO COME DOWN TO THIS, THOUGHT VASKO Popadic.

He stood on the balcony of his home on the Bulgarian coast, looking out at the stillness of the Black Sea. He'd been there a week. Popadic liked to move between his residences often, and usually only stayed somewhere a week or two. When there was trouble, when he had a target on his back, he moved more often. Moving was a habit he learned during the Bosnian War, where he also learned how to fight, and supply the black market with whatever it required. The war was where he honed his smuggling skills, and he'd spent his life after the war building one of the bigger drug trafficking clans in the Balkans. He'd learned an important lesson early in the war. Kill your enemies before they have a chance to kill you. But as he faced the Black Sea, he realized he'd misjudged Alex Riba and the Spanish Syndicate.

Popadic wasn't as trim as he once was, during the war. He'd always been short and thick like a fire hydrant. Now, he was a little thicker, but most of it was hard muscle. He had a bald patch on the top of his head, the white circle surrounded by thick dark hair that hadn't departed yet.

The patio doors opened behind him, closed, and another man stepped onto the balcony. Popadic turned. Zelek Siroky wore a brown suit over his burly frame. He wore a thick beard and mustache, and his dark eyes focused on Popadic.

"You called," Siroky said. He stopped near the balcony rail next to his boss.

"Somebody hit one of our drug labs. Blew it to hell."

"Which one?"

"Lab 3."

"And?"

"Your brother is dead, Zelek."

Siroky stiffened. Popadic only saw Siroky's eyes change; the facial hair covered too much of his face. The burly man's eyes didn't show sadness. They showed fury.

"Who did this?"

Popadic faced the water again. He leaned on the rail with both hands clutching the gold-plating. His thick fingers were rough, calloused; they were hands that had killed many during the war.

"I thought I could handle this myself," Popadic said. "I didn't want anybody alarmed. I never suspected we'd be looking at a war."

"You *know* who did this?" Siroky clenched his jaw tight.

Popadic turned to the other man. He and Siroky had been together since the war; they were trusted friends and confidants.

"The man responsible is Alex Riba. He's the leader of the Spanish Syndicate." Popadic explained how Riba came to him with the idea of a merger. He wanted access to Popadic's resources to help get into the Eastern European market. The aggressive moves of the Central American cartels were pushing Riba out of Western Europe.

"I turned him down," Popadic explained further. "It wasn't even a consideration. I didn't think it was important enough to tell you or anybody else. Now, he's trying to get back at me by declaring war. All right—it's war. We need to figure out how we respond."

The burly man stepped closer to Popadic and leaned into his face.

"You should have *warned* us, Vasko."

Popadic didn't flinch or move back. "Yes."

"They killed my *brother*."

"I'm sorry, my friend."

"How did they do it?" Siroky finally moved back, turned, and began to pace.

"A missile attack," Popadic said. "The lab burned to ash. So did most of the valley."

"They have a strike team here?"

"I don't know how large."

"We need to find this team," Siroky said, "and kill them. Hunt them like rabid dogs!"

"You're in charge."

"I'll look for them *myself* if I have to."

"No need for that," Popadic said with a slight smile Siroky couldn't see. He knew his old friend was in no shape to go hiking through no-man's-land.

The drug boss added, "Alerts need to go out. I want every lab, training camp, all of them, on alert. Tell the crews in the cities to remain vigilant. Riba may hit them too."

"Consider it done," Siroky said. He pivoted again to face his boss.

"Go," Popadic said.

Siroky nodded curtly and left the way he'd arrived.

Popadic turned back to watch the stillness of the Black Sea. He watched the water. It looked peaceful; the opposite of how he felt. But he hoped enough meditation, and enough *action*, would give his inner spirit the same stillness as the water.

———

"RAVEN'S ON THE MOVE."

"Did he get out of Spain?"

"Yes."

Martin Bennett closed his laptop and sat straight in his chair. The open windows of his upper-floor office let in the sounds of crashing waves and the cries of seagulls. He wore a short beard now, and island living gave him a permanent tan.

"Where's he heading?"

"No idea."

Bennett faced his number two, Jonas Wasser. Wasser was a tall, broad, spike-haired German who spoke perfect English. He wore narrow, black-framed glasses.

"He might go home to Stockholm. He has a contact there. Oscar something. Oscar *Morey*. The old gangster."

"I'll tell our people to look for him there."

"What about the CIA in Madrid?"

"Currently trying to convince the Spanish government they didn't have a hand in Raven's escape."

Bennett chuckled. "That will keep them spinning for a while. We need Raven free."

"But we also—"

"Need to make sure Riba doesn't think we're fake."

"Yes."

"Do you have any ideas?" Bennett asked.

"I've been in touch with Gustav Burian."

"And?"

"He's available for work."

Bennett pressed his lips together. "Raven better be as good as he used to be if we send Burian after him."

"What if we do nothing?" Wasser said.

"Riba will wonder why we're not taking action. I won't be able to lie to him about Raven's whereabouts. He probably has his own people watching for him too."

"Do I call Gustav again?"

"Do it."

"All right. But he may actually *kill* Raven."

"He won't."

"You're playing chess with real lives, Martin. If this goes bad—"

"I'm the chess *master*, remember? You let me worry about whether it goes bad."

"Raven's not going to be happy."

"Raven will address his complaints to *me*, he always did."

"You sure this is the right way to go?"

Bennett glared at Wasser. He was stating his objections in a different way, but each statement had the same impact. He thought they were going too far. Maybe they were, but Bennett always knew where the line was, when *too far* became actual reality. They weren't there yet. Close, but not yet.

"It's too late to turn back," Bennett told him. "We have the team in the Balkans, and Riba on a short fuse. We're going to need to speed things up at the rate we're going. And Sam Raven is the nuclear torpedo I'm launching into the middle."

"Only one problem," Wasser said.

"*Now* what?"

"How are you going to explain the bombing to Raven? You know him better than I do, but I know him well enough. He's going to demand an account for the CIA people as well as the civilians."

Bennett nodded. His expression turned grim. "He and I will have that conversation, too. How it turns out—well, we'll have to see."

16

GUSTAV BURIAN WAS BORN IN THE CZECH REPUBLIC AND CAME from a bad neighborhood. His criminal path ultimately led him into the freelance assassin role, and he was good at his job.

He wasn't a big man, topping out at five and a half feet bang on, and his slight appearance made him anonymous. He faded into any crowd. He was the Everyman. The one nobody noticed.

His latest assignment had him in Lisbon. Burian sat in a stolen car on a street of narrow homes with only a foot or two between them. He wore dark clothes, a dark jacket, and black gloves. They were lousy homes, as far as Burian was concerned. At least he didn't have to live in them. But his target did. And his target wouldn't have to put up with the narrow space much longer.

Burian's target was a man with a big mouth, a man who planned to testify against his employer on an embezzling case. The target witnessed said embezzling and blew the whistle. The cops didn't think he was under a direct threat, so he had no protection. It was going to be a fatal error.

It was dark, pushing six p.m., and the street was lined with other cars. Lights burned within homes; people were settled in for dinner. Streetlamps along the street provided plenty of light, and when the target passed under the beam of one of those lights, Burian went into motion. He opened the car door, stepped out, and grabbed for the suppressed .22-caliber autoloader under his coat. The gun had an extended trigger guard to accommodate his gloved fingers. He'd had the gun built for him by an expert gunsmith in the Sicilian underground. The pistol bore no manufacturer markings or a serial number.

The target wore a long overcoat and walked with haste. Burian wasn't worried about the coat. The hard-nosed FMJ bullets in his pistol would more than penetrate the fabric.

He crossed the street, watching the target. His dark clothes helped conceal him in the shadows the streetlights didn't reach. He and the target were going to meet a few feet from the door of the target's home. When he reached the sidewalk, a slight turn left put him face-to-face with the whistle blower. The man paused, started to move to the side, but Burian didn't continue. He raised his gun. The target never had a chance to scream.

Burian pulled the trigger rapidly. The pops from the .22 barely made a noticeable sound, producing only a slight echo along the street. Three shots center mass. A fourth between the target's eyes. Burian pivoted and ran back to his car. He didn't hear the target fall.

After starting the engine, Burian eased into the street. No screeching tires, no racing engine, nothing to indicate a speedy getaway.

Now he had to ditch the stolen car. It was another night on the job.

He drove to an alley where he'd parked a back-up car. Once he switched to the rental, Burian continued his drive.

This time, out of the city. He was heading north. He took the on-ramp to the motorway and sped up.

Fifteen minutes into the drive, his phone rang. He picked up the cell from the center console.

"Yes?"

"It's Wasser."

"You need me after all?"

"I'll send you the information. Get back with me when you've had a chance to look it over."

"Okay."

Burian put the phone down and continued driving. He wasn't going to interrupt his escape from Portugal to talk to Wasser. He'd do so only when he was clear and back on home turf.

CLARK WILSON WATCHED his computer screen. The face of his boss, Christopher Fisher, filled the monitor.

"He really left us in a lousy spot, didn't he?" Fisher said.

Wilson took his time responding. Fisher was the Deputy Director of Operations, Wilson's boss, and, like him, a close associate of Raven's. Fisher had been Raven's chief prior to his promotion to DDO, at which point Martin Bennett took over leadership of Ground Branch's covert activities. Raven was closer to Bennett. But Wilson knew Raven had nothing but good things to say about Fisher.

Wilson said, "CNI has registered their displeasure with me, and I'm sure you've heard about their formal protest, right?"

Fisher laughed without humor. "Oh, they've made it clear they aren't happy, for sure. It's going to take a long time to heal this rift, I think. And not only with Raven. They're furious about our surveillance outpost, which is understandable, and we'd be upset too. But Raven makes it worse."

"I've made it clear he isn't under our control, nor did we have anything to do with his escape."

"A Band-Aid. Won't go very far."

"You're right."

"But we can't worry about him. He's following his own agenda, and we'll cross paths with him when the time comes. What I want to know is what you've been doing at the embassy. What's the latest?"

Wilson sat in a private office in the basement of the US Embassy in Madrid, where the CIA kept a small staff. The office walls were bare white, the lights almost too bright, but Wilson needed workspace, and the office had been the only one available.

Wilson had told his assistant, Paul Heinrich, to take care of matters at HQ until he returned. And then there was the conversation with his wife, which hadn't gone well. He'd explained the situation in general terms, unable to be specific, as usual, and while his wife didn't demand he come home, the unspoken hostility in the words she did use still rang in Wilson's mind. She wasn't happy, but Wilson's commitment outweighed personal considerations.

"I've been going through the personnel files of the people who died in the explosion," Wilson said, shifting his attention to written notes. "Each one was an expert in anti-drug activities, and they were focused on the narcotics traffic from the Galician clans on the Iberian Peninsula."

"So Spain and Portugal," Fisher said.

"Right. It's where they started, but not where they finished."

"What do you mean?"

"Some of the clan activity led them to Alex Riba and the Spanish Syndicate, based here in Madrid. There'd been a few clashes between Riba's group and one of the other clans. They began looking into Riba more than the others when the rumors surfaced he might be talking to terrorists, and then somebody blew up the store."

"You're pinning this on Riba then?"

"It could be anybody they looked into," Wilson said, "but the bombing didn't take place until they turned their attention to Riba, and Sam Raven entered the picture."

"And Sam—"

"Is after Riba specifically, yes."

"Did he tell you why?"

"He did not. We didn't have a lot of time when we talked. Said it was for his own reasons."

Fisher sighed. "Raven isn't going to arbitrarily decide to go after somebody. He has to have a reason."

"Um—"

"What, Clark?"

"I *might* have found it."

"What is it?"

Wilson consulted his notes. "Terry Ryker was the leader of the surveillance team. The last report he filed mentions another name in association with Riba. It's an American. One of us. Or *used* to be one of us."

"Jesus, Clark, who?"

"Martin Bennett."

"You're serious?"

"Ryker left a big question mark next to the notation, but according to a recorded conversation between two of Riba's people, Bennett's name came up."

"In what context?"

"Not sure. And Ryker died before he learned more. But he's positive they talked about Bennett coming aboard in some capacity."

"There's your motive for the bombing."

"But how did Riba find out?"

"We don't know yet. He *did* find out. And I bet that's why Raven is poking around too."

"You want me to try and reach him?"

"You mean you haven't already?" Fisher said.

"Only his cell, which he didn't answer. We can start pinging the contacts we know of and tell them we're looking for him."

"He *knows* we're looking for him after he slipped away from Madrid. I *need* to know how he did it, frankly. It's impressive, as usual. I think he'll get back to you when he's ready. You can ask then. Anything else? You look like there's more on your mind."

"What if Raven doesn't know? About Bennett, I mean."

"Not our problem. What I want you to do is dig into Bennett. See if you can find anything to explain what Ryker left behind. Bennett has been off the radar for a long time. Find out what brought him back on the scene and see if you can find where he is currently. It might be a big misunderstanding. We don't have the audio Ryker referred to. We don't have video. We have *nothing*, Clark. It all went up in flames."

"Okay. I'll dig some more."

Fisher scheduled their next check-in for the following day and ended the video call. Wilson looked at his notes.

Deception. Hidden motives. Friends working for enemies. Moral gray areas. All part of the spy business. Wilson shook his head. It was one thing to chase after bad guys for planting a bomb. It was another to find out a former ally allowed the bombing to happen. What exactly was Bennett's role in the Riba syndicate? There was no misunderstanding—Fisher was grasping at non-existent hope. Bennett had *something* to do with the operation, and Raven dealt himself in to discover the truth too. Raven *had* to know.

It was the only reason he'd have kept his mouth shut about it. He didn't want the CIA to know. He didn't want Bennett's old friends and colleagues to know. Because traitors hurt more than their country.

Wilson had to keep looking. He had to follow the evidence. And if Martin Bennett had gone to the dark side, if he'd allowed the deaths of not only CIA personnel but innocent people, the former CIA man would find Raven had no room for forgiveness, no room for compromise, and wasn't interested in mercy.

17

ANYBODY LOOKING TO HIRE RAVEN OR ALERT HIM TO A situation worthy of his attention dealt first with Oscar Morey. If Oscar determined the contact wasn't a threat, he passed word to Raven, who then used his own discretion in arranging a meeting. Raven trusted Oscar enough to often meet a contact after only a minor review. It was a topic Oscar often brought up. He thought Raven took unnecessary risks when setting up a meeting. But Raven, Oscar decided, would have to learn the hard way. After the evidence Oscar planned to show him about Abby Fox, maybe he'd get the point.

Oscar lived in Stockholm, same as Raven, but had a *real* house as opposed to Raven's houseboat. His home sat on the coast of Tranholm, an island in the Lilla Vartan strait. Mainland Stockholm was a short boat or chopper ride away. Oscar had access to both modes of transportation.

Oscar had once been a major player in the European underworld; the proverbial godfather of an organized crime family. Those days were a memory now, and a fading one. Now he dealt information instead of guns and drugs.

Sometimes, he used the information he gathered in unusual ways.

Oscar walked down the short set of steps into the basement of his house. He'd build his "intel center" there, and a young man and young woman ran the computer gear.

"You called?" Oscar said.

The young man turned from his bright monitors. He was thin with frizzy hair, and his name was Tito. A former pickpocket who once tried to lift Oscar's wallet, he now worked to further Oscar's pursuits after being convinced street life wasn't the best choice for a *long* life.

"We got it," Tito said.

"The whole thing?"

"It's cued up if you want to see it." Tito's hand, on the wireless mouse, hovered a cursor over an icon.

"Do I really need to?" Oscar asked.

The young woman, at her own terminal, swallowed a sip of coffee before chiming in, stepping on Tito's answer.

"Don't, Daddy. It's gross old people sex."

Tito laughed. Oscar frowned at his daughter. He had wanted at least one son; what he had instead were three daughters, of which Linnea was the youngest and the one who shared her father's larcenous mind. He figured it was better to keep her close by than risk her going off on her own. Like her mother, she was a tall and skinny blonde.

"Just you wait, young lady," Oscar said.

Tito asked, "What do I do?"

"You got clear faces?"

"No doubt who it is."

"All right. Send it to the Minister of Defense. Tell him if he doesn't stop fooling around on his wife, we'll leak the footage to the net."

"Consider it done." Tito began typing the email.

"We have a guest on the way," Oscar announced. "My

friend, Raven. We'll show him the video we have and I'm sure he'll need a few other things."

"Wow, I finally get to meet him," Linnea said.

Oscar excused himself. According to the time, Raven should be halfway across the strait.

———

THE BOAT RIDE wasn't as choppy as Raven expected. He sat behind Oscar's driver and watched the scenery. He'd seen it all before, but Stockholm always left an impression. And while he wished he was going home to his houseboat, he had to stay on task. Find another link to Alex Riba. Find out if the rumor about Martin Bennett was true.

An anonymous tip sent Raven off on his current mission, a tip that provided very little information. Raven would have ignored the message had Bennett's name not been part of it.

He watched other boat traffic, small crafts running from the mainland to outer islands. Blue water, a lot of green along the two coastlines in view. He preferred the hustle of Stockholm; Oscar liked the solitude of Tranholmen. There were less than four hundred people on the island. Most liked to keep to themselves. Oscar was one of those who preferred privacy to social activity. He'd found the perfect spot to plant roots. And it was a far different life for Oscar than when Raven first met him. Raven's life remained the same. The only change? He was older. They both were. But Oscar didn't have a war to fight. It wasn't time for Raven to stop yet.

Rule One: no roots.

Maybe someday. Not now. His houseboat made for a decent domicile, but he never failed to note it had no real foundation. It sat on *water*.

Oscar's dock grew larger as the boat cut through the Lilla

Vartan. The jetty was one of many sticking out from the edge; it was the only one without more than one boat.

Oscar had a two-tier backyard, the side of the house that faced the water. Large swimming pool on the bottom level, a raised patio with marble columns dividing it from the pool, then the house itself. Raven had only visited once before, more years ago than he cared to remember; he hadn't stayed long.

The breeze whipped at Raven's face. His departure from Madrid would certainly entertain Oscar, and as the boat driver throttled back and cut the motor, Raven rose to help get the boat tied to the dock. He leaped onto the wooden planks, tossed the driver the rope, and tied the other end to the hook on the edge of the dock. Water lapped at the boat with a light slapping sound. As the driver stepped onto the jetty, Raven turned to the sound of Oscar Morey's footsteps.

Oscar followed the sloping steps from the house, which ran beside the patio level and pool. "Looking good, Sam!"

"I feel like hell."

"Why?"

"I've been in the same clothes for two days!"

Oscar laughed and the two men embraced. Oscar was a solid mass of muscle in a stocky frame. He wore sandals, a white polo shirt, and tan cargo shorts.

"You're way too casual," Raven said.

"The benefits of never leaving the house. You should try it."

"Business first. We got a lot to go over."

"Let's get you cleaned up and fed. Then we can talk."

With the boat driver trailing behind them, Raven and Oscar headed up the steps to the house.

18

OSCAR'S WIFE ESTHER WHIPPED TOGETHER A MEAL FOR RAVEN, and Oscar sat with him at the kitchen table. The table was in a crescent nook overlooking the water.

"How'd you get out of Madrid?" Oscar asked after listening to Raven's update.

"By the skin of my teeth. I arrived on my jet with my usual flight crew, but I left them behind. No way I could get through the airport. Instead, I took the car and left the city, called in one or two favors, and off I went. You can imagine I won't be going anywhere near Spain for the near future."

"And your jet?"

"I told the crew to come to Stockholm and stand by."

"What about Abby Fox?"

"I thought she may have died in the blast, but Clark Wilson said he saw her run."

"She did."

"What's your proof?"

"The video."

"The *what*?"

"Finish your food."

Raven ate faster.

OSCAR'S DAUGHTER Linnea ran the video in the basement. They watched on a large wall screen.

"See how she drops behind you prior to the explosion?"

"I didn't notice," Raven said.

"The blast at this point blots out the view, but when we switch to this other camera, further down the street and behind you, and zoom in—"

"There we are. But it's grainy."

"But you can tell who's who."

"Okay."

"Look at her take off down the alley."

Raven watched. He saw himself falling, trying to find cover as the explosion flung debris, chunks of brick, and glass throughout the street. Abby Fox dashed left, into the same alley Raven had stumbled into. But he didn't make for the alley until at least forty seconds after her.

Oscar told Linnea to freeze the picture. She did.

"What do you think?" Oscar said.

"Looks like she survived."

"It *looks* like she set you up."

"How?"

"Next block, Linnea."

Raven asked his question again, but Oscar held up a hand. Raven stopped talking.

The video changed to the opposite end of the alley. No more zoomed-in grainy footage. The shot was crystal clear, and the camera was close enough to capture Abby perfectly. She ran out of the alley, climbed into a car parked on the curb, and sped off.

"She had a *car* ready?" Raven said. Disbelief flooded his face.

"She led you there. Led you to be killed, Sam."

Raven concealed his surprise with a frown, but Oscar saw through the façade.

"You weren't supposed to walk away from there."

"Makes no sense."

"You sure? Alex Riba's syndicate blows up a CIA front at the same time a rumor leaks about Martin Bennett's association with him. How much you want to bet the CIA, and you, at the same time, were digging into the truth of that rumor? Think they tried to kill two birds with one stone?"

"Jesus…"

"It looks like your old boss—"

"Stop, Oscar."

"The video doesn't lie, Sam."

"Does the car belong to Abby?"

Oscar asked his daughter. The young woman read off her computer. Her answer was short.

"It's a rental, hired under a phony name, and the alias turned up a dead end."

"Where is she, Oscar?"

"Home in Paris."

"You're serious?"

"What do I always tell you about not checking people out thoroughly?"

"You vouched for her," Raven said.

"I'm not foolproof. All I know is what's on the record. Your friend Bennett knows I'm the connection to you—"

"And he used her to set me up. This keeps heading for the worst-case scenario."

"I'm sorry, Sam."

"Sounds like I need to get to Paris," Raven said.

He waited until dark.

When Abby Fox finally exited her flat building, she paused in the alcove, glanced left and right, and stepped onto the sidewalk. She wore jeans and a leather jacket with tennis shoes and her long hair bounced on her shoulders. Had the situation been different, she'd have earned more than one glance from Raven. He followed her from the other side of the street and had to watch his step, keep one eye on her while making sure not to crash into any of the other pedestrians on the sidewalk with him. It didn't take long to determine her destination—the corner store. She went inside. Raven watched the door shut behind her and turned around. He made his way back to the flat building.

Another set of eyes watched him do so.

No doorman. He ignored the lobby cameras and took the elevator to Abby's floor. Oscar's people had found her address. He knew where to go. Off the elevator on the fourth floor, he proceeded to 406 and removed a set of lock picks from inside his jacket. Thirty seconds worth of work and he had the knob and deadbolt undone. He entered and locked the door behind him. The apartment was dark and quiet. Raven navigated through with a small flashlight and found the place empty. Turning the flash off, he made himself comfortable on the couch and sat in the dark. He held the Nighthawk Custom .45 on his lap. He didn't expect Abby to be gone very long.

Fifteen minutes later, a key scratched in the locks.

Raven clicked off the safety on the .45.

The door opened and shut. The kitchen light snapped on. Abby busied herself pulling items from a bag and stowing them in the refrigerator. Raven remained in partial darkness. The kitchen light threw a small amount of illumination on him. He watched for her. She'd either exit on one side of the kitchen where he was, or go the opposite way toward the bedroom.

She came around to his side.

Abby stopped short, sucking in a startled breath. She flicked on more lights. Raven held his gun on her casually, but his finger touched the trigger.

"Hello, Abby."

"You're not dead."

"Surprised?"

"I wondered."

"Your client didn't tell you?"

"How much do you know?" she asked.

"I saw video of you getting into the other car. Have a seat. We need to talk."

She took a chair on the opposite side of the room, within reach of a bookcase.

"Hands on your lap, Abby. You make a move and I'll kill you, okay? There won't be another warning."

"I know your reputation, Raven."

She placed both arms on the chair's armrests and crossed her legs at the ankles.

"Start talking," he said. "Who hired you?"

"A cut-out."

"Don't bullshit me, Abby."

"I'm not lying! I don't know who. I was contacted by a representative of the client."

"What were your instructions?"

"Get to you through Oscar Morey. My client knew you were looking for Alex Riba, whoever he is, and told me his name would be the key to catching your attention. Then I was to get you to that street in Madrid. They didn't tell me why. I had no idea there'd be a bomb, I swear. I thought they had set a trap, or something. I was only supposed to lead you there."

"And everything you told me? The pictures?"

"Bogus."

"And you had the car waiting."

"Of course!" she said. "How else was I going to get away?"

"You say you didn't know about the bomb, yet you knew to put some distance between us before the blast?"

"The alley was my marker. They said something would happen when you passed it."

"This is cute," Raven said. "If I was a little dumber, I'd believe you. Who hired you, Abby?"

"I told you—"

"You always go through *representatives* on your jobs?"

"When the client wants to stay behind the scenes, *yes*. You know how it works."

Raven laughed. "I most certainly do *not*. I don't take jobs under those conditions."

"I didn't know there was going to be a bomb," she repeated. "I didn't agree to lead a man to his death, nor did I agree to watch almost sixty civilians get killed in the blast. Not to mention I might have died too. I *certainly* didn't agree to *that*."

She had a point, Raven decided. Instead of threatening her, he could try to get her on his side. Whoever the *cut-out* was might have left a trail. Oscar and his crew could build a lead from even the slightest trace.

"I'm going to put my gun away," Raven said. "I'll trust you not to make any threatening moves."

"Why the truce all of a sudden?" Abbey asked.

Raven holstered his gun under his left arm. "Because you're right. They lied to you. I'm frankly surprised they didn't try to get rid of you as a loose end once they found out I was still alive."

"Who says they won't?"

"What do you mean?"

She scoffed. "You need to start *thinking*, Raven. They might get the idea you'll come looking for *me*."

ANOTHER SET of eyes watched Raven enter Abby's flat building.

After his escape from Lisbon, Gustav Burian, the assassin, took a call from Martin Bennett's number two, Jonas Wasser. Wasser promised to double his usual fee if he detoured to Paris and waited for an opportunity to kill two people, Abby Fox and Sam Raven. Burian did not know the woman, but he knew of Raven, so for this job, he brought in help. After securing an empty office across the street from Abby Fox's building, Burina began his watch. The woman walked a lot, and never went far—a block or two in either direction, as she was close to stores and a couple of restaurants. She drove little. When he watched her depart for her corner store, he expected another long night of nothing happening. But then he spotted Sam Raven crossing the street. When Raven went inside, Burian knew this would be his opportunity. Wasser and Bennett had guessed correctly. Raven wanted a face-to-face with the woman, for reasons he didn't care about. It was none of his business. His job was to eliminate them both, and now he had to prepare for action.

"WHAT DO you suggest we do now, Raven?"

The question broke him from his thoughts. Because, yeah, he wasn't thinking. And the reason he wasn't thinking was because his old friend Martin Bennett might have gone off the deep end, gone to the "dark side," and the idea of him betraying all he'd ever fought, and nearly died, for left Raven in a state of stunned disbelief. It was clouding his judgment. Abby was right. He had to get his head in gear if he was going to find the answers he wanted.

"I suggest," he said, "we join forces and get to the bottom of this."

"Really? A minute ago, you were going to kill me."

"I still could," Raven said, "if you're lying to me."

"Let me tell you a secret, Raven. Abby Fox isn't my real name. My *real* name won't mean anything to you, but it used to be on the employee list of the CIA's Russia desk. Get it?"

"I'm starting to."

"Word is out on the target of the Madrid bomb. The people who hired me killed CIA officers, and that makes me more upset than almost getting killed myself."

"All right."

"We'll work together as you suggest, because I'd like to see whoever did this at the end of *my* gun."

"Then I have some bad news for you. The man responsible used to be CIA too. In fact, he used to be my boss. Does the name Martin Bennett mean anything to you?"

Abby gasped. Her face paled.

GUSTAV BURIAN EXITED the office building and hurried along the sidewalk to a car parked curbside. He whistled twice to signal the driver. This way, the driver didn't open fire with the autoloading pistol hidden on his lap once Burian opened the passenger door and dropped onto the seat.

The driver was local talent, a contact of Burian's. His name was Pavel, and he was from the Czech Republic too.

"We go?" Pavel asked.

"Not yet. They're in the woman's apartment."

Burina reached under the seat to withdraw a compact submachine gun from concealment. He checked the chamber for a cartridge, then rested the weapon on his lap. He watched the front of the flat building through the passenger mirror.

Going inside for a direct assault was out of the question. There were too many ways to get trapped. It was better to wait till the pair hit the street, however long it took.

———————

"You knew him?" Raven said.

"*Knew* him?" Abby said, raising her voice. "I almost *married* him!"

"Your real name is—"

"Guess."

"Callie Webb."

"Bingo."

He'd never met her, but remembered Martin talking about her in the few times they spoke after Raven left the CIA. He'd been out of place with the world after his departure and keeping in touch with old friends helped ease him through the transition to civilian life. Once his new life took hold, he lost touch with everybody. Now, his old team was dead, Mara was MIA somewhere; she didn't want to see him again, and Bennett was an enemy.

An enemy. He hated to use the word when referring to friends. The unfortunate thing was, Bennett wasn't the first. He wouldn't be the last, either.

He spoke to Abby again.

"Why the change? Why are you working freelance?"

"None of your business," she said. "And I'd appreciate it if you called me *Abby*. It took a lot to bury the Webb identity.

You don't know how hard it was, and still is. I'm not going back to it."

Raven nodded. "Okay." He understood—a little. Something had happened to force the change. Something bad. He had his secrets, too, the stuff he never talked about. Only the ghosts of battles past understood. "Abby Fox" had her ghosts too.

"They paid you?" he asked. It was time to get back on track.

"Yes."

"Probably through a shell account, but we can trace it."

"How?"

"My friend Oscar. He's in Stockholm. If we leave now—"

"You have a plane?"

"Yes. It's a Cessna Citation and it's very nice. You can even watch a movie while we fly. Or sleep. I'll be busy updating Oscar."

"I need to pack a few things. Promise not to shoot if I stand?"

Raven promised.

ABBY TOOK fifteen minutes to throw clothes and other items in a tote bag. She filled a second bag with weapons and ammo.

Raven held the door open for her as they stepped onto the sidewalk. There were far fewer pedestrians to contend with now, and fewer cars too. Raven led her up the block to where he parked his rental.

When he heard an engine rev on the street, he turned to look.

The black sedan speeding their way would have looked

like any other car, except for the man leaning out the passenger window with a sub gun.

"Down!"

Raven threw himself at Abby Fox, taking her to the rough concrete. She screamed as he landed on her, and screamed again when the buzz-saw noise of the firing submachine gun sent a swarm of angry hornets their way. The salvo hit a light pole and smacked the brick wall to their left. Sharp bits of brick stung Raven's neck. The car picked up speed and flashed by.

Raven, still atop Abby, looked up. There was no way to chase the car, and he wasn't going to run into the street and shoot back. Screaming bystanders captured his attention, but none appeared hurt. They rose from where they'd hit the deck, talking in jumbles, shaken, but he saw nobody down or wounded. He stood and helped Abby to her feet. She brushed off the front of her clothes.

"Well," she said, "now we know."

"Know what?" Raven was looking in the direction the car had gone. He rubbed the back of his neck. One or more bits of brick had fallen down his back.

"I'm a loose end," she said.

19

ABBY MOVED FAST TO KEEP UP WITH RAVEN. HE WANTED TO BE gone before the police showed up. They reached his car and drove away. He made a phone call to tell his flight crew to get ready for takeoff.

She thought about what he said—about Marty. Was it true? Had her ex not only arranged the bombing, but used her to get Raven to the scene of the explosion? *Did that mean he knew who about her new identity?*

Yes, they'd almost tied the knot, but she broke off the engagement. She found out some things about Martin— thankfully before it was too late. The decision to leave him was the ignition point for her new life. Callie Webb had to disappear.

But she'd learned the hard way that the past always stayed with you. A name change didn't wipe away history. It was a fact she was still trying to come to terms with.

Neither she nor Raven spoke as he drove. She glanced at him. He was focused on the road, checking the mirrors, remaining at the speed limit. Abby faced forward. A small grin pulled at her mouth. Of all the night's revelations, she'd never forget the biggest surprise.

There were worse things in life than having Sam Raven land on top of her.

"What's happening with our mercenaries?" Alex Riba asked.

He spoke into a scrambled telephone while seated on his couch at home. The lights were low. Most of the room was in shadow.

Martin Bennett answered on the other end of the line.

"Louis Perry tells me they found a bunch of Popadic's troops getting onto helicopters. They think they were a search force. There were three copters. Then Perry and his men hit, and now there are zero—unless Popadic has more. We'll see."

"He'll send more out to find them. Perry's team may run out of luck very fast."

"I told him so," Bennett said. "He's confident they can hit all the targets we laid out for them."

"Popadic will send people *here*, too," Riba added.

"You better get busy then."

"Don't *you* have all the answers."

"It's what you're paying me for."

"Don't let it go to your head, Martin."

Bennett chuckled. "You know my background. I've been moving pieces around this global chessboard longer than you've been breathing, Alex."

"Just make sure you don't screw up and end up in checkmate."

"Stay cool and it will all work out."

"What about Sam Raven?"

"You worry about Popadic. I'm taking care of Raven. He's handled."

Riba's woman, Alecia, appeared in the doorway. She looked fresh from a shower and wore a too-small negligee for her voluptuous proportions.

"I have to go," Riba said. He wanted to say more, but arguing with Bennett was like yelling at a rock. He hung up without a goodbye. Placing the phone scrambler on the coffee table before him, he stood and went to her.

"Bed's all ready," she said.

"Lead the way, my darling."

The negligee covered even less of her rear end. She was nice to follow. He liked how her buns and thighs rippled as she walked.

Riba undressed in the bedroom and sat on the edge of the bed. Alecia positioned herself behind him, on her knees, and began massaging his shoulders. Her warm touch, the heat of her body, the scent of her perfume and the scratching points of her fingernails felt good, as usual, but he didn't experience the usual reaction this time.

When she noticed, she stopped.

"Are you okay?"

"No," Riba said. He sighed. "There is much on my mind tonight."

She leaned down to nibble on his neck. Some of her long hair touched him. He groaned softly, but it was all the reaction he mustered. The feel of her silk-covered breasts on his back did nothing for him.

Damn Bennett! Mouthy son of a bitch!

He stood up and helped her off the bed. With a smack on her plump behind, he told her to sleep in her room. He wanted to be alone. He didn't watch her leave.

THE SAME BOAT driver took Raven and Abby across the strait to Oscar's. Abby wore a baseball cap to keep her hair from flying around her head.

"You live here?" she asked.

Raven gestured back toward receding Stockholm. "In the city, yeah." It was all he was willing to commit to. He liked to keep the location of his houseboat a secret.

"Maybe Paris isn't the best place. This sure is an upgrade."

"I like it," Raven told her. He faced forward again. He wanted to focus on what was ahead, not think about what lay behind. Another staple of his life, but not a rule like the other two. What was behind and forgotten sometimes jumped ahead to be dealt with again. And again. But Raven found, no matter how much he reviewed the past, outcomes never changed. Someday, he'd get the hint, and stop trying to change what was set in stone.

The ride was a little bumpier this time, forcing Raven to stay seated and grab for handholds when the bumps came in rapid succession. He noticed Abby didn't grab anything. She took the roughness as part of the ride, a fact of life she couldn't change. Or so he thought. Maybe she didn't care one way or another. He was willing to trust her to help but didn't want her on too long of a leash. He preferred to keep her close in case she attempted any skullduggery. *You're paranoid*, he thought. Or maybe his hypervigilance was a sign he'd been in the fight too long and it was time for a break.

Oscar, once again dressed in a polo shirt and shorts, albeit different ones than last time, met them at the jetty. The boat driver tied up the craft as they talked.

"I'm Oscar Morey," he told Abby, putting out a calloused hand for her to shake. She told him her name.

Raven said, "I hope you can trace whoever wired her money for the Madrid job."

"Always business with this guy," Oscar remarked to Abby. She only grinned in reply.

The walk up to the house impressed Abby, and she said so to Oscar. He told her he barely used the pool, but his wife and daughter liked it very much. He'd done enough swimming in his youth, he added. "It's time for me to rest the old bones," he said.

"You'll only get fat and die, Oscar," Raven said.

"I'm already fat and dying a little every day," Oscar said.

Raven wasn't sure if he should laugh or not. Oscar hadn't sounded like he was joking.

In the basement, only Tito waited for them. He sat in front of his computer station eating spaghetti out of a bowl. He said, "Howdy, boss," with his mouth full.

Oscar addressed Abby. "What did you bring for us to look at?"

Abby set her bags on a nearby table and unzipped one. She pulled out a small laptop and powered it on. After entering her password, she logged onto her bank and handed the computer to Oscar.

"My payments are transferred to this Swiss account," she said. "The most recent one is from the client who hired me for Madrid."

"We'll find him," Oscar said. Tito set aside the bowl and took the laptop. Abby stood beside him. He frowned at her.

"I'm not going to rip you off," he said. "There's no fun in that."

"Still," she said. "I'm your new shadow."

"Don't argue with her," Oscar said.

"Won't argue, boss."

Oscar gestured for Raven to follow him, and the pair left the basement.

20

OSCAR GRABBED TWO BOTTLES OF BEER FROM THE KITCHEN. Raven noticed it was the *second* refrigerator in the kitchen and contained nothing but bottles of beer. Oscar apparently never wanted to run low. He and Raven went out to the pool to sit at a table. A tall umbrella stuck out from the middle, high enough to block the sun but not the view of mainland Stockholm across the strait.

Raven decided there were worse places to be. He should enjoy the peace before the war heated up to a level he might not be ready for.

Oscar's bulk filled the chair he sat in, his legs forming a V as he drank a mouthful of beer.

"All we do is talk on the phone," he said. "I never see you."

Raven agreed it was his fault they hadn't spent any time together in so long.

"You're too busy for your own good," Oscar said. "You gotta tap the brakes now and then. All your running around isn't good for you."

"This one is a little different, Oscar."

"My point exactly. This isn't like the last jackass who

went off the rails. Martin Bennett means a whole lot more to you, which means you can't be objective. You got an emotional angle on this one."

Raven related his conversation with Abby on the subject of not thinking when it came to this particular crusade.

"She has a point."

"And I don't need a lecture from you about it, Oscar."

"I'm only telling you to take it easy. This kind of betrayal —it cuts deep. It hurts, Sam. Trust me. It's the kind you don't recover from. It'll stay with you. So, take it slow. It only ends one way. There's no sense in rushing to get there."

Raven looked at his beer. He hadn't touched it. He tipped back a mouthful and watched the water.

"You act," Oscar said, "in everybody's interest but your own."

"When I do something for myself, something bad happens," Raven said.

"Do me a favor. Stay a few days. It might take that long, anyway, to make the connections you're looking for. We'll find a spare spot for Abby, too. She can bunk with my daughter. We'll keep her close by. I'm not sure if I trust her."

"I'm not sure, either, but I'm giving her the benefit of the doubt for now."

"Will you stay?"

Raven drank more beer. The view across the straight was nice—Stockholm created an oasis, it seemed. The low skyline showed an environment of unlimited potential. A place to recharge. It usually was. But he hadn't spent a lot of time at home, lately.

"We'll stay as long as it takes," Raven said.

"Should be a week. Maybe a day or two less."

Raven chuckled to himself. "Whatever you say, Oscar."

Raven had a restful forty-eight hours at Oscar's place, but Oscar had to admit, after two days, it didn't seem likely they'd make the trace and connections they assumed they would.

"How they moved the money I have no idea," he admitted to Raven and Abby. "We've tried every trick we know. This Bennett guy is good, Sam."

"He learned from the best, and created new tricks of his own," Raven said.

"Tracing the money may not be the way to find him," Oscar continued. "For now, it still looks like finding somebody who knows where Riba hides, and making him talk, is the way to go. Or—"

"Or what?"

"If you want to blow up some of Riba's labs, whack a few of his guys—"

"I don't want a war of attrition. I want to hit the heart of the beast. There has to be somebody we can waterboard. Break a few fingers. You're saying there's nothing?"

"Riba has a lady working in Western Europe, she's French, kind of a big deal—"

Raven's cell rang and interrupted Oscar. Raven told his friend he needed to take the call. It was Clark Wilson calling from Madrid.

Abby asked Raven not to mention her name.

Raven took the call outside, slipping into the woodshed beside the pool for more privacy.

"Clark."

"Where are you, Sam?"

"Stockholm. Am I still on the naughty list?"

"Send the CIA a case of scotch and we may love you again."

"That bad?" Raven couldn't help but crack a grin.

Wilson lowered his voice. "A lot of us are impressed. How'd you do it?"

Raven thought of the risks taken by the Madrid cops who sprung him from the custody of the CNI.

"Magic," he said.

"Tell me when it's over?"

"In person. Oscar tells me I need to slow down a little. What do you have for me? I hate to say we've hit a dead end here, but it looks like we have." He gave no details. Explaining would bring Abby into the conversation.

"I know you're looking for Martin Bennett, Sam. The surveillance team in Madrid was looking for him too, which is why I think they were taken out."

Raven said, "Okay."

"I've been digging into Bennett's history since leaving the Agency, and a couple of things jumped out. He's had regular contact with three other ex-Agency guys, all high-level managers in their day. Bennett worked closely with all three."

"Got names?" Raven asked.

"One is a DC lawyer, then there's a senator. The third made his money in angel investing and lives like a king on the Riviera, big yacht and all. The lawyer is Jagger Malone, the senator is Leon Carter, and our playboy finance guy is Corey Gordon. Now with Malone, Bennett had the least contact. The other two he talks to a lot. Since you're overseas, Corey Gordon may be the best place for you to start."

"How do we handle the other two?"

"I'm going to ask my assistant at the office to call Callen Cord. Remember him?"

Raven indeed remembered the tough freelance operative well. Cord had helped him a great deal on a recent mission in

Paris, no less. He told Wilson he thought Cord was a good choice.

But he wanted to know more about Bennett's three pals.

"Do you think they're involved in whatever scheme Bennett has going?"

"The contact suggests they could be. My money's on co-conspirators. And there's only one way to find out."

"Are you able to forward anything, or am I on my own?"

"I gave you names. Anything more and the boss will be as pissed at me as he is with you."

"Okay, Clark. I'll take it from here. Thanks."

"Anytime," the CIA man said.

Raven ended the call and left the woodshed. He had to update Oscar and Abby. Time for a trip to the French Riviera…

21

CLARK WILSON, STILL WORKING OUT OF THE EMBASSY basement in Madrid, hung up from his call with Raven, then picked up the phone again. He called his office at CIA headquarters. His assistant, Paul Heinrich, answered on the second ring.

Wilson took a few minutes to update Heinrich without mentioning Raven's name. As far as Heinrich knew, Wilson was only relaying information the CIA needed to help solve the bombing in Madrid. He asked Heinrich to schedule a meeting with Callen Cord and see if the freelancer could lend them a hand, at his usual rate, or more, if required. Wilson didn't need to talk to his boss to know they'd want to spare no expense in getting to the bottom of what happened. Heinrich agreed, though he noted he'd have to wait until morning. It was nighttime in the US. Wilson said okay and hung up. He was glad Heinrich reminded him. He had planned to call his wife next. Better to wait till the sun rose on the other side of the world. She was mad enough he was still in Madrid. Waking her up would leave her even more upset with him.

COREY GORDON WAS a rich American playboy and didn't care who knew it. He was a late bloomer though. Most of the playboys who haunted the French Riviera were younger, living off the excess of Daddy's money, and whatever they scraped together based on their own business acumen or social media expertise. But Corey Gordon wasn't the only over-fifty rich dude hanging around, so he had no trouble fitting in. Saint-Tropez, where he docked his yacht and owned a top-floor condo, was a party town. Even during the off-season, like now, there was always something going on. And there were plenty of women for him to pick through too. He had a tremendous number of options. He'd stopped counting how many he'd taken to bed; they all blurred together after a while. One woman had the same parts as any other. He was well aware it was his money and power the women liked; since he'd lacked both prior to getting rich, he wanted to make up for lost time.

Everybody on the Riviera was judged by two things. The location of their apartment, whether it had a view of the shimmering Mediterranean or not—and, for men especially —the size of their yacht. Every season some son of a bitch from Hollywood, Qatar or Saudi Arabia showed up in a new yacht—usually a *big* yacht—and the competition for biggest yacht was fierce. Some were as big as a city block, and not a small city, either.

Gordon wasn't on his own large yacht at the moment. The craft was safely docked with many such others, waiting for the next big party on the ocean when the season began. His condo not only overlooked Saint-Tropez, and the Med coast, but sat atop one of the tallest buildings in the area. His pool was on the roof. He was, literally, king of the hill. Not even the oil barons could top him.

He stood on his balcony like a conquering king over-looking his domain. Dressed in a white terrycloth robe, holding a glass of vodka with ice, he enjoyed the afternoon breeze and the crystal-clear blue water.

He'd traveled a long way to this reward, and he was grateful for every moment.

He lived the opposite of his previous life as a CIA officer. His career had never been exciting; he'd sat behind a desk for ninety percent of it. A few international posts. A little intrigue during the early days of the war on terror. He made the most of his time by making the contacts needed to wisely invest the money he saved. Those investments paid off; now he lived on his own terms. Nobody could take it from him, and it mattered not a bit if he ever invested another penny. He had enough to live on for the rest of his life.

But Corey Gordon had a problem he didn't foresee. There were eyes on him, watching his every move, waiting for a chance to strike. The eyes belonged to Gustav Burian, the Czech assassin. Burian was waiting for Raven and Abby Fox to join the party. And Corey Gordon didn't have any decorations for the occasion.

IT MAY HAVE BEEN OFF-SEASON in Saint-Tropez, but it didn't mean the place still wasn't crowded. Raven and Abby arrived at their hotel by taxi, dressed for the role of a rich couple looking to get away from it all. They checked in to the large two-bedroom suite Raven booked prior to their departure from Stockholm. Abby tested each of the two beds to see which was softer. They were equal, so she took the bedroom which included a master bathroom.

She found Raven on the balcony. There was no water from where they stood, only the city built on sloping hillsides. Lots of white roofs. A few of the buildings and homes had personal touches on display, but the white color ruled.

"Can we see him from here?" she asked.

"Lean over the rail and contort your body to the left, and maybe."

"But he's close."

"Yup. We can walk there."

"Tonight?"

"Why not? We shouldn't waste too much time. I'd like to try for a peek at the place first and look at his yacht. See what kind of security he has."

"I didn't think you were much of a sea-going guy the way you grabbed the handles on Oscar's boat."

"You like falling in the ocean?" he said.

"It's only *water*, Raven. Some people even *drink* it."

CALLEN CORD, freelance operative, lived in a small apartment in McLean, Virginia. When Paul Heinrich of the CIA called and asked for a meeting, he made the appointment for lunch at a burger place he liked downtown.

Once a highly decorated CIA officer, he now worked on his own, often for Western intelligence agencies, but now and then for less savory types. His government employers allowed him to mix with certain undesirables because he brought back useful information the West had an interest in learning. His duplicity was a carefully guarded element to his line of work. Should those he betrayed ever learn about what he did, they'd cut his throat.

He wondered what kind of risks the CIA had for him this time.

Cord sat in a booth near the open kitchen where the scent of grease was strongest. He had his back to a wall, and a full view of the entrance and exit. And the smell didn't bother Cord. When Heinrich arrived, the CIA man's nose twitched when the scent hit him.

"Don't like the smell?" Cord said.

"Do you?" Heinrich asked.

"Reminds me of home. My old man had a place like this when I was a kid. I used to cut fresh potatoes for french fries. I'd come home smelling like grease and pickles and let me tell you, you could shower for a year and not get the smell off." Cord laughed. He had fond memories of growing up and liked to talk about them.

"I hope the food is good."

"Don't worry. Best burgers in town."

The pair ordered from a young waitress with a doughy face and then turned to business.

"You hear about Madrid?" Heinrich opened.

"A few things."

Cord wasn't used to dealing with Heinrich, but he knew the CIA man's boss well enough. Heinrich was younger than the others Cord dealt with, but his age didn't mean he wasn't capable. He looked a little out of place at the diner in his black suit and white shirt though.

"There is a possible connection here locally," Heinrich said, "and we'd like you to investigate." From the briefcase he'd carried in with him, Heinrich handed Cord two glossy photos. One showed the lawyer, Jagger Malone; the other showed Senator Leon Carter. Cord let out a low whistle.

"You know them?"

"Carter, yes," Cord said. "Who doesn't? One of the biggest defense hawks on Capitol Hill. Or the biggest *warmonger*, depending on who you ask. The other guy, ex-Agency, am I right?"

"They both are."

"Carter? Really?"

"It's not a secret, but not talked about much, either."

"These two—"

"Not directly involved, but they may lead us to the man who orchestrated the bombing. We'd like you to have a conversation with them. Do not apply *any* pressure should they refuse to cooperate, am I clear?"

"No. You expect they'll volunteer information that could land them in prison? Or worse?"

"If they resist, withdraw. If we have to get rough, we'll find another way."

"Okay." Cord wasn't in the mood for smacking lawyers around anyway. They tended to be litigious in such matters.

"But there's another thing."

"Right," Cord said. "Who am I asking about?"

Heinrich leaned close. "Martin Bennett."

Cord's eyes widened. "Are you serious?"

"Yeah." Heinrich sat back again.

"I *worked* for Bennett."

"A lot of guys did."

"All right, I'll go ask these two. But, wow, this is a blow. Bennett's gone dirty?"

"We really don't know. We want the answers as much as you do."

"Who's got this covered elsewhere? Surely, it's not only me."

"Unofficially? Sam Raven's on the other end."

"Good. I like Raven."

"He worked for Bennett too."

"We all got skin in the game then."

The waitress returned with their meals, and Cord hoped he still had enough of an appetite despite the grim news. After a couple of bites, Heinrich agreed the diner made the best burgers in town.

22

LOUIS PERRY AND HIS MERCENARY TEAM WERE NEARLY FED UP with the Balkan forest.

The four men were becoming a touch paranoid after looking out for so many dangers during the three days of their mission so far. There weren't only the forces of Serbian drug lord Vasko Popadic to watch out for, but other bandits as well. But it was the third day of their five-day mission, and they were still alive. They wanted to keep the streak going.

Perry and Finn lay prone on the edge of a clearing where half a dozen Popadic troops were preparing to move out. They checked weapons, packs, assorted pieces of gear. The men carried light automatic rifles—old-school Soviet AKMs, by the look of them—with one toting a heavy machine gun. It was their leader who held Perry's attention. He was thicker than the rest, perhaps "burly" was a better description. And when Perry caught a full look at the big man's face, he knew this kill would hurt Popadic more than losing a processing lab or a few helicopters loaded with two-legged cannon fodder.

"Recognize the big guy?" he whispered to Finn.

"Yup," the other merc said.

The burly man was Popadic's close confidant, war buddy, friend, Zelek Siroky. His picture had been among the many of Popadic's associates provided by Martin Bennett. The mercenaries had their faces memorized.

"If we can get rid of him..." Finn let the statement hang.

"Yeah," Perry agreed. He clicked off the safety on his rifle. He figured the distance to be about thirty yards. Finn took aim as well. If one missed, the other would succeed.

The other two mercenaries on the team, Luke and Kit, had taken a similar watch position on the clearing's east side. This time, Perry used the com link to communicate, but only did so by pressing the transmit button on his belt pack twice. The two beeps signified Perry was ready to open fire and Luke and Kit should do likewise when the fireworks began.

Perry took up the slack on his rifle's trigger and felt the break. At the same instant, the rifle fired. The sharp crack of the shot filled the air, followed by Finn's shot. The battle was on.

ZELEK SIROKY HAD INSISTED on going out with the search party after the mercenary team blew up three helicopters' worth of troops. He managed to convince Popadic they needed to reduce the size of the search parties, send each team out separately, and spread out the search pattern. The boss hadn't liked the idea of his friend going into harm's way but knew Siroky wouldn't take no for an answer. The mercs had killed his brother at the processing lab, and the burly man wanted their blood in exchange.

Siroky hadn't seen real combat since the war, but his camo uniform fit his stocky frame well, and the AKM he carried felt natural in his grip. He and his crew had been working a search pattern for twenty-four hours; as he woke his men with loud shouts and told them to hurry and eat and pack up, he was certain they'd run into the mercenaries within a few hours. He'd soon have his revenge. And then they'd take the fight to Alex Riba and the Spanish Syndicate and show them *nobody* messed with Vasko Popadic and lived to talk about it.

Breakfast and the morning routine of his men took an hour. A final inspection of gear and weapons, and they were ready to move out.

Then the first shot split the air.

The *zing* of the bullet passing his head told Siroky he was the target. He hit the ground as another shot passed overhead, yelling for his men to take cover and return fire. But they faced an enemy they couldn't see. The forest was thick, imposing, and easy to hide within. No matter. Siroky had faced similar conditions during the war.

With the AKM rifle set to full-auto, Siroky returned fire, aiming in the direction the first two shots had originated. The rifle kicked against his shoulder with each controlled burst, and he shifted his aim with each pull of the trigger. His men turned their guns in the same direction, and then more enemy fire came from the east side of the clearing. Two of his men screamed as bullets found them, and Siroky yelled for gunners to fire in the new direction. Some tossed grenades, and the sudden explosive blasts shook the ground and rattled eardrums. Smoke from hot barrels filled the clearing. Siroky was flat on his belly, with only the natural terrain providing minor concealment. His big body still made a target if the other side managed to get a clear shot. He pitched a grenade of his own into the forest and followed it with a sustained burst. When the grenade exploded, he hurried to eject his empty magazine and lock a new one into place. Bullets from the enemy continued to fly overhead. They were too far away for precision shooting, or they were shifting positions to avoid the return fire. Either way, staying put was not an option. It was only a matter of time before he was hit. And the rest of his men—the four who remained. Siroky yelled for a man near him to drop a smoke grenade. When the canister popped and filled the clearing with white smoke, the shooting stopped a moment. Siroky shouted for everyone to follow him, and the search party rushed to the west side of the clearing. They'd engage the enemy within the forest. And even the odds a bit more.

"SMOKE!" Finn yelled.

Perry rushed a reload and locked a new magazine into his rifle. He shouted for Luke and Kit to retreat to him and Finn. The Popadic troops were running into the forest, which called for a change in strategy. They couldn't let the search party get away only to fight them again later. Perry wanted them gone so he and his men could focus on their next objective.

When Luke and Kit reached them a moment later, Perry led his men away from the clearing. He kept a picture in his mind of what Siroky and the Popadic troops might be doing. They would have reached the forest by now. Siroky knew the direction of the first shots, and he'd lead his men where he figured Perry to be. Perry wanted to head south, cut west, and circle around the opposing force. It was tough going. The heavy forest and its natural obstacles kept them from running hard, but Siroky and his men faced the same hurdle. And if they spread out too far, Perry would lose sight of his team. But they hustled, boots pounding the soft ground, their heavy breathing evidence of exertion. Perry made the westbound turn gradually, then raised his left arm to order a halt. He and the others found cover. Time to watch and listen.

THEY KILLED MY BROTHER!

Siroky kept the phrase on repeat in his head. He wasn't going to lose sight of the goal. *Revenge.*

He had four men left, trained fighters; how many did the enemy have? He didn't let the lack of an answer slow his assault. With his men in a line behind him, they navigated the thick forest with care, watching every step. The last thing Siroky needed was for somebody to slip and twist an ankle— or worse.

Siroky raised a hand to halt the line. He dropped low with his finger on the trigger of the AKM. He listened. The forest was quiet—even the critters and forest sounds had gone silent when the fight started. The enemy was close. But how close? Siroky looked with his eyes, but his ears did most of the searching, reaching out to hear foreign sounds, the sounds of armed men loaded with gear same as his. They *had* to be close.

One way to find out.

Siroky plucked another grenade from his combat vest. He caught the eye of the trooper a few feet to his left and gestured with the grenade. He wanted them both to throw one, see what happened. The soldier did as instructed, and Siroky pulled the pin. He pitched his high and to the right. The other soldier tossed his in the same direction. The second grenade smacked into a tree and deflected—no matter. The explosive pattern would have the effect Siroky wanted. The twin blasts rattled his ears and the forest. Somebody shouted, and a burst of automatic gunfire raked across Siroky's position. Tree trunks splintered, leaves tore; one of his men cried out. A broken branch landed on Siroky's back. He ignored it and fired the AKM in return, a left-to-right pattern. They were *very* close. Siroky yelled for his men to rush forward, and he was the first to rise and run. He screamed loudly, his battle cry echoing, joining the fury of automatic weapons fire as both sides finally clashed in the same spot.

PERRY FLINCHED when a grenade glanced off the side of a tree and sailed toward him and his teammates.

He shouted, "Incoming!"

The first grenade landed behind them, detonating and showering Perry with bits of forest debris and dirt. The second went off close by—not close enough to hurt, but enough to startle. Perry opened fire first, his Galil 5.56mm rifle spitting lead in rapid succession. The others joined him. Then Perry heard a man yelling, not in pain, but in a rush. A war cry. Getting louder. And then the Popadic force broke through.

Perry ran for the burly man, swinging the Galil's butt-stock toward Siroky's face. The big man ducked and rolled into Perry, taking him down to the ground. Perry landed on his back. With the wind knocked out of him, he struggled to get a breath. Siroky smashed him in the face with the stock of the AKM, and then shifted to get distance in order to fire. Perry rolled. Siroky's burst kicked up dirt where Perry had been. Perry swung his legs in a sweeping kick, connecting with the big man's belly. Siroky howled, falling onto his belly, rolling through thick leaves as Perry tried to get his rifle into action once more, but it was caught under him. Siroky stopped on his back. As the burly man rose and tried to aim again, Perry snapped his right hand to his thigh holster. He snatched out the Glock 9mm and raised the gun. Siroky's big head appeared in the sights. Perry fired once, then again and again. The big man took the hits in the face and chest and pitched over. Perry holstered the pistol and continued to struggle to breathe as he reloaded his rifle. Another Popadic trooper took Siroky's place. Perry stitched him stomach to chest with a short salvo of 5.56mm tumblers.

Luke Richards, the tall merc with the shaved head, shot one Popadic trooper twice in the chest, then pivoted right. Another gunman pushed through thick foliage to get the drop on Finn. Luke fired twice more. The gunner uttered a strangled cry and dropped beside Finn.

"You need another set of eyes," Luke snapped.

"Why bother when I have yours?" Finn said. He scanned for further threats.

"Where's Kit?"

"I lost sight of him in this mess."

Kit Jordan, the strong silent one, was only a few feet away, locked in a hand-to-hand struggle with a Popadic trooper bigger than him. Kit slashed at the man with the barrel of his Galil, breaking the contact; then the trooper pulled a knife and lunged. Kit sidestepped, bringing the stock of his rifle down hard on the gunner's back. The blow didn't stop the man. He turned, slashed with the knife, and Kit kicked him in the balls. The thick combat boot delivered a crushing blow, long enough to stun the gunman, and give Kit time to pump the last rounds in his rifle into the gunman's chest.

"Never bring a knife to a gun battle," he told the corpse.

Perry finally caught his breath, rose halfway, and searched for more targets. But the shooting had stopped. Only the smell of discharged rounds and the cry of a wounded man filled the air. Perry ran to Siroky's body. He started patting his pockets. He heard his men calling out and shouted a reply. Two shots cracked—the wounded man stopped making noise. Shortly, Luke, Kit, and Finn found him. The three looked rough, faces bruised, uniforms covered in mud, but they weren't hurt.

"Start checking the bodies," Perry snapped. "We need anything we can find about other search teams and where they might be looking. Any bad guys still alive?"

"I popped the last one," Kit announced.

"Get going. I want to be out of here in five minutes."

23

COREY GORDON'S FAVORITE NIGHTS WERE PARTY NIGHTS.

Or, in his case, *private* party nights.

Yeah, it was off-season. But there was still action in Saint-Tropez. Instead of going out, Gordon wanted to bring the party inside. He'd called a local "modeling agency" and asked for three women. He welcomed the first guest at ten minutes past nine in the evening; the second showed up ten minutes later. They were both dressed in sexy LBDs, both already lit on either alcohol or drugs. Either one was fine with Gordon, but he was missing the third. A redhead. The first two were blonde and brunette, respectively; Gordon had also hired a redhead. As he poured the champagne and turned on the music, he checked his watch. Had she bailed at the last minute? He'd never met a working girl in Saint-Tropez who ditched a client…

A knock at the door.

There she is!

He left the blonde and brunette dancing in the center of the living room. He hoped they didn't spill their champagne on his polished tile floor. Reaching for the doorknob, grinning like an idiot, anxious at the anticipation of sharing *three* girls for the night, he opened the door. A frown replaced the grin. A blonde-haired woman stood in the doorway, decked out in black like the other two, but black *pants* rather than the tight-fitting almost nothing the other two wore. Plus, she wasn't a redhead.

"No, I asked for a redhead," Corey Gordon told the woman in the doorway. "I already got a blonde. Why the hell am I paying so much if the agency can't keep it straight?"

"Party's over," the woman said.

Corey Gordon noticed the woman had her hands behind her back. He'd missed the detail when he answered, so focused on her not being the girl he asked for. Ancient alarm bells in the back of his mind—the type of early warning he hadn't experienced since his CIA days—started going *bong bong bong* very loudly.

Whoever the woman was, she wasn't there for a party.

At least, not the kind of party Corey Gordon wanted.

ABBY FOX BROUGHT her Glock-17 from behind her back and pointed the muzzle at Gordon's belly. "Inside," she ordered, stepping forward to force Corey Gordon back into the living room. He didn't argue, moving backward with both hands out, even the one holding his drink. He didn't try to toss the champagne in her face. Abby awarded him points for that; he wasn't stupid. But his lack of action probably had more to do with Raven entering immediately after her. He was also dressed in black, and the big .45 autoloader in his hand added an imposing force to his already impressive appearance.

"What is this?" Gordon said.

More points, Abby decided. He didn't stutter.

The two girls stopped dancing and examined Abby and Raven through glassy eyes. Raven went to the stereo and turned off the music. Abby put away her gun and took out a roll of gray duct tape. She herded the women to the side of the room. They shuffled and almost fell and tried to protest in a language she didn't understand, but they listened to her demands. She taped their hands behind their backs, wrapped their ankles, and finished off with a strip across their mouths.

Abby turned her back to the women and took out her gun again. Corey Gordon's eyes darted between her and Raven.

"Tell me what this is!" he demanded. "Are you robbing me? There's no money here."

"We don't want money," Raven told him.

Gordon turned his back to Abby to focus on Raven. "*What* then? I'm not a mind reader!"

NOW RAVEN TOOK OVER.

"I know you aren't a mind reader, Mr. Gordon."

"Wait—"

"Hmmm?"

"I know your face."

"Then it won't take long to remember my name."

"Raven! Sam Raven!"

"Congratulations. You haven't pickled your brain beyond repair."

Another flash of realization crossed Corey Gordon's face. He spun to look at Abby.

"And you—"

"Corey," Raven snapped. "Forget about her. Turn around. Look at *me*."

Gordon turned back to Raven.

"You're not here to rob me," Gordon said, "so what *do* you want?"

"We need to talk," Raven said. "I want to talk about Martin Bennett."

Gordon glanced at the champagne in his left hand. He shrugged and drank the amber fluid down in one gulp. Raven didn't stop him from setting the empty glass on a narrow table placed against the back of a couch. The front room had a nice setup. Open space first, polished tile floor; then a set of couches and love seats facing the wrap-around windows of the second section of the room. The windows looked out on the ocean, and there wasn't a spot on any part of the glass. Corey Gordon kept Windex in business. The walls had tasteful art mounted here and there. An open doorway near Abby revealed a set of stairs to the roof, and the pool up top.

"Do I get to sit down?" Gordon asked Raven.

"No. Stand where you are. Nobody ever forgets *all* the tricks, Mr. Gordon."

"Joke's on you, *Mr.* Raven. I did my best to forget *everything*."

"Tell me about Martin Bennett."

"Well, there's a lot. Can you be more specific?"

"Are you aware he's now affiliated with a drug cartel out of Spain?"

"Are you...serious?"

Raven didn't reply. His silence supplied the answer.

"Oh, wow, you aren't kidding. Um...I need another drink."

"Don't move."

"But—"

"Step away from the table. Further. All right." Raven said to Abby, "Get the glass and give our friend a refill."

Abby left the two taped-up women, who watched the

scene with wide-eyed fright, but made no noises. Abby kept her gun in her right hand, fetched the champagne from the wall bar, and moved behind Gordon to refill the glass. Raven allowed the financier to pick up the glass once Abby moved back to the women.

Raven narrowed his questioning. "What have you done for Martin the last few years? CIA knows he's been talking to you."

Gordon, so far, hadn't tasted his refill. He looked past Raven but answered.

"We only knew each other briefly on the job," he began. "Once I started my business, investing and money management, he found me again. He had cash, Raven. A lot of cash! My job was to make it grow."

"Did you?"

"It took a few years. He's not the richest man in the world, but he ain't hurtin', either."

"How did he get the money?"

"Don't ask, don't tell. It wasn't my concern. Could have been an inheritance, for all I know."

"You had no other interaction?"

"You think I'm involved with a drug cartel?"

Raven gestured around the room. "You tell me."

"No, I *earned* all this! The *honest* way." Finally, he drank a little champagne.

But Raven noticed his hands were shaking.

"Where can I find him, Gordon?" Raven asked.

"No idea. We've only met a few times and the rest of our interaction is telephone or email."

"Video calls?"

"No. Never. He won't do it."

"How often do you talk to him?"

"Lately? Last six months? Not much."

"I want to see his accounts," Raven said. "I want to know

who else may have access, how, and whether any of the data tells me where to find him."

"Why don't I call him?"

Raven liked the idea, but Bennett wasn't dumb enough to let anybody have direct access. Any phone number would go through a variety of cut-outs and redirects before reaching the man himself. Gordon hadn't exaggerated. He indeed forgot much of the basic tradecraft he practiced at the CIA. He should have known better than to suggest a phone trace. Raven told him so, adding, "We'll find him through the accounts. We *always* find people by following their money, remember?"

"It's a bit hazy." Gordon took another drink.

"What do we do with the women?" Raven asked.

"Hey, now, what you want won't take long, then I can get back to my party, right? Who needs a redhead. By the way—"

"Forget about the redhead, Gordon."

"Um, yeah. Guess it doesn't matter, does it?"

24

CALLEN CORD WORE HIS BEST SUIT TO THE MEETING.

He wanted to look like a real client, after all.

The Law Office of Jagger Malone occupied a suite in Downtown DC not far from the Washington Monument. He was on the third floor of a plain white building, but it fit Malone's personality. The outside didn't matter as long as what counted was inside. The office itself was clean and even had current magazines in the waiting room, with a very efficient secretary who answered calls and did paperwork without skipping a beat. Cord waited with his legs crossed, ignoring the magazines. He was focused on how to open the conversation with Malone, because he also knew the other aspect of Malone's personality: he'd go off like a rocket if he thought somebody was wasting his time or insulting him.

When the secretary stopped long enough to answer an intercom buzz from Malone's office, Cord took note. Then she told him to follow her and left her desk with Cord trailing behind. She opened Malone's inner office door after two taps of a knuckle, announced Cord, and allowed the freelance operative into the inner sanctum. The door closed behind him, and Cord fought the urge to think she'd locked him in a cage with a hungry tiger.

Malone stood, offered his hand, and introduced himself. Cord crossed to shake hands and give his own name. Malone may have been pushing seventy, but he looked trim and sharp in his tailored suit. His grip had strength, and his thin face and sharp jaw line didn't betray any softness whatsoever. Malone gestured for Cord to sit. Both men did so, and Malone cleared his throat.

"What problem brings you to my office, Mr. Cord?"

It was hard not to note the condition of the office. Malone didn't go for flash, even in his private work area. A set of battered gray filing cabinets lined the wall to Cord's left. Picture frames of Malone's family sat on top of the cabinets. The desk was clean. A set of pens, desk blotter with calendar, telephone—very spartan. Only what he needed. Blinds covered the window behind him, and they were closed. Cord wondered if Malone ever opened them, or if keeping them closed was a carryover from his CIA days. You didn't want the window open in case a sniper shot at you from the rooftop across the street. Some habits are hard to break.

Cord answered Malone's question. "I represent a group of gentlemen who work for the government. You may know some of them. They have offices at a big building in Langley."

"Excuse me?"

Cord continued. "This isn't an official visit. I'm not on the payroll. I'm doing a friend a favor. But they have a few questions only you can answer."

"I should wring your neck, young man. You come in here to waste my time?"

"Not at all, Mr. Malone. It's only a conversation. A few questions."

Malone said, "I don't have anything to do with those

gentlemen at Langley any longer. What in the world do they want with me?"

"They have a concern about a man named Martin Bennett. Records indicate the two of you have had regular telephone contact, and they'd like to know what you discussed."

"Martin Bennett is no friend of mine," Malone bellowed. "In fact, I only talked to Bennett long enough to tell him to take a fast train to *hell*."

"Really?"

"And to stay out of my life, but I figured that was a given."

"Why?"

"I'll tell you what. I never want to hear the name Martin Bennett ever again, and to make sure I don't, get ready for an earful, young man."

Cord smiled. "I'm all ears, sir."

"Everybody thinks lawyers are scumbags, correct?"

"Not everybody. I like mine."

"Yeah, because he's *your* scumbag. It's like those public opinion polls about Congress. As a group, Americans *hate* Congress, but they *love* their individual representatives. Makes no sense. It shows how most people aren't bright enough to *exist*, let alone *vote*."

"I get it," Cord said.

"Well, I work hard *not* to be a scumbag lawyer. Believe me, I had my moments back at the Pickle Factory. I'm trying to make up for that."

Cord stifled a laugh. No matter how many times he heard "Pickle Factory" used as a euphemism for the CIA, he found it funny.

"I do honest work and don't cheat my clients," Malone continued. "Then Martin *fucking* Bennett comes along. He wanted my legal take on a personal project. Do you want to know what kind of project, Mr. Cord?"

"I do."

"I had such an objection to his idea, I'm throwing attorney-client privilege out the Goddamn window, because if the boys on the seventh floor are onto him, you're going to need to know certain things."

Cord waited.

"Bennett still wants to save the world. He thinks he can do a better job working on his own than he could as part of an official government agency. It's the kind of stuff you talk about at the bar when you're pissed about the red tape you gotta cut through, but the smart guys knew it never went further than talk. Well, Bennett wanted to do it for real, and wanted to know what legal trouble he might face by doing so. I told him he was nuts. Worse, he kept thinking I might want to throw in with him, this time with none of the restraint we had to deal with you-know-where. Again, I told him to kick rocks. Then he tried offering me money, and then I *really* told him what I thought, and haven't heard from him since."

"How did he plan to go about assembling this private army?" Cord asked.

"Freelancers, mercenaries, selected recruits. He said he had the money to make it happen, but I never asked how. He said he wasn't the only one involved, I'd be part of a 'secret council' or some shit, can you believe it? I told him I wouldn't ever take part in turning his God complex into reality."

"What do you mean by *God complex*?"

"Bennett's problem at the office was thinking he was this grand chess master who could move pieces around a board, make sacrifices, and still come out the winner. Home base had to step in so many times to deal with him, I'm surprised he kept his job as long as he did. Were you one of his shooters, by any chance?"

Cord nodded.

"Then you must have more than one story about how Bennett tossed you to the wolves and you only survived because your teeth were sharper."

"There were tough spots, but I never blamed him," Cord said.

"Right, because he was loyal to you boys, wasn't he? Always looking out for his men, right? But I'm telling you, Mr. Cord, there were times he didn't expect you to come home, and it was just another day at the office. If you survived, it was because you were good. If not, you were another cog in whatever scheme he was working to accomplish his mission."

"Interesting."

"A sobering thought, isn't it?"

"Would this attitude of Bennett's extend to civilians?"

"Now it's *my* turn to ask what you mean."

"The Madrid bombing."

"That was *Bennett*?"

"We have a strong suspicion." Cord explained the investigation, Bennett's alleged connection with the Spanish Syndicate, and the Madrid bombing and its aftermath.

Malone's bluster faded. His face took on a look of grave concern. Even his tone of voice softened when he replied.

"My goodness, he's gone mad."

"What's your guess?"

"My guess? He hasn't *joined* the drug syndicate, Mr. Cord, he's trying to *destroy* it. And whatever his reasons are, he's not unwilling to let innocent people and CIA employees die to further his goal. Which means he'll do something *worse* if anybody tries to stop him. You must be careful, son, seriously."

"I'm only talking to you. We have others, overseas, collecting more clues. Sam Raven, for one. Remember him?"

"Good man, that Raven. I was one of the people who pushed him out the door after he got his ass captured in Afghanistan for the second time. Hated to do it, but he got sloppy and it cost us. Ask him about it."

"Based on what you told me, I'm going to have to update him in person."

"Who else are you talking to?"

Cord said, "Senator Carter."

"Leon? That son of a bitch. Yeah, he'll be one of Bennett's inner circle. Bet on it. Those two were simpatico back in the old days. Be ready for trouble when you talk to him. Maybe, you know, take appropriate steps."

The old spymaster isn't dead, Cord thought. He figured Malone's words were very good advice indeed.

"Do you know where Bennett's hiding?" Cord asked.

"Start looking at private islands. I know he bought one. Bad guys always have private islands, don't they? He tried to get me to come out and see him. That's all I know about it."

"I'll tell my client." Cord rose. Malone did too.

"Good luck, young man. Wish I could do more."

"You've done more than you know, Mr. Malone."

25

CORD RETURNED TO HIS CAR AND CALLED HEINRICH AT CIA headquarters. He cracked a window to let air in, which also let in the street sounds. Moving cars, rumbling buses. Cord turned up the volume on his phone to hear better. Heinrick didn't interrupt his story, took careful notes and asked questions. When they finished, Heinrich summed up Cord's reaction to Malone's tale in three words.

"This is crazy."

"I know it's nighttime in Madrid, but this is worth waking up Wilson for."

"Hell, it's worth going straight to the DCI."

"Any word from Raven?"

"He talks to Clark, not me," Heinrich said.

"Make it known I'd like to join him. After I deal with Senator Carter."

"Do you think you'll need help with Carter?"

"Extra muscle, you mean? Not at all. I know how to handle goons like Leon Carter, don't worry. You just get this info to Wilson."

"On it," Heinrich said.

A GENTLE NUDGE woke Alex Riba, leader of the Spanish Syndicate, from sleep. He opened his eyes. There was no need to be afraid of the nudge. He knew from whom it came. Alecia stood beside the bed, holding a cordless phone.

"What is it?"

She was hard to see in the dark room. He reached out and turned on the nightstand lamp. The light lit the corner of the room, but left most of it in darkness, still. Alecia wore her hair tied back and a thick white robe with pink trim.

"It's Popadic," she said quietly.

"At this hour?"

She shrugged.

"Okay." He took the phone. She turned and left the room. Riba said hello as she pulled the bedroom door closed.

Popadic answered curtly.

"It's time we talked, Riba."

Riba grinned despite the sleep fog he felt. His pulse spiked with anticipation. He sat up in bed, resting against the wooden headboard, and said, "Okay. Let's talk."

"We can blast each other until there's nothing left, but it won't do either of us any good. Maybe it's best if we come to an agreement after all."

I got him right where I want him. Riba didn't know how, and wasn't going to ask the Serbian drug boss, but it was plain Bennett's mercenaries did more than Riba thought possible. They made Popadic *hurt.*

Excellent. Very good indeed.

"I agree. Violence is pointless, and only costs money. Is it safe to say you're now open to a merger?"

"What are your terms?" the Serbian drug lord asked. He spoke without energy. He sounded defeated. *We hurt him bad,* Riba thought.

"Same as before," Riba said. Now wasn't the time to gloat. He'd made his point, Popadic realized his error, and now it was time to make peace. He continued, "You keep one hundred percent of your business. You allow us access to the Balkan Pipeline and take a seventy-thirty split of our product. I'm not trying to take over. I need the Eastern European market. We won't duplicate each other. I'll supply the merchandise you don't, and we'll both prosper."

"All right."

"We should meet to put this agreement in final form."

"On one condition."

"Which is?" Riba asked.

"I want your strike force. I want them dead."

"Of course. They're mercenaries. They mean nothing to me."

"Get with your people and we'll settle on a meet. In the meantime, tell me where to find these mercenaries."

"They'll be delivered on a silver platter, Vasko."

"You know where to reach me."

The line clicked in Riba's ear. He turned off the phone and set it on the nightstand. He didn't turn off the light.

The clock on the nightstand read three a.m. He wasn't getting back to sleep now, but he didn't want to leave his bed either.

The Balkan Pipeline. It was the prize. The secret route Popadic and others like him used to transport drugs, guns, whatever they needed to move into other parts of the world. It was in the no-man's-land of the Balkans, a death trap for any authorities attempting to close it down. And Riba needed it because he had more than drug smuggling in mind. To save his cartel, he needed to offer certain parties access to the pipeline so they could go where they wanted without detection. Certain parties who believed in striking at who they called *infidels*. And they were willing to pay large sums of money for the opportunity.

————————

ABBY REMAINED in the front room with the blonde and brunette. Corey Gordon led Raven into his private office, where the financier turned on his desktop and let Raven watch over his shoulder. Raven still held the .45, and didn't let Gordon forget the gun's presence. After a few minutes of watching the financier behind the computer, Raven began to wonder if the gun made any difference. Gordon was so focused on calling up the accounts Raven wanted to see, he didn't pay attention to Raven or the pistol.

"Here is Martin's folder, and his accounts." Gordon opened the files, all spreadsheets, and highlighted each one. "This is money currently invested, here are dividends from past investments, and here is his total cash, liquid, as of this moment."

"Very substantial," Raven remarked. "I should have you manage my money."

"I'm good at my job."

"All right, I see the amounts, now tell me what happens on the other end of the cash."

"These are Swiss accounts with the usual private arrangements," Gordon said. "I'll make deposits or transfers based on standing instructions, but I can't tell you what happens after I do something. There's no way to trace the account activity from here. You understand, right?"

"Which is why you're going to forward this to my buddy in Stockholm."

"But—"

"Corey?"

Raven didn't have to add anything. The threat behind his tone did the work.

"Okay. Um…I can give you Cloud access. Your own password and username and you can poke around all you want."

"And as soon as I'm gone, you'll lock me out. Then what do we do, Corey?"

Gordon turned in his seat to look up at Raven. Now he saw the Nighthawk Custom pistol, and he gulped before speaking. "We've come this far. And you're telling me Martin is engaged in illegal activity. I don't need anything illegal on my conscience, nor do I want Interpol or any other law enforcement outfit digging into my shit because they think I co-conspired. You can have it all, I don't care."

Raven took out his smartphone and called Oscar. The big man wasn't available, so Raven spoke to Oscar's daughter instead. He told Linnea the username and password info Gordon provided, and watched Gordon make the Bennett accounts accessible from the Cloud. Raven gave her the rundown on what he wanted. Trace the account activity to the other end, where Martin might be found, then use his internet data to track his location. It sounded easy; it wasn't. Like the telephone, there were many ways to cover one's tracks in cyberspace, but there were more weaknesses to exploit. He hoped Oscar's people were up to the challenge.

"Okay, Gordon, get up. Let's go back to the other room."

"What's that noise?"

Raven heard it, too.

The whipping rotor blades of a helicopter.

Getting closer…

26

GUSTAV BURIAN, THE CZECK ASSASSIN, SAT IN THE HELICOPTER cabin with two hired associates. They were what he called his Corsican Cannon Foder. Crooks for hire who didn't care what the job was as long as they received compensation. Burian paid them up front, provided each with a CZ Scorpion submachine gun, and said, "Let's go for a helicopter ride."

The blacked-out chopper blended into the night sky but made a lot of noise. Such sounds were familiar in Saint-Tropez. Nobody would bother with the chopper's presence until the shooting started—and Burian had a way of even delaying frantic calls to the police. The sub guns he and the Corsicans carried had suppressor tubes attached. But when Sam Raven let go with his .45, *if* he did, was when people might notice the helicopter wasn't like the others they often saw and had nothing to do with a jet-set billionaire making a late-night rooftop arrival at his private residence.

The pilot started out with a pass over the ocean, then swept left, over the city, bright lights below blurring as the chopper arced toward Gordon's building. Lights around the rooftop pool served as a beacon. The pilot aimed for the lights, and shortly the balcony came into view. The chopper flew closer. Raven, Abby Fox, and the financier would hear their arrival, but Burian had no way of avoiding the early warning. It was the reason he'd brought along the Corsican Cannon Fodder. They'd go in first.

Closer. The tall steel-and-glass structure towered above its neighbors. The balcony loomed large, steel railing up front, the wrap-around window on the other end. Burian threw open the port side cabin door, secured his rope, and yelled for his compatriots to do the same. As leader, he wanted to be the first one down, and he examined the wide balcony for positions of cover. Picking out his landing spot, he waited for the pilot to slow to a hover. He tossed the loose end of the rope; it uncoiled quickly, slapping onto the concrete deck of the balcony. Burian stepped out and slid down the taut nylon rope faster than he thought he would. His stomach was still somewhere in his throat when he touched down. The Corsicans followed quickly, CZ Scorpions up and ready. Burian fired through the wrap-around glass. The panes shattered, spreading out onto the balcony, as well as into the condo itself. His men rushed forward searching for targets.

ABBY FOX DIDN'T STOP to ask why a helicopter was approaching the condo.

After the drive-by murder attempt in Paris, there was only one reason.

She jammed her Glock 9mm in the waistband of her black jeans and pulled a knife from a rear pocket. Flicking open the blade, she spoke hurriedly to assure the blonde and brunette she wasn't going to hurt them. Their wide eyes watched her cut the tape around their ankles. The blade cut smoothly, with only a flick of Abby's wrist. She stowed the knife and helped the women stand. She did not cut the tape at their wrists.

"Where's the bedroom?" Abby asked.

The chopper noise increased. The windows began to vibrate. Almost there. Abby's mind raced. How many gunners were aboard? She had to get the women clear.

The blonde took the lead. Running awkwardly in her heels, trying to balance with her hands behind her back, she hurried across the room to a hallway. Abby nudged the hesitating brunette after her and followed close behind. Once in the wide master bedroom with its ridiculous oval bed in the center, Abby told them to get on the floor and stay put. She pulled the door shut and ran back down the hall to the corner. Taking a knee, Abby took out her gun and waited for the fireworks. A peek around the corner revealed three shooters fast-roping onto the balcony. Their combat black blended with the night sky behind them, but their silhouettes gave away movement.

The wrap-around glass and balcony doors shattered under the impact of a suppressed salvo of sub gun fire. A mess of broken glass landed outside and spread across the floor inside. The bullets coming through the opening smacked into the walls, destroying Corey Gordon's knickknacks and pockmarking his expensive paintings. Larger chunks of glass fell out of the metal window and doorframes and crashed into pieces on impact. Abby ducked back. She had eighteen rounds in the Glock-17. Eighteen rounds against three men with sub guns. Only one spare magazine, because who was expecting a war? She couldn't hold them off alone.

Where's Raven?

Abby looked across the living room to the doorway

Raven and Gordon had gone through. The door was partially closed, and she couldn't see inside. Were they finished with the account files?

Hurry, Raven!

The first two gunmen ran into the condo.

COREY GORDON KNEW ENOUGH to scoot back from his desk and slide underneath as the gunfire in the living room wreaked havoc. He was shaking.

"Do you have any weapons?" Raven asked. He kneeled behind the desk, resting his gun on the edge, pointing at the door.

Gordon stuttered but answered. "Are you *kidding*?"

"Don't move till I come get you."

"What if you get killed?"

"Punt."

Gordon wailed as Raven ran to the door. He'd left it partially closed when he and Gordon entered the office. Abby spotted him; she held up three fingers. Lights mounted on sub guns snapped on and filled the darkened living room with powerful beams. Raven dropped to his belly, but his gun tapped the doorframe as he moved. *Aw, hell!* One of the light beams swung his way. The gunman fired, his suppressor turning the shots into rapid thumps, splintering part of the doorframe, and punching a clean hole through the door itself. Chunks of the doorframe landed on Raven, but he had no time to deal with them. He tried to get a sight picture and return fire, but the bright light's glare made focus impossible through his squinting eyes. Another beam swung toward the door. Raven fired anyway, two shots, a pause, two more. The blasts were loud in the small room, but he achieved the desired result. The beams swung away as the shooters sought cover.

Abby opened fire, her first double-tap taking down one gunman. He fell back with a useless burst drilling through the ceiling and his light beam tumbling wildly as his dead hands lost their grip on the Scorpion. Raven still had spots in his eyes, but he fired twice more. Both shots hit nothing. The shooter he aimed at vanished behind a balcony-facing love seat.

Another suppressed burst of enemy gunfire slammed into the doorway. Raven moved back further along the wall. Corey Gordon, still squirming under his desk, kept up a whiny and screechy soundtrack to the gun battle. Raven *almost* wanted to shoot him out of spite. But he knew a darker truth. If he and Abby didn't end the fight soon, he and the playboy financier would be trapped in the office with no way out.

Raven recharged the Nighthawk with a spare 10-round magazine from the pouch under his right arm. Abby kept up a steady stream of fire, spacing her shots a few seconds apart, but the lack of kills meant she had the same problem as Raven. *The damn lights!* But they were keeping the enemy at bay. They didn't have a fix on Raven and Abby either. It was almost a stalemate. The light beams continued to streak across the living room, and when one showed a solid silhouette behind it, Raven took his chance. The gunner was moving to a new position, but he never made it. Raven fired.

The pistol discharged once, twice; flame flashed from the muzzle on the second shot. The silhouetted gunman pitched over, crashing onto a glass coffee table before thudding onto the carpet. Raven backed away from the door some more as return fire shredded the frame. Further impacts on the door forced it back, exposing Raven to the full beam of light attached to the enemy's gun.

Raven fired blind. The light didn't shift away. Abby's Glock cracked. The beam swung away as the gunman fell. Raven held his position. The light glowed behind one of Gordon's couches. It didn't move again.

"Raven?" Abby called.

"I'm here!" he shouted back.

Raven leaped to his feet and cleared the doorway. He ran to the nearest body to check it, confirmed the man was dead, and moved to the second. Abby was beside the third when Raven reached her. She took the light off the dead man's gun and shined the beam on his face.

"He's the one from Paris," Raven said. He'd only had a short glimpse of the man during the drive-by attempt, but it wasn't a face he'd forget. "Get a picture. I'll get the other two."

As Raven used his smart phone to snap one picture and then moved to the other gunman, noting the Corsican features of each man, Corey Gordon emerged from his office. He leaned in the wrecked doorway to survey the damage.

He left the doorway and began slapping light switches, bathing the room in brightness.

"This is outrageous!" He scanned the room, the ruined fixtures, the holes in the walls. Then his face paled. "Where are the girls?"

"Bedroom," Abby snapped.

Corey Gordon ran down the hall.

Raven put his phone away after checking the pictures he took. They were clear, the faces visible. He put the phone away and went to Abby.

"We need to go."

"What about—"

"Let him deal with this."

Corey Gordon returned with his arms around both girls.

He'd freed their wrists, but the tape remained stuck to their skin. They looked shaken and confused but they weren't hurt.

"This is awful!" the financier yelled. "Just—oh, my, at least the liquor is okay." He glanced at both frightened girls. "We can move the party to my yacht. What do you think?"

Raven scoffed. Abby stifled a laugh. Both headed for the door.

"Hey, Raven!"

Raven stopped and turned back.

"Get the bastard!"

Raven grinned. He followed Abby out to the hall.

27

LOUIS PERRY WASN'T SURE ABOUT THE MEET. YES, HE AND HIS crew needed to resupply, but the remains of the bombed-out village he examined from afar looked more like a trap. A place to get stuck. But the idea of a night sleeping *inside* rather than out also had an appeal.

"I'm not sure about this," Finn said.

Perry looked at his teammate. He'd said out loud what Perry was thinking. The merc leader examined the faces of Luke and Kit. They wore their doubt plainly.

"Why did the boss tell us to meet the resupply team here?" Kit asked.

"Easy to find on a map," Perry said. It was a guess, but more than likely the truth. The resupply team wanted to be in and out as fast as possible.

Most of the old village was overgrown with tall grass. Flimsy wooden structures remained. Perry didn't trust any of them to be safe to occupy. They didn't need walls falling down on them while trying to cook. Or sleep. The best option looked like the stone-walled church at the far end of the crumbled street. The roof looked intact. At least the building wouldn't have a high probability of falling over if the wind blew too hard.

"The church is the place to hole up," Perry said. "Short wait till tomorrow morning."

"Says you," Luke said.

"We stay in formation, do a security sweep, and then make camp in the church."

"Should be warmer than outside," Finn said. The nights had been cold for sure.

Luke said, "Don't like your tootsies freezing?"

"Stop it," Perry said. "Let's go."

The four mercenaries moved forward at a slow pace. They carried everything with them from their original base camp, and their packs bulged with weight. They stayed to the left side of the crumbled road, checking behind every plank of wood, every smashed brick wall, every ditch. The remains and ruins of the old village were a stark reminder of the reality of the Balkan war. It didn't take much to wreck what somebody spent a lifetime building. In the end, the cockroaches inherited everything. The four men scared away a few wild critters, but nothing to worry about. The only thing they thought about were two-legged threats, and there was no end to the amount they'd face if they stayed in the Balkans any longer. But Bennett had two more targets in mind. He'd explained about them during Perry's last check-in and promised a resupply of ammo and food for the extended stay. And, of course, there'd be a bonus.

Before they cleared the first block, the mercenaries knew they were alone. Perry directed them to the church, but they didn't drop their guard. Each man kept his rifle ready in case of surprise. But the only surprise they found was a solid oak door at the church entrance, which led into a sanctuary with bare wooden planks for a floor, and no pews. No icons. No cross at the forward altar. Some of the stained-glass windows were broken. The interior was an empty shell. Well, plenty of room for the guys to spread out and get some rest before the next phase of the mission.

"Check the place," Perry called. His voice echoed. He cut left, into the room where the candles had once been. He stood a moment remembering his childhood and the Catholic church his family had attended. He'd left religion behind a long time ago, but he had a strong sense he should return as he gazed at the empty room and the debris scattered across the floor.

Two short hallways split from the altar in either direction. One was lined with offices, and the remains of bedrooms lined the other. Only one of the rooms contained an intact metal bed frame. The rest only held more junk tossed aside by whoever last looted the place.

Luke found the ladder to the bell tower. He reported the bell was intact if anybody cared. Perry noted it would be a good lookout spot. The merc leader checked for other exits but found none. As he walked along the walls, he decided the church was perfect. No back exit, no side exit; the only way in or out was the front door.

Perry gathered his men together at the steps of where the altar had once stood. "We'll keep watch from the front windows, four-hour rotation. Two-hour rotation overnight. The truck should be here by nine a.m. tomorrow and then we go back to war."

"Unless somebody intercepts the truck," Luke grumbled.

Perry let it lie.

CANS OF STERNO burned under the pan in which Luke cooked the team's dinner, using a mix of MRE rations from everybody's packs. Kit had the watch at the front, and as the sun went down, reported nothing of interest. He did spot a couple of jackrabbits running through, but they didn't stay for dinner.

Later, Perry had trouble sleeping, and not because he kept his rifle next to him and his Glock in the thigh holster on his right leg. He lay on top of his sleeping bag staring at the rafters holding up the roof. How the church had survived the war while the rest of the village suffered and rotted, he didn't know, but maybe, in war, one side or the other knew when to exercise restraint. Blow up a house, but don't hurt the church. Did it make sense? To Perry, the answer was no. If you were going to destroy one building, destroy them all. God wasn't going to do any favors for you because you spared a church but destroyed a house with three kids hiding inside. As a man who had seen too much war in his lifetime, he knew there were soldiers who believed the opposite was true. It was okay to kill an enemy in war, but don't blow up God's house, or there will be trouble. War didn't make sense. But it wasn't Perry's job to philosophize. It was his job to fight the wars his was hired to fight.

Presently he dozed off until Kit woke him for his part of the night watch.

MORE COOKED MREs over the Sterno the next morning. Perry took over the morning watch out of sheer anxiousness. He kept pacing as he ate from his metal plate, checking his watch over and over—sometimes only seconds apart. Finally, he took over at the front window to have something else to occupy his mind.

By eight a.m., he told the others to find positions outside and watch for the resupply truck. Finn and Kit covered the road passing the church. Even in its crumbled state, with weeds and grass growing through the cracks, it was the only route available to the truck. Luke climbed the ladder to the top of the bell tower for a 360-degree view over the village. The team stayed in touch via the wireless com links they wore in their left ears.

From the church entryway, Perry said, "When the truck arrives, only I will meet it. The rest of you stay hidden."

Kit replied, "You expect trouble, boss?"

"No," Perry said. Not true. And he hoped they didn't think he was lying. "I'm in charge, so I should meet the truck. Plus, I have the password."

Good save, he thought. One that should assure his men all was well. And maybe it was. But Perry had a feeling, ever since searching the church upon their arrival, something wasn't right. Why the extended mission? Hadn't they met their goal? What did Bennett expect to gain?

Why didn't I tell him to go to hell?

The deal was five days only.

No merc ever *doesn't* expect a double cross, especially when working for somebody like Martin Bennett. Perry had done enough secret work for Bennett's private intelligence group to know the former CIA man kept the cards close to his chest. It was the familiarity with the group that made Perry say okay, he realized. Bennett had never cheated him before. Why would he now?

Am I talking myself out of being paranoid?

Sounds like it.

Perry decided to calm down. He'd feel better once the truck delivered the needed supplies. They were low on food and especially low on ammunition.

"Truck is coming," Finn reported. "South end of the road. Approaching the rear of the church."

Perry didn't move from the front steps. "What can you see?"

"Standard US deuce-and-a-half. Covered back, canvas canopy. Two men in the cab."

"They armed?" *Hell, they'd be dumb if they weren't...*

"Passenger has a Kalashnikov," Finn said.

"Okay."

Luke reported spotting the truck from the tower. "One minute ETA," he added.

Perry said, "Kit, come closer to the church."

"Already moving, boss."

Perry jacked a cartridge into the chamber of his Galil 5.56mm rifle and left the steps. He went to the corner of the church close to the road, but only peeked around.

I have no reason not to trust Bennett...

But I also can't shake my doubts.

"I'm coming closer too," Finn said.

"Copy," Perry replied.

Luke above. Finn behind. Him and Kit in front.

We have it covered...

But doubt still clouded Perry's mind.

"Be ready for anything, boys," he said.

The chugging truck came around a bend and straightened as it neared the church.

THE MAN in the passenger seat of the truck said, "This road is terrible." His name was Simeon, and he took a hand off his AK rifle to grasp a handle on the doorframe. The bumps and jolts were constant, rocking the truck back and forth.

The driver, a man named Bogdan, did not reply. He was focused on navigating the ruined road. It beat the dirt paths they'd followed to get here, but no matter how he tried to maneuver around the worst of the damage, the jolts didn't stop. He hoped the gun crew in back wasn't too beat up.

Their boss, Vasko Popadic, had selected Bogdan and Simeon for the mission, and the two men eagerly awaited the chance to avenge fallen comrades. How the big boss managed to find the mercenaries, neither knew. How he'd managed to trick them into thinking they were being resupplied was also a mystery. But they had a mission to accomplish. The questions could wait.

"I see one," Simeon reported. "At the corner of the church."

"Where are the other three?"

"Is he the only one left?"

"We were told there'd be four."

Simeon gripped his rifle with both hands again. Bogdan slowed and finally stopped the truck beside the church. He engaged the handbrake and shut off the motor.

———————

PERRY SHOULDERED his rifle and aimed at the passenger. The man sat still in his seat, watching Perry through his open window.

"Nobody move," the merc leader called out. "I'm supposed to ask for a password."

The driver stuck his head out his side and yelled, "The sun sets in the west..."

Perry finished the phrase. "Only when the earth runs backward."

A stupid phrase, to be sure, but there'd be no faking it.

"Can you stop pointing the artillery at us?" the driver asked.

Perry lowered his rifle.

Finn said in his ear, "The cover on the truck is shifting."

"You sure?" Perry kept his voice low.

"I ain't hallucinating."

Perry raised his voice to address the drier. "Only the two of you?"

"Yes," the passenger answered. "We thought there were four of you."

"There are. Start unloading. Leave the cases on the ground. We don't have all day."

"We could use some help," the passenger said.

"I'm busy," Perry said.

I really need to be wrong.

The rifleman in the passenger seat set his weapon on the cab's floor and jumped out. He shut his door. The driver exited as well and walked around the front of the truck.

"Far enough," Perry said.

"We have two cases of ammo and one case of MREs," the driver said.

His accent...

"Go get 'em," Perry said.

Bennett employed many freelancers, Perry reminded himself. In the Balkans, some were sure to have a Serbian accent. Perry moved back from the corner. He listened as the two men went to the rear of the truck. They wore street clothes and running shoes. Both were of medium height and thin. Perry's mind raced to find a threat. His heart rate was up. He heard the pounding of his pulse in his head.

"Got 'em covered," Finn reported in his left ear.

FINN LAY on his belly in thick grass, his Galil 5.56mm rifle braced and ready to fire. The driver and passenger reached the back of the truck. The driver reached for the zipper holding the back flaps of the canvas cover closed. Finn had seen the back portion move as if somebody touched it from inside. He breathed fast and felt sweaty. It wasn't warm enough for him to sweat while lying still. The driver lifted the zipper, stepping onto the rear bumper to pull it to the top. He jumped off and yelled, "Now!"

Finn opened fire. His blast ripped into the canvas, tearing into bodies as men with rifles attempted to exit. Two tumbled to the ground. Somebody poked out an AK and fired back. Finn fired another salvo and his rifle clicked empty. The driver and passenger rushed around either side of the truck.

"Hostiles coming out!" he yelled, reaching for another magazine.

More gunfire crackled, coming from above; it would be Luke, in the bell tower, shooting down at the attackers.

LUKE FIRED a burst through the top of the canvas canopy, then shifted his aim. The man from the passenger seat was going back for his weapon.

The bell tower was solid like the rest of the church, but he had to watch his step. One wrong move backward and he'd fall through the hole. A rope far below connected to the big cast-iron bell behind him.

Shots from the front smacked into the passenger before he reached his AK. Perry, who was closest to the enemy, had joined the fight. Luke shifted back to the men exiting the rear. What happened to Finn? Six, seven, now eight gunners jumped out and split in every direction for cover. Luke tracked them and fired. One fell in the street. The others ran out of sight. Luke cursed. Somebody fired back at him, and Luke flinched as the rounds hit the bricks, clanged off the bell, and chunked into the wooden support beams holding up the pyramid-style top of the tower. He fired again, leaning over to see his targets, and the first bullet hit him in the chest. He didn't feel the other impacts as he cried out, instinctively moving back, but then he fell, fast, through the hole and to the floor below. He didn't feel the impact.

KIT BROKE cover and ran along the street, eyes on Perry, firing as he went. None of his shots connected with the rush of gunners leaving the truck. Perry kept shooting. The truck driver stayed low on the driver's side, hauled a pistol from behind his back, and fired twice at Kit.

Kit's feet left the ground as he tripped on a protruding piece of road. The fall saved him from the pistol shots, but the landing knocked the wind out of him. As he struggled to breathe, ignoring the pain of the landing, he lifted his rifle to aim. The driver fired again, and Kit stopped moving. He stopped seeing, too. Everything went black.

PERRY WATCHED KIT DIE. Kit's body lay still, face on the pavement, the back of his head blown open by the pistol shot. Perry left the corner, ran around the front of the truck, and swung around the left fender to blast the driver point blank. Then he raised his rifle at the gunners across the street. Finn's covering fire took out one shooter, and Perry tagged another in the chest.

The Galil locked open, empty. Perry reached for his Glock. He lifted the pistol, but never had a chance to fire. A salvo of automatic fire stitched him groin to chest. Perry fell onto the road.

FINN PITCHED a grenade and watched it sail toward the enemy. He fired his rifle. Several gunmen ran at him, others covering their rush. The exploding grenade tossed a few bodies onto the road, but not all. The three in the lead kept coming. Finn fired his rifle, but only hit one. The gunner in the lead reached him and hosed the mercenary with a full-auto burst, which emptied the magazine in a few short seconds.

Finn's body jerked with the hits, but when the gunner's rifle clicked empty, he wasn't dead. He tried to lift his rifle once more, but it was too heavy. The Serbian gunner drew a pistol and finished the job with one shot.

28

MARTIN BENNETT WATCHED THE RIPPLING OCEAN. THE blazing sun above created shimmers in the distance.

He stood on a sloping paved roadway in front of a steel rail which followed the winding road to the mansion atop the hill behind him. The Caribbean island he used as his home base was only two miles in length, the mansion on the south end, a flatter portion with an airstrip on the north end. In between the airstrip and hilltop mansion was open space tended by his grounds crew, who doubled as a security force. He hired former spec ops shooters with green thumbs.

The paved road extended from the airstrip, up the south hill to the mansion, and Bennett's fleet of electric golf carts shuttled guests to and from. He didn't have many guests visit though. The airstrip was primarily used for his private jet. But, sometimes, one liked to entertain associates...

A rocky edge lined the coast of the island. Anybody who attempted to land by boat was going to have a very bad day. By Bennett's estimation, by the time any landing force cleared the rocks, they'd be cut to ribbons by his security force.

But Bennett wasn't thinking about a potential attack on home base. His mind instead contained thoughts of problems and their possible solutions. The operation against Riba and Popadic was nearing its end; from here, he had to tread carefully. He turned to his left as one of the electric carts rumbled his way, silent except for the sound of tire rubber making contact with the asphalt. His number two, Jonas Wasser, sat behind the wheel. He stopped the cart two feet from Bennett.

"Riba's on the phone," Wasser said. He handed Bennett a wireless phone, part of the scrambler unit in Bennett's office. The ocean was quiet. Bennett wouldn't have to go inside. He pressed the button to take the connection off "hold" and raised it to his ear.

"Yes, Alex?"

"It's done."

"Is Popadic satisfied?"

"He says so."

"What's the problem, then? You think he's setting up a double cross?"

"Wouldn't you?"

"Of course! But the difference here is our show of good faith. We gave him something he wanted, now we work together to make everybody happy."

"Trust will take time," Riba said. "I suppose."

"I've seen bitter enemies bury the hatchet to the betterment of both sides many times, Alex. Now—what about this meeting?"

"We need a neutral area."

"Agreed," said Bennett.

"A show of force, just in case."

"I also agree. Popadic will want one too. But we should set a limit. Neither of us needs to bring an army."

Bennett waited for Riba to respond. He wasn't used to

hearing the Madrid drug boss so subdued. Where was the *machismo* he wore on his sleeve?

"What about your island?" Riba asked.

"What about my island?"

"Can we use it for the meeting? It's remote, unfamiliar to both sides. Nobody will pull any tricks when they're in the middle of nowhere surrounded by ocean."

Bennett smiled. He showed Wasser the smile. "Yes, Alex, it's a fine idea. And I have my own security force here. They will be a further deterrent."

"I'll get back to you."

Riba clicked off. Bennett turned off the hand unit and passed it back to Wasser. He laughed.

"What's so funny?" Wasser asked.

"I've been thinking we need to watch our step as this plan comes to an end. Instead, we'll have both Riba and Popadic here, on our turf, with a limited number of soldiers who will be well outside their comfort zone."

"How long do we have to prepare?"

"Not sure," Bennett said. "Riba will talk to Popadic first and sell him on the idea. But we should start right away."

Bennett swung into the passenger seat of the golf cart. Wasser made a U-turn and began the ride back to the house.

Bennett had the mansion built to his own drawings and specification. He liked the Spanish colonial look; the mansion covered two hundred square feet, two stories, with white walls and dark red tiles on the roof. It was the best reproduction of the Spanish colonial style he could manage. A low wall surrounded the front of the mansion, wrapping around both sides. The wall provided defensive cover should an attack force *somehow* gain access to the island. The wall had cut-outs for machine guns. The weapons were currently stored, but ready in seconds' notice if the security force required them.

The golf cart bounced over bumps in the road. It wasn't as smooth as Bennett would have liked.

"Our men in the Balkans…" Wasser said.

"Yes?" Bennett had been expecting Wasser to voice his disagreement. The time had arrived.

"Do I have to say it?"

"This time I agree," Bennett said. "Perry and his men deserved better. They were good men. You have to understand, Jonas, this is our biggest and most important mission yet. We're trying to save *billions*. Save them from a nuclear disaster, Jonas. Perry and his team, and the CIA officers and civilians in Madrid…their losses will be nothing compared to what will happen, and how many will die, if we fail. We *cannot* fail."

Wasser said nothing more for the remainder of the ride.

SENATOR LEON CARTER followed a regular morning routine. He rose before his wife and was sitting at the kitchen table watching the morning news on the kitchen TV, and planning his own agenda for the day, when she came down to make breakfast. Black coffee, toast, two scrambled eggs—every day, without fail. Carter preferred the eggs be cooked with a dash of butter, with a warmed spoonful of mild salsa on the side to mix with the eggs. After he finished, he kissed his wife goodbye and went out to the porch. His driver was always waiting at the curb with the car running—a black Lincoln Town Car with a luxurious back seat. Carter had no idea when the driver actually showed up. All he knew was when he left the house at eight a.m. sharp, the driver was waiting.

He didn't recognize the driver holding open the back door.

Leon Carter was on his third term as an Ohio senator.

He'd earned "The Hawk" as a nickname from those in the military and defense industry. His support for military budget increases and the defense needs of the US and its allies were often the talk of Hill gossip. His opponents had another name for him: The Warmonger. It wasn't original or creative (neither was The Hawk, he'd readily admit) and he disliked it a great deal. He was accused of wanting to get the US involved in every conflict on the planet "in the name of freedom!" Not true. He advocated such when US interests faced a threat. Since the US was spread so far across the globe, most conflicts reached a point where they crossed a boundary and posed a danger to US assets. He'd explained such so many times, on many television programs, yet nobody understood, especially the losers who spent all day whining on Twitter.

Carter wore a tan overcoat over his black suit, his white hair close-cropped, a briefcase in his left hand. He reached the sidewalk and frowned at the driver.

"Where's Hamilton?" he said.

"Sick, sir," the substitute said, offering to take the briefcase while the senator made himself comfortable. Carter refused. There weren't any secret documents in the briefcase, but it was an old habit he wasn't about to give up. He'd carried briefcases during his CIA days that the government expected him to defend with his life. He saw no reason to stop despite the change in careers.

Or had he? It was a question Carter often asked himself. Not only was he still involved in US defense policy, but he also sat on the Senate Intelligence Subcommittee. Intelligence and defense. He'd spent one part of his career on the front line, and now he spent the second half of his career trying to smooth the path of those on the front line. The ones who had his old job. It was tougher for them than it had been for him; they needed all the help they could get.

Carter settled back in the plush leather backseat. The driver pushed the door shut—gently, Carter noted, the way he liked—and resumed his place behind the wheel. The engine purred smoothly as the driver accelerated from the curb. Carter took a deep, relaxing breath. He had a full agenda for the day, but his evening was free—so far. He wanted to keep it open. He wanted to be home at a decent hour so he and his wife could watch her favorite show. It wasn't *his* favorite show, but spending time with her while she watched helped keep her off his back and complaining about how they never spent any time together.

Carter looked out the tinted window at the passing scenery, sights he saw every day, almost didn't notice anymore because they were so familiar...and then he saw store fronts, street signs, businesses he didn't recognize. He looked forward. They weren't heading for the Hill. He didn't recognize the route the substitute driver was taking.

"Hey. What's your name? This isn't how we get to the Hill."

"Shortcut, Senator," Callen Cord said, before he pressed the accelerator to the floor.

29

CALLEN CORD LISTENED TO THE SENATOR SCREAM AND YELL AS he sped onto the freeway and turned up the volume on the dashboard infrared scanner. He wanted an extra second's warning in case there were cops hanging around. Eventually the senator lowered his tone and began making threats, and not discreet threats, either.

"Pull over and let me out of this car, or I will gut you like a fish and etch my initials on your kidneys!"

Cord chuckled. The man had a way with words.

Carter yanked on the door handles several times. He pulled on the handles, then shoved his body against the door. Nothing. He grabbed his briefcase and slammed it against the thick window glass once, twice. Nothing. Breathing hard, Carter set the case down again.

"You're only going to hurt yourself, Senator."

"What is the meaning of this?"

"Martin Bennett sends his regards."

Carter froze in his seat, but the words had the effect Cord intended. He finally stopped struggling and remained still.

But Cord didn't think for a moment the senator was finished with the fight. To make sure he cooperated, Cord brought along a bag of tricks. They were contained in a tote bag sitting on the passenger seat beside him. Carter had yet to notice the black bag.

Cord stayed on the freeway for an hour, then turned off and followed a route into the forest. They were somewhere in Virginia. He'd picked out the spot for the interrogation in advance and drove the route twice. He knew every inch of the road. He also knew Carter wouldn't know the area. Cord would have liked to have rendered the senator unconscious for the drive but planned to save such treatment as a consequence to his resistance, if the senator didn't behave himself.

"Where's Hamilton?" Carter asked.

"Mr. Hamilton will be fine," Cord told him. "He's taking an extended nap."

"I swear, if you've—"

"Senator, we both know you're not the man you once were. Let's save the tough guy rhetoric for the senator floor and Fox News, okay?"

The senator didn't respond.

THE MAIN QUESTION on Carter's mind was what the driver meant by using Martin Bennett's name. Was Bennett cleaning house? Had something gone wrong with the Riba operation? But how—Riba and Popadic were going to meet at Bennett's island. Bennett had a plan to dispose of them both. Carter tried to come up with an answer. His competing thoughts only produced a brain fog he couldn't cut through.

He decided to try and get the driver to explain more.

"Are you going to kill me?"

"You sound nervous, Senator."

"Answer me."

"I don't intend to."

"So you might? Is that what Bennett wants?"

"I don't know what Bennett wants. I'm not working for Bennett."

Carter shivered as a chill ran up his neck. If it wasn't Bennett who had arranged this kidnapping—

They knew! The Agency discovered the plot, identified participants, and now they were taking action. How had he not heard about it through their contact inside the Agency? What was his name? Harris, Carter remembered. Victor Harris. The kid who worked on Clark Wilson's staff. But why was the CIA acting? The FBI should have—

Another chill. Carter began to realize the dire situation in which he was in. He'd have to make a decision. Fight the interrogation, or give up the works? Turn informant. Because if the Agency was handling this in-house against the usual protocol, they might not hesitate to make sure the participants vanished. They'd leave him in a ditch some-where, make it look like a heart attack. Carter tried to sit still and be cool, but he was fidgeting, suddenly uncomfortable on the soft bench seat on which he sat.

"How much further?" Carter asked. The bluster was gone, replaced by acceptance.

"Not long now. Enjoy the scenery."

CORD PULLED OFF THE ROAD. He followed a rough dirt path to a small clearing. The forest surrounding the clearing was thick. He stopped the car and grabbed the tote bag and set it on the fender after getting out. Carter pulled on the door handle inside, but the back doors remained locked. Cord wasn't worried about him getting out. Child locks weren't easily defeated, even by former spies who found themselves at the mercy of the kind of people they once sent out to handle the dirty work while they sat comfortably behind a desk.

Cord paused before unzipping the tote. He didn't want to be bitter or angry, but his conversation with Jagger Malone left him in a state of conflict. Not only had Bennett played fast and loose with lives, but here sat Leon Carter who encouraged it, continued to support it, and thought his status as a senator left him above being held accountable for it. Stopping Bennett and his inner circle wouldn't change anything. Covert operators lived with the fact they were expendable; one could do everything right, and still not make it home. But the natural order of things was better than being thrown to the wolves by a man who fully expected his people not to return, in exchange for advancing a private agenda. Chasing personal glory. Cord had a lot of questions, and he hoped to get some answers.

First, he needed Carter docile. He unzipped the tote and took out a Taser gun. Priming it, he held it in his right hand while popping the door locks on the driver's side armrests with his free hand. Carter finally wrenched open his door and climbed out of the car.

"Now, you listen—"

Cord fired the Taser and sent the prongs into Carter's belly. The older man did not have a medical condition that put him at risk of a heart attack from the electric shock. Cord had checked to make sure. Carter stiffened and opened his mouth to scream, but nothing came out. Cord grabbed the man before he fell to the ground. He might have been safe from the electrodes, but bashing his head on a rock was an event Cord wanted to avoid.

Cord clutched the senator under his arms and dragged

him away from the Town Car. The heels of the senator's shoes left a trail in the dirt. They'd been brightly shined when Carter began his day; now, a layer of dirt replaced the shine. Cord propped Carter against a fallen tree trunk, used a roll of thick tape to wrap his wrists and ankles together, and then sat on the ground with his tote bag. Carter would need a few minutes to come out of the zap. He was breathing okay, though. Cord only had to wait.

Carter woke with a start and struggled against the tape. "This wasn't necessary!" he told Cord. "We aren't animals!" But Cord only held a bottle of water to Carter's lips and let him drink. When Carter pulled his lips away, Cord put the bottle down.

"Question and answer time, Senator."

"What do you want to know?"

Cord laughed. Carter grimaced. The senator may have decided it was better to cooperate, but Cord wasn't certain. "We know about Bennett's private army," the freelancer said, "and his inner circle."

"Then what do you want *me* for?"

"Tell me about why he's working with the Spanish Syndicate."

"Who talked? The whole thing was supposed to be secret."

"You know how it works, Senator. We grab somebody, they trade information for money; somebody comes forward, makes a statement—"

"All I know is Bennett has a plan to destroy the syndicate. Alex Riba is nearly broke. He's made an arrangement with outsiders to save his ass."

"Another cartel?"

"Are you delirious? No. Not another cartel. *Terrorists*. A jihadist group called the Islamic Union."

Carter frowned. "We wiped them out."

"Years ago, yes. But we missed a few, apparently. They've reformed and they have a plan to hit Europe *hard*. Riba is providing assistance—or plans to."

"What kind of assistance? Guns?"

"Safe passage into Europe via the Balkan Pipeline. The smuggling route nobody can close down. They'll move back and forth with no resistance, my friend. Bennett figured out a way to stop them."

"How?"

"Riba needs an alliance with a Balkan drug gang to make it happen. He's finally scored the merger he needs. They're about to meet to seal the deal. Bennett will kill them both and put an end to the entire conspiracy."

"Senator—"

"I'm serious. That's the whole story."

"What was your responsibility?" Cord asked.

"My job was to stay in touch with our contact at headquarters. Pass information back and forth between him and Bennett."

"Who?"

"You don't know as much as you say, do you?"

"Or I want you to confirm what we already know. Place your bet, Senator. Otherwise, I'll dip into my bag of tricks." Cord pulled a hypodermic needle and a glass vial from the black bag. "I can make this difficult, or we can do it—"

"Yeah, yeah, the *easy* way." Carter sighed. "His name is Victor Harris; he works on Wilson's staff. We haven't said much since things got hot. Harris had second thoughts after the Madrid situation. Wait, he's the one, isn't he? He *talked*."

"Probably," Cord said. "Go on."

"Harris got squeamish after the bombing. He called Bennett direct. He needed, I guess, reassurance. Bennett asked me to have a chat with him, talk him off the ledge."

224 | BRIAN DRAKE

"Where's Bennett holding this meeting?"

"I don't know."

Cord held up the needle.

"I'm not read in that far!" Carter said. "I have no idea."

"Where's the island?"

"The what?"

"Bennett's private island. Where is it?"

"I don't *know*."

"Senator—"

"You *must* understand," Carter said, "our contact was minimal. No more than necessary. I haven't seen Bennett's face in years. He could be living in the attic above my garage, for all I know."

"You have to do better than this, Senator."

"Or what? You give me the needle? You'll get the same answers."

"All right."

"All right *what*?"

"We're going back to headquarters. Some other people want to talk with you further."

"You can't be serious."

"Yes, I can. We're going to want to see Harris too."

Cord put away the needle and vial, threw the bottle into the bag, and stood. Taking out his phone, he stepped away from Carter. Cord kept his back to the senator as he made his call, reaching Paul Heinrich at headquarters to give him the update.

If Bennett had learned of a new terror plot, Cord decided, he should have brought the information to US authorities. Instead, he wanted to be a hero. What had Jagger Malong called it? A God complex. Bennett wanted the glory and was willing to sacrifice as many lives as possible to achieve it. Now Cord understood a bit more. Bennett had always wanted the glory. Wanted to be the big hero.

Cord ended his call with Heinrich and returned to Carter. He cut the tape at the senator's ankles and helped the man stand.

"Don't give me any trouble," Cord said.

"Let's get in the car and get this over with."

Cord helped him back into the Lincoln.

30

Raven and Abby remained in Saint-Tropez, confining themselves to their hotel while they waited for Oscar and his people to find a lead within Bennett's financial data. It also helped them remain out of sight while the cops and Corey Gordon took care of cleaning up the financier's condo. How Gordon explained the matter to authorities amused Raven, but he didn't think about it much. He had other things on his mind.

Raven had decided to stay in Saint-Tropez because his constant flying from one place to another was starting to add up. He could save a little money by staying put and then leave from Saint-Tropez for wherever he and Abby needed to go. There was a chance Oscar and his crew would come up empty as well. Then he'd have to make nice with the CIA to finish the job. He didn't want the Agency getting to Martin before he did. He wanted to look Bennett in the eye and ask for the truth. What he'd do after learning the truth, he had yet to decide. There was always the obvious answer, but Raven had his doubts about pulling the trigger on somebody he'd once been closer to than his own family.

Raven awoke to the smell of brewing coffee. Abby made it to the kitchen before him. He wasn't a coffee drinker but appreciated her enthusiasm for it; when he got up before her, he made sure to have a pot ready for her when she emerged from the master bedroom. Meanwhile, he brewed his tea. He wondered if she'd do the same courtesy—and then he heard the kettle whistle. Yup. Time to get up. He showered and dressed and wondered if they should go outside today. The cops had been in and out of Corey Gordon's condo the last few days; they had to be done by now. What became of Gordon himself, Raven didn't know. Perhaps the party on the yacht never ended.

"You might need to warm it up a bit," Abby announced from the balcony lounger as Raven entered the kitchen. But the water in the kettle remained hot enough. He poured a mug, dropped bag of Irish Breakfast into the steaming water, and stepped out to join her. She sat on the low-slung lounger near the balcony rail. Raven wished they had a view of the Mediterranean, but the sprawl of buildings wasn't a terrible sight. They were out of direct sunlight and had the advantage of the day's warmth and brightness without any glare. The wind off the water blew strong yet didn't disturb them as the gusts blew elsewhere than their side of the hotel.

"Any word from Stockholm?" Abby asked.

"I haven't checked my phone. Still need to wake up."

"It's been a busy few days," she said. "I'm wiped out too."

"You know you've been at it too long when—"

Her laugh cut him off. "Never. I'll keep going till I drop. Or somebody drops me."

"Always a cheerful thought," Raven said. He was about to sip his tea when he heard his cell phone chime from inside. He set his mug on the small table next to Abby and went back inside.

When he answered, Clark Wilson spoke on the other end.

"I'm heading back home," the CIA man informed him.

"What's the latest?"

"Our pal Cord speared a whale. Get a load of this, Sam…" Wilson took his time explaining what Cord had learned from Malone, confirmed through Senator Carter, and passed on to the Agency for the rest. Wilson told Raven that Carter and his Agency contact, Victor Harris, were in custody and facing fierce questioning. By all accounts, they were also cooperating. The DCI wanted Wilson back in the US to oversee the interrogations.

"Do you remember this Islamic Union group the senator mentioned?" Wilson asked. "There were so many of those jihad groups they blur together for me."

"Remember? I still have nightmares."

"Well, they're back, and Bennett thought he could solve the problem himself."

"And what we're left with are a bunch of innocent people dead, and who knows what coming next."

"No kidding. I'll let you know if I have anything when I talk to these guys myself," Wilson said. "What's happening on your end?"

Raven told Wilson about his adventure with Corey Gordon.

"Why risk getting his own guy killed?" Wilson said.

"Bennett didn't think that far. He wanted *me* out of the way. He sent Burian to do the job. Trying to hit us while we spoke with Gordon was an accident. An accident which worked in our favor. Gordon was pissed and gave us everything, which may lead us to Bennett's front door."

"Don't place all your bets on tracing IP addresses," Wilson said. "Jagger Malone told us to look at private islands. There are too many for a fishing expedition. It would take weeks to investigate them all, and we don't have that kind of time. See if your people can find a larger than normal expense and see where the purchase was made. It will narrow down the search."

"We're running out of time, for sure," Raven said. "I'll get with Oscar and mention it."

"I guess that's all for now. I should be landing in a few hours."

"Stay in touch. Thanks for your help, Clark."

"This involved both of us, and more. We're close to the end, buddy, hang in there."

Raven promised he would and ended the call. Abby wanted to know what Wilson said. Raven tasted his tea; just right. He leaned against the balcony rail and gave her the update. She didn't ask a question until he finished. When his words trailed off. When the gravity of the problem finally caught up with him.

"YOU OKAY, RAVEN?" Abby asked. He'd gone silent, staring into space, his eyes far away. The thousand-yard stare into infinity; he was trying to see into the past.

The Islamic Union. Afghanistan. The capture. The hole. The torture. The trade. The end of one life, the beginning of another, cut short; the war without end, ghosts of battles past, and the locket around his neck. A flood of memories he wanted to wrestle to control, but they instead flowed through his mind, like multiple movies playing at once. Events he could never control, decisions he couldn't change. Many decisions he hadn't wanted to make, but he'd had no choice. He was forced to choose bad options over very bad options. Memories where nothing was right—all of it was wrong, and left Raven standing on a balcony in Saint-Tropez wishing more than ever for a do-over. How do you come to terms with what you can't control, but have to suffer consequences for? Decisions made by others, events unfolding as life carried on with its business, oblivious to the pain caused by those forced to adapt.

A perpetual circle of questions, and no answers, all leading to the same place. He was where he was and that was the end of it. He might choose to be somewhere else, but it wouldn't change what he faced. The war would always be with him.

The man at the center of those memories…a man who'd sent somebody to kill him. A man he'd called a friend. A man whose actions demonstrated none of those feelings were mutual. Raven was a tool. Bennett didn't think of him, or any of the other operatives Raven had known, as people. They were things. Easily replaced. Nothing special. A means to an end.

Raven leaned against the balcony rail with a now cold mug of tea in hand and thought he knew pain. And not physical pain with its visible scars. He had those and learned to live with the marks. He knew mental pain too, from loss, the kind you never truly healed from but learned to live with, and carried with you, perhaps in a locket, as a reminder of what had been, what might have been, and what wasn't any longer.

What he felt over Bennett's betrayal—and knowing how far back the betrayal began—wasn't something he could grasp. Bennett had turned on many, not only Raven, but Raven had a front row seat. The wound was raw, reached deep, and he'd only know the extent of the damage after a period of time, when he could finally reflect and take inventory. Now? Too soon. Nothing was real. Everything was a lie. Who could he trust? He had no doubt—he was alone in the world, and in the war without end.

What was the point?
Did he matter?
Did anything he did matter?
"Raven?"
He didn't look at her.
"No, Abby, I'm not okay."

31

SHE SAID, "IF IT MEANS ANYTHING, NOW YOU KNOW WHY I LEFT him."

Raven still didn't turn.

"I discovered the hard way what kind of man Martin was," she continued. "Once, a couple of friends of mine died on a mission. Martin said it didn't matter in 'the grand scheme,' whatever that was. The final straw was what happened with you in Afghanistan. I was in the house when he and Jagger Malone talked about you, Raven. About trading those two terrorists for you. They were mad at the president for making them do it. Martin said your loss would be a rally point. They'd go after the Islamic Union hard, and he'd get another Intelligence Star for the win. But trading you didn't get him that. It's when I decided to drop him and drop out."

Raven remembered the jet ride home.

All Bennett had talked about was the president's orders. He said nothing about working to get Raven home; instead, he talked only about those who wanted Raven gone. He'd been one of them. Only the president's orders had pulled Raven out of the hole. Bennett hadn't lifted a finger.

"Are you listening to me?"

"Yes," he snapped. "This is what happens when you buy the lie."

"What do you mean?"

"They tell you it's for king and country, freedom, peace, all that happy shit. In the end, it's just a bunch of assholes playing politics. I feel like a fool."

"But look at what you've done since, Raven. Aren't you living up to the—"

"What difference have I made?"

"As a whole? Probably not much. For certain individuals? Probably more than you think."

"I should have died in that hole."

"What?"

"Never mind."

"You want me to leave?" she asked.

"I want to know what your intentions are."

"I'm staying," she said, "till the end. If you fail, I'll have a target on my back for the rest of my life. This way, one of us gets him. Right?"

Raven's phone rang again. He looked at the screen.

"Who is it?" Abby asked.

"It's Oscar."

VASKO POPADIC DIDN'T LIKE the way his people looked at him.

They were angry, distrusting of his decision. He didn't blame them. But he hoped they'd mellow once they heard his entire plan. He'd yet to explain every detail. The truth was he was not, would not, and had no intention of surrendering to Alex Riba.

And the room was extra quiet without his old friend Zalek Siroky.

His associates stood close to the edge of a large table, upon which Popadic had spread a map of the Caribbean, so his crew had knowledge of where he was going.

"I'm making the trip alone," he told them.

"Without protection?"

"They'll kill you!"

Popadic raised a hand to quiet the objections. *Maybe they aren't as mad as I thought*, he decided. "I will bring two soldiers. Riba will have two as well. The host of the meeting does not want to deal with a mass of armed men on his island."

He took out a felt pen and drew a red circle on the map to show the location of Martin Bennett's island. "Just south of Jamaica," he told them. "I'll land in Kingston and take a boat the rest of the way."

"With Riba?" one asked.

"No. By myself. Riba will take another craft."

"You must kill him before, or after," another of his people stated. "There will be an opportunity—"

"Not yet," the Serbian drug boss interrupted. "My friends, we are not surrendering. We will wipe out Riba to avenge ourselves, our comrades, our fallen, and pay him back for his treachery. When the time is *right*," he insisted. "And then we will take over *his* cartel and be unstoppable. But this can only happen if he thinks we are now pursuing peace. He will fall into a false sense of security, and when the moment comes, we will strike.

"We are Serbian, after all," Popadic continued. "We never forget or forgive. We won't forget this time, either, what was done to us. We will have our revenge."

There was another phrase Popadic could have used, one

he'd learned long ago. Never let an enemy live long enough to enjoy what he thinks is victory.

MARTIN BENNET STOOD at the edge of his private runway. He stood near part of the rocky edge where his crew constructed a jetty. It was where Riba and Popadic would park their boats for the very short meeting Bennett intended to host. One where they wouldn't set one foot in his home. They'd barely touch the runway tarmac behind him.

Two plastic dummies stood in front of him, representing the two drug kings, as if they'd stepped off their boats and onto the island. When Bennett stepped away, four members of his security team, also standing near their boss, raised submachine guns, and opened fire. The weapons crackled on full-auto and caused immediate destruction. The two dummies split in two and collapsed. One rolled off the edge and plopped into the water. The gunmen stopped firing. Bennett turned to face the men.

"Good," he called. "I can't promise where they'll be, or if they'll cheat and bring more than two guards, but this is how we're going to do it."

"You were awfully close, sir," one said.

"I felt it," Bennett told the man, grinning. "I'll do my best to get further away. You make sure not to miss."

While the men cleaned up the wrecked dummies and swept up their spent brass, Bennett started back up the paved path to the house. Jonas Wasser met him halfway, and Wasser's face looked grim.

"What is it?" Bennett kept walking.

Wasser fell in step beside him. "Corey Gordon."

"What about him, Jonas?"

"He left a message. He's not happy." Wasser explained the shooting at Gordon's condo.

Bennett stopped and faced his second-in-command. "Well," he said. "Isn't that unfortunate."

"He may have told Raven—"

"Everything, yes," Bennett said. "He'll be going through my accounts to find this place."

"He was supposed to go after Riba. You said he was—"

"I misjudged. Instead of Riba, he focused on me." Bennett cursed. "Of course, he would. I should have known better. He wants to know if I've really gone dirty."

"What do we do?"

"We wait. Raven will find his way here, then he and I will have a talk. I will explain my actions, and he'll do whatever he sees fit."

"He may—"

"Kill me? Not when I'm surrounded by guns, Jonas." Bennett gestured to the crew on the tarmac. "Even Raven can recognize when the odds aren't in his favor."

"Then he'll wait."

"Only if I can't convince him what I did was the right thing. Once I tell him of the re-emergence of the Islamic Union, he'll understand."

"Are you sure?" Wasser said.

"No. But I'd like to think Raven will still see me as an authority figure. If not now, he will when we see each other."

"Make sure you're armed."

"You're paranoid enough for the both of us, Jonas."

Bennett continued toward the house.

32

Oscar Morey said, "Are you sitting down, Sam?"

"No. Give it to me straight."

"We found him. Bennett purchased a small island south of Jamaica. And we've been watching the chatter from Riba's associates, the ones you weren't interested in. Riba is flying to Jamaica for a meeting, which will be held on Bennett's island. A Serbian drug boss named Popadic will join him there, and this whole scheme has been about the two of them merging."

"It's about more than that," Raven said, and began filling in the gaps provided to him by the CIA.

Oscar listened, but as Raven continued, he sounded less confident. Eventually, Oscar interrupted.

"Hey. You aren't getting weak, are you?"

"Hold on."

Raven went inside, shut the door to the small bedroom, and sat on the edge of the bed. "Tell me what to do, Oscar. I'm out of answers."

"It's easy, but you can't see it."

"Show me."

"Remember what he took from you."

Raven processed the words. Martin alone wasn't responsible for his dismissal from the CIA. But had he remained at the Agency, his life may have gone in a different direction. The event sparking his war without end may have been avoided. How much of what took place was truly the fault of CIA management thinking he had become a liability?

"I can't blame Bennett for everything," Raven said. "He wasn't responsible."

"Not what I mean. He took your trust. He took advantage of your ideals. Of course, the CIA isn't all bad. Did you have a problem with Fisher when you worked for him?

"No," Raven said. Christopher Fisher remained Deputy Director of Operations; he was Clark Wilson's boss, and Raven still had a good relationship with him. But he'd been closer with Bennett. Bennett's management style and the bond he forged with his men were much different from Fisher's way of doing things.

But Fisher wasn't the bad apple.

Raven told Oscar he had a point.

"You've never lost your nerve before, Sam. Don't lose it now. Go to Jamaica and finish this."

Raven said okay.

It was time to show Martin Bennett the meaning of *payback*.

ALEX RIBA STARED out the window at the outline of the Jamaican coast in the distance. Between him and Jamaica was nothing but blue ocean.

The private jet's engine droned through the cabin. He felt light in spirit. A lot of work had brought him to this point, and he wanted to enjoy the moment of victory—it was close.

It hadn't been easy, the risks taken were huge, but his gamble paid off. Soon he'd have access not only to Eastern Europe, but the coveted Ballan Pipeline too. He was going to save his empire.

Riba had never quit before, and he wasn't quitting now. When he first found himself in the underworld of drug smuggling as a young man, he'd been a simple courier, a worker-bee for the organization he now controlled. Taking steady advantage of several opportunities—coupled with removing those who competed for the same posts—made him more than a number, and the late boss of the Spanish syndicate took notice. Soon Riba controlled entire sections of Madrid distribution, and the boss gave him more responsibility and more territory as time went on. He solved problems with negotiations first, and then violence if talks failed. The strategy had paid off once again.

He wouldn't have considered the Eastern Europe market had the Islamic Union not approached him.

Representatives of the jihadist organization contacted him while on holiday in Barbados. They had a problem, and thought he might help them solve the issue. The Union needed a path into Europe. Yes, borders were open because idiot globalist politicians wanted unchecked immigration, illegal, of course, to replace their populations with those who might not think as much. But while porous borders helped the terrorists move, selectively, and not in huge numbers, the Union needed another way inside those in authority had no control over. They had a plan in the works, Riba figured; what their plan was meant nothing to him. He liked their money. Money he could use to get his organization out of the red in which it now found itself. The Union knew he was desperate; they'd done their homework.

Riba looked for a solution. He and his advisers knew right away the Balkan Pipeline was the answer. But to use it, they needed to merge with one of the Balkan drug clans. The protection the clan provided would allow the Union operatives safe passage. No need to worry about bandits or other hostile forces. But which clan should they approach? After much discussion and debate, they identified Vasko Popadic as their best option. Riba considered Popadic their *only* option. He didn't want word to leak about his connection to the Union. If they took too long to make a connection, a third party could discover the need Riba had. It helped that the Spanish Syndicate was facing financial issues; but money problems wouldn't cover up the truth for long.

What to do if Popadic refused? Violence, of course. But Riba had another problem. He didn't have the manpower or resources to declare war should the Serbian clan boss refuse.

Enter Martin Bennett.

Bennett didn't approach as quietly as the Islamic Union. He was blunt, direct, decisive, and said he had the answer to Riba's manpower problem. The former CIA man made his past quite clear; it piqued Riba's interest. Bennett proposed hiring mercenaries to go into the Balkans and fight if Popadic refused. How Bennett learned about the deal, Riba didn't ask—his excitement overruled such thoughts. Once agreeing to Bennett's proposal and payment, Riba began talking to Popadic and his people, leaving out any mention of the Islamic Union. Didn't matter. Popadic refused, Bennett sent in the mercenaries...and they made the Serbian hurt enough to return to negotiations. Assuming all went well, Riba planned to reach his Union contacts and tell them to get ready to visit Eastern Europe.

The Jamaican coast grew larger in his window. Soon the pilots turned left, and he'd lost sight of the island. He'd not see it again until he stepped off the plane.

Riba scanned the quiet cabin. As agreed, he had two shooters with him, sharpshooters who knew how to fight.

He figured Bennett's security force would provide plenty of deterrence should Popadic try and get rough—Riba certainly had no plans to cause trouble. He was about to have his cake and eat it too. His excitement grew as the jet continued its course. They'd be on the ground soon, and then sort their business quickly.

If there was time left over, Riba wanted to see the sights in Kingston.

33

Vasko Popadic also rode in a private jet, but he wasn't as comfortable, or as excited. His face showed the strain he battled within.

He paced the cabin, cursing every time he bumped one knee or the other against a seat. The aisle was narrow. His two bodyguards didn't try to interrupt him, but they did glance with concerned eyes now and then.

Popadic's mind was full of what-ifs and self-accusations.

Why hadn't he attacked Riba first? Strike before the Madrid boss organized his mercenaries.

Simple, he remembered. His review of Riba's forces, based on data from local informants, said the Madrid boss didn't have the power or money. Why else ask to merge if his cartel was healthy? Riba was on the ropes. Everybody knew. Any counterattack on what he had left would have finished him.

So why didn't you?

There were others he could have gone to; why me?

What's so special about me?

He wondered why he hadn't pressed harder to retaliate. He put too much focus on the mercenaries, finding them, rooting out the cancer within before expanding the fight. He should have sent a team of his own to Madrid to hit back at Riba directly. At the same time.

I had to save our infrastructure first!

Bullshit! He messed up, miscalculated, end of story. Too caught up in the moment. Now he expected to get even with a sleight-of-hand trick.

What if Riba had help?

It was another question he had no answer for.

Was it a third party *not* part of the Madrid drug scene? Somebody he could use to his advantage. Turn against Riba? He'd know soon enough. Striking back before he understood more would only invite trouble from the alleged third party.

And waste more resources.

Finally, Popadic found a chair. Sitting wasn't comfortable, though. He had a CZ-75 9mm autoloader holstered behind his back; the gun pressed against his skin, the bulk of the weapon digging into his back. He followed the rule about bodyguards, but nobody said anything about not having his own weapon.

Pacing in circles was pointless, and by ruminating, he'd dull his edge when he needed it most—during the meeting. He rotated the chair to look out the window to his left. They were still over the ocean. Another few hours before touchdown.

Popadic faced forward with a grim set to his face. He'd survived worse during the war, when the fighting was almost over, and he was half-starved, low on ammo, and facing an enemy on two sides. Croats on one, Bosnians on the other—Operation Storm, 1995. The largest land battle in Europe since WWII and Serbia was on the losing end. The enemy had gone mad; no atrocity was off the table. He'd have been lying if he said they didn't have a reason.

Popadic reminded himself he'd seen worse. *Survived* worse.

He'd survive this, too.

He wasn't starving or low on ammo this time. This time, he had a bigger army behind him.

THE WIND off the ocean almost pushed Martin Bennett off his feet. But he remained resolute, standing straight, watching the water. He was waiting for the boats.

He wore his best suit for the meeting. It was going to get dirty, perhaps torn, but he thought the impression was important. It was a light gray Brioni with a white cotton shirt and black tie. While a portion of his security team held their ready position in the trees behind him, he stood with hands clasped behind his back and watched the water.

Riba telephoned an hour earlier and said he was on his way. Another hour, max, with Popadic close behind.

Very soon it would be over, and his actions would leave Riba and Popadic's organizations in disarray, and the Islamic Union in the lurch, ready for a final hit to take them out of play.

The reformed jihadist group had a nuclear bomb. How Western intelligence missed the development he didn't know, didn't understand. But his sources found out and backed the intel with pictures and hard data. He knew where they were hiding the bomb. They wanted to smuggle it into Western Europe via the east and needed a way to do so without detection. When Bennett's informants explained how they wanted to go about the effort, he planned to interdict. By doing so, he wanted to destroy two major drug operations and the Islamic Union. It would be his biggest win ever. And the CIA and other Western agencies would know they had another player in the Good Fight to contend with, one who wasn't afraid to do whatever it took to win. Unlike them, with their red tape, bureaucratic nonsense, and errors. Like not discovering the Union's bomb in the first place.

He'd wanted an extra edge, an X-factor neither side was prepared for. Sam Raven. The anonymous tip putting Raven in action came from Bennett, by proxy. But while Raven started out looking at the Spanish Cartel for his answers, he changed course and instead began looking for Bennett. Why? What prompted the change? Something confirmed the "rumor" Bennett planted; somehow, Raven learned the truth. Had the CIA team in Madrid known more than he realized? If so, it made the Madrid bombing a miscalculation, for sure. It had seemed like the proper move at the time. A way to keep on Riba's good side. But now? He wasn't sure his purposes were served the way he wanted. Raven wasn't an asset any longer, albeit a secret one; Raven was coming after *him* directly.

There'd be no admitting errors to Jonas Wasser, of course. He'd never subject himself to Wasser's *I told you so* response. Things happened in the heat of battle; you adjusted and adapted and kept fighting. It was the only way to win.

And winning, this time, might require another justified sacrifice.

If he had to kill Raven to win, he'd do so. He wasn't going to let past loyalties get in the way, either. Where Raven might hesitate, he'd not.

One thing he'd been right about though. Raven was still the man Bennett remembered. He'd survived Gustav Burian and, likely, found the location of the island. He'd found Leon

Carter and Victar Harris; they remained unreachable, which meant the CIA or FBI had them in custody, and his money was on the CIA. They'd want to keep the situation under wraps, under their control, for better or worse.

The wind off the ocean blew harder. Bennett remained at his post.

34

RAVEN HAD NEVER VISITED JAMAICA BEFORE, AND REGRETTED this wasn't going to be his chance to explore the island. He had a mission to finish, one more personal than the one which sparked his war without end. There'd be time to rest later. If he survived.

Jamaica had a pleasant surprise waiting upon arrival. Per Wilson's notice, Callen Cord met Raven and Abby at the airport. He told them he was the official non-official liaison for the Agency. He then admitted he had an investment in Bennett and the case and now wanted to see a payoff. Raven understood. After Cord told him the story of *his* side of the investigation, Raven was glad to have him. Bennett betrayed them both; they *both* wanted a final confrontation with the man who many had called the chess master during his prime.

Another benefit to having Cord on the team: he knew how to drive a motorboat; in their case, a twenty-footer with a cockpit for one. Raven and Abby sat in the stern partially covered by a collapsible canopy, protecting them from splashes on either side and behind. The ride was bumpy, and Raven was not amused. Abby bore the discomfort stoically.

She hadn't said much on the flight to Kingston. Raven wondered what was on her mind. But he asked her a different question, instead.

"Did Martin know who you really were when he hired you?"

"I don't think so," she said. "It was one hell of a coincidence."

"Or kismet."

"If you believe in that."

"What do you think he'll do when he sees you?"

"He'll stop short of ordering us shot, I'd say, when he first sees me."

Cord stood at the controls in the narrow confines of the stand-up cockpit. He did a sort of dance with the bumpy ride, adjusting his stance, bending at the knees, to roll with the choppiness and keep on track. He was following a navigation screen; they'd plotted the GPS coordinates to Bennett's island, and Raven hoped he didn't have an early-warning system. Or mines. Or any countermeasures that would cut the mission short before they finished. He wondered if they'd get there before Riba and Popadic. He wondered if it mattered.

Oscar arranged with a Kingston contact for the boat and their weapons, but while Raven was content to let Cord and Abby wield the HK MP7s, he wanted only his Nighthawk Custom Talon .45 autoloader for the time being. He wanted to talk to Bennett first. Try and understand the scenario in which they found themselves. Try to understand the past. His gut told him he was a fool; he had to have answers before the shooting started. He hoped he had a chance to hear the answers. He had enough mysteries in his life, events he replayed trying to find coherence, a narrative flow, a reason why. Too many of those events were like scrambled eggs—a jumbled mess, spread about, with no rhyme or reason. For once, Raven wanted to know the *why* of the matter.

The twenty-footer continued across the ocean, no land in sight.

Yet.

NOTHING but the best for his guests.

Bennett arranged for two sleek, powerful speed boats to collect Riba and Popadic. The two arrow-shaped crafts arrived within minutes of each other. They each docked on one side of the jetty, and Bennett stood with a big smile as first Riba, and his guards, then Popadic and his pair advanced along the jetty to the solid rock of the island.

"Welcome!" Bennett yelled over the waves and wind. "Good to see you!"

Bennett grinned as Alex Riba smiled. The narrow jetty forced all six men to remain close together, but he had to wait. He wanted them closer. On solid ground. Opening fire now might give Riba or Popadic a chance to get back to the boats. Not even the drivers would want to stick around through a shootout.

Riba reached Bennett first. They clasped hands.

"This is the big day," Bennet told the boss of the Spanish Syndicate.

He didn't notice the change in Popadic's expression.

Vasko Popadic had what might be called a *sudden realization* the moment he overheard Bennett's greeting, and watched the two men shake hands. Did Riba have help? Yes. And the help came from this Martin Bennett. They were *not* meeting on neutral ground. Riba lied. They were in the lion's den, and there was only one way to deal with this kind of treachery.

He snapped an order to his men to prepare their weapons. The pair hauled compact submachine guns from under their bulky long coats.

Bennett and Riba both watched with surprise as Popadic moved faster toward them, raising his voice as he stepped closer.

"You two *know* each other! This is not neutral!"

"Wait!" Riba shouted back, holding up both hands. The Serbian bodyguards had their weapons out, muzzles aimed ahead. Riba's bodyguards went for their autoloaders, and the guns stayed level. Nobody fidgeted. Those holding the guns, anyway.

Alex Riba was losing control and knew it. *Everything* was riding on this meeting. To see it crash and burn before they began talking sent him into near panic, and it showed in his strained voice. He spoke like a desperate man, a man desperate to save his life.

"No! Vasko, that's not what's going on. What do you think—"

Popadic hauled out his CZ 9mm and shot Riba in the belly. The man from Madrid stopped midstride, let out a choked gurgle nobody heard, and fell to the ground.

Bennett thought, *This is not what I planned*, as he dived right, landing in a shoulder roll to get out of the way as he shouted for his security team to *fire, fire, fire!* He almost didn't need to say the words; the crew knew what to do, because the bodyguards were starting to shoot too.

The Serbians with their SMGs fired as Popadic ran between them, trying to get back to the boat he'd arrived on. The SMGs didn't stutter their death song for long. The crackles of M-4A1 semi-auto rifles from the section of tress center of the island chopped them down. They fell as they tried to move backward along the jetty. Both bodies slipped over the side and into the water.

Riba's two bodyguards had no time to react to the six gunners emerging from the trees. They died next, cut down by short bursts fired by two of the security team. One lost his handgun. The weapon skidded across the concrete to stop a foot from where Martin Bennett lay.

After landing on his left shoulder and rolling, Bennett came to rest on his belly and rotated to face the fight. The bodyguards were down; both sets; Popadic still fired his pistol, but Bennett barely registered the cracks of his shots. One of his men went down. The others returned fire. Bennett watched Popadic do a jerk left, then right, as 5.56mm slugs ripped through him. Then he fell, bouncing off the hull of one of the boats, to splash into the water with his bodyguards.

Gonna have to tip the boat company, Bennett decided. He heard Riba moan. The Madrid boss wasn't dead. Bennett rose, straightened his now dirty suit, and picked up the gun lying ahead of him.

Riba lay on his back, arms out, legs spread, like a snow angel on blacktop. His face twisted in pain, he didn't notice Bennett kneel beside him until Bennett said, "Sucks, don't it?"

Riba yelled, his body stiffening. "I'm hurt bad."

"Yup."

"All our work—"

"No, Alex. *Mine*."

Before Riba fully registered what Bennet said, the former CIA man stood, extended the pistol, and shot Riba through the head.

Bennett directed two of his men to get rid of the boats and pilots. If they knew what was good for them, they saw nothing, and would remember nothing. Then Jonas Wasser radioed from the balcony of the mansion. One of the other security team members took the call. He handed the radio to Bennett.

"What is it, Jonas?"

"A third boat is heading our way. Three people aboard."

"Armed?"

"Not that I can see."

"It's Raven," Bennett said. "Bet on it. We're going to have a busy day, Jonas."

Bennett gave the radio back to his trooper. He glanced at the wounded man. He was on his feet with the help of two others. They'd get him squared away. Bennett couldn't concern himself with the man's condition at the moment.

Raven had finally arrived.

But Bennett's earlier resolve departed for a moment. He wasn't sure what to do except wait. He tucked the pistol behind his back. It pulled at his belt, but keeping his pants up was the least of his worries right now.

35

"HERE THEY COME!" CORD SHOUTED.

Raven and Abby leaped from the stern to the tote bag near their feet. He handed her one of the MP7s while taking another for himself. The weapons were loaded and locked. The two speed boats heading for them moved fast, then made wide turns to their starboard side, avoiding the twenty-footer. Raven grabbed for a handhold. The combined wake rocked them from side to side. Raven watched the speed boats continue on.

"What was that about?" Abby said.

Raven had no idea. He told Cord to hold steady and grabbed a pair of binoculars from the console. He moved to the bow, bracing his body against the port gunwale. The zoom-in showed him all he needed to know. The "meeting" was a ruse to get Riba and Popadic in the same place. From the bodies on the ground, to the activity of the armed men, and finally Bennett's lone figure standing in wait, Raven knew the fight was already over. The table was clear for another meeting. The one between Raven and Bennett.

Raven stayed at the bow as Cord cut the motors and the boat drifted to the jetty.

"Martin!" Raven called.

"Sam Raven! Come on up! Bring your friends!"

Raven jumped onto the jetty to tie up the boat. Cord and Abby off boarded with MP7s in hand. Raven only carried his pistol still in the shoulder harness under his left arm. Bennett did not seem surprised to see the firearms. He didn't appear to have his own, but three men behind him did, US M-4A1s. And while they had young faces, Raven saw experience in their eyes. The trio knew how to use their tools.

"Thanks for clearing the bodies," Raven said as he stepped onto solid ground. But Bennett wasn't looking at Raven. His eyes were fixed on Abby.

"Hello, Martin," she said.

"Callie?"

"Callie is dead. I'm Abby Fox to you."

"Wait...what?"

Raven grabbed Bennett by the arm, which jerked the former CIA man's gaze back at him. "Your mistakes started in the beginning, Martin."

Bennett jerked away, moved toward Abby; he stopped when she pointed the HK MP7 at his gut.

"I don't understand. Callie, I—"

"You had no idea, did you? A lot changed after I left you, Martin."

Bennett's face turned grim as Abby kept her gun and eyes on him, and they weren't friendly eyes, or neutral eyes. He saw hatred there, anger, nothing good. Bennett went back to Raven.

"What do you want, Sam? A showdown right here? We just had one."

"I want to talk, Martin."

"We should talk in private. Come up to my office?"

"Only you and me. Anybody else, you get it in the back."

"You haven't changed a bit."

Bennett started for the house. Raven nodded at Cord and Abby. "Keep and ear out," he said, then followed after Bennett.

———————

"Care for a drink?"

"No."

"Mind if I—"

"Sounds like you're celebrating, so go ahead."

Bennett poured vodka over ice at his corner bar, then crossed the carpet to his desk. Raven stood and refused the seat Bennett offered. Bennett sat behind the desk and leaned back a little to meet Raven's eyes with his own.

"It wasn't supposed to happen this way," Bennett began. "I had wanted you to go after Riba, weaken his organization further. Would have wrapped it up sooner. Would have saved me trouble today."

"I was supposed to be a secret weapon?"

"You got an anonymous tip about an American working for Riba, right?"

"A tip said the American might be you."

"Where do you think the tip came from, Sam? You only knew because I told you—by proxy. Before long we would have intercepted you and filled you in on the rest. What changed?"

"Madrid. The CIA team heard your name too."

"Ah ha. So the Agency—"

"Knew from the beginning, but it took a while to assemble all the parts."

"In the meantime—"

"I decided the hell with Riba. I was going to find *you*."

"And here you are." Bennett swallowed some vodka.

Raven stared at him.

"Is there more?" Bennett asked. "You were never shy before. Don't be shy now."

Raven finally had his chance to ask *why* but couldn't get the word out. Watching Bennett behind his desk reminded him of the old days—before the war. Before his life changed.

Finally, he spoke.

"Tell me why, Martin."

Bennett drank a little more. "It's the spy business. That's all. That's why."

"You're saying if you're not a sociopath you're not a good spy?"

"I'm saying, in the spy business, ruthlessness is the only attribute you *must* have if you're going to win. I threw you guys into tough spots because it was the *only* way to win. You lived or you didn't, based on your own skills. I'm sorry about Madrid. But I needed to keep my cover. Riba needed to know he could trust me, otherwise none of this would have been possible."

"Exactly *what* have you achieved, Martin?"

"How much do you know?"

"Everything. From the Islamic Union to your little massacre outside."

"Then why do I need to explain myself? Why do you think I did all this? Because of eight billion people, Sam. That's the world's population as of this moment. Eight *billion*. At least more than one million were threatened by the Union and their home brewed nuke. You *must* understand."

"I don't understand dead civilians in Madrid."

"Oh."

"I don't understand trying to kill me when you said you *needed* me."

"Chess master, remember? Riba would have suspected I wasn't fully committed if I blew up Madrid but left you alive. You'd live or die based on your skills, as always, and you did —congratulations. You're still one of the best. Also, if you thought Riba was bringing out the big guns to stop you, you'd work harder."

"Another mistake," Raven said. "Because of Burian, Corey Gordon gave up everything."

"I'm not worried. Look what I've accomplished. The Islamic Union has no way—no *safe* way—into Western Europe now. Can the CIA or SIS say that? No. Because while they were sleeping, I was out trying to prevent a disaster. *Me*. Not *them*. CIA missed a home brew nuke, Sam. They may have blown a mission here and there, but the nuke sniffers aren't stupid. Yet they still missed this one."

"You think they'll forgive the deaths of their people because you're a big hero?"

"Goddammit, Sam, you're naive. The CIA has made more friends with killers than you can name. They were used to catch more killers back when you were in diapers. Look it up. In the '70s and '80s when some Mideast terrorist nut would shoot a bunch of Americans, we sent people to *recruit* those terrorists instead of killing them. Turned them double. We collected valuable intelligence on entire terror *networks* because of those double agents. Because it was more important to focus on the big picture—the whole board—rather than fuss over individual victims. No, Sam, you'll be the only one who cares about the dead in Madrid once the CIA learns the full story of my work."

"I see no matter what," Raven said, "you're sticking to your story."

"There are no rules, Sam."

"I can think of two," Raven replied.

Bennett downed the remainder of his vodka and stood. He set the glass on the desktop.

"Did you get what you came for?" he asked.

"I did."

"And?"

"How do I know there's really a nuke?"

Bennett laughed. Pulling open a desk drawer, he extracted a file folder, a thick one, and dropped it on the desk. "All there. On paper so it can't be hacked. I have people everywhere, Sam. Informants exactly where they're needed. You should join me. We'll be unstoppable, Sam. It'll be the old days again."

"Until you decide to leave me in a hole somewhere."

Bennett frowned.

"Afghanistan, remember? Your former lover tells me I kept you from getting another Intelligence Star."

A red flush crawled up Bennett's neck.

"Sam, you son of a *bitch*."

Bennett's right hand flashed behind his back but tangled in the flaps of his coat. Raven moved faster. He whipped the .45 from his shoulder harness and had the gun extended as Bennett finally hauled out his pistol. Raven fired once. The blast echoed; he knew they heard it outside. Bennett dropped back into his chair with a red hole in his forehead and bits of blood, bone, and brain splattered on the wall behind him. His eyes remained open, staring at nothing. Raven wondered if they'd ever seen anything at all, or only what Bennett wanted to see.

Shouting. Running—heavy footsteps on the hallway floor. Raven hurried from the desk to the wall beside the doorway. He kept his finger on the Nighthawk's trigger. The two troopers who entered swept the room with the rifles; one yelled an emergency call into his radio when they saw

Bennett's body. A voice on the other end of the radio told all units to stand down and wait for instructions. It was a voice of authority; one Raven didn't recognize. The two troopers lowered their M-4A1s and approached Bennett's desk.

"Hold it."

Raven lined up the closest trooper in his sights. Neither attempted to lift their guns after they turned toward the sound of his voice.

"Your boss is dead. Don't die for nothing," Raven told them.

"Raven!"

He risked a glance at the new arrival, a man he didn't recognize but one who carried no weapon.

"I'm Jonas Wasser, second-in-command here."

"Looks like you're first-in-command now," Raven told him. "What would you like to do, Jonas?"

"Martin and I argued many times about his choices. I can tell the Americans everything they don't know. The rest of the inner circle, for example. Martin didn't work alone. *We* didn't work alone."

"Your men won't try to shoot me or my friends?"

"I've given the stand-down order. You're free to leave. But—"

"What?"

"Got the number for the CIA?"

"I can do better than that." Raven put away his .45. "Let's call a buddy of mine and he'll send a ride for you. Oh, and I need that folder on the desk."

"Take whatever you want," Wasser said.

Raven went to the desk. Wasser dismissed the two troopers. Raven decided he might as well use Bennett's phone—he was in no position to object.

HE MIGHT AS WELL HAVE BEEN WALKING through a fog, the way he felt. But Raven didn't have time to question his mental state. Bennett was dead; his partner in crime was going to talk; the job was done. Except for the nuke. He had a favor to ask of his friends who waited at the jetty, and he hoped they'd agree to join him. Raven still had accounts to settle with the Islamic Union. He'd go alone if he had to.

They watched him as he walked for the paved lane from the house. Bennett's troops were doing their own thing now, clustered elsewhere to figure out what to do now that their circumstances had changed.

Raven reached Abby and Cord. Cord said, "What happened up there?"

"The spy business," Raven said. He tried to explain the conversation as best as possible, but found he was rambling, trying to make sense of what didn't make sense. Finally, he said, "There was no other way."

Abby said, "Did he say anything about me?"

Raven shook his head.

"Now what?" Cord said. "What's the computer for?"

"Information on the nuke the Islamic Union allegedly has," Raven said. "We need to go through it and get the CIA to sign off on going to collect it. I don't want to leave this in Agency hands."

Abby and Cord said nothing.

"Will you come with me?" Raven said. "I could use the help."

"You don't have to ask," Cord said. "Ride or die, brother."

"Abby?"

"Let's finish this," she said.

Raven nodded. He decided he wasn't alone in the war after all. If he hadn't had Abby and Cord, there was always Darbo, Liz, and Roger to call. He had Oscar in his corner.

They were a good set of friends to have.

36

THREE COMMANDOS DRESSED IN BLACK, CARRYING AUTOMATIC rifles and other tools of combat, moved at a quick pace through high brush. The overgrowth had once been properly maintained by area farmers, but they were long gone, only the shells of their farms remaining. Nature was reclaiming its own. But squatters had taken refuge in some of those shells. Squatters otherwise known as *terrorists*.

Sam Raven walked point, his danger scan constant, looking for threats within the high grass, behind trees. Low branches whipped at his face, but he ignored the discomfort. His SIG-Sauer SG-553 was tucked into his right shoulder and ready for use; his companions, similarly armed, remained in his peripheral vision to the right and left.

Raven checked the GPS unit on his left wrist, whispered, "Halt," into his digital com link, and the trio of night fighters kneeled. The high brush concealed them.

"Twenty yards from the fence," Raven said. "Spread out."

"Going left," said Abby Fox, who broke off to vanish into the forest.

Callen Cord, the third member of the team, turned right, heading for higher ground.

The mission was simple. A high-stakes nighttime raid on an abandoned fruit farm in the western region of the Caucasus. Recover the homemade nuclear bomb. Head south for a secured airfield where representatives of the US government's Nuclear Emergency Support Team (NEST) would take charge of the weapon.

The intelligence regarding the nuke was strong, but Bennett's files weren't perfect. Raven had no idea how many enemy Islamic Union troops they faced.

Raven waited a moment while his teammates slipped away. He took a deep breath, let it out slowly, and rose to a low crouch. He moved forward once again. Twenty yards to the fence. The wooden posts finally came into view. He stopped and dropped flat to examine the fence. The structure looked weak, the posts rotting in sections, but he'd still have to get over the wire barrier.

The glow of the moon provided minimal illumination. The target was an abandoned farm. Like the rest of the area, it had seen better days. The main house, not much more than a one-story cottage, sat to the right of a large barn, a few useless tractors here and there. The enemy force had cleared the brush between the cottage and barn. Bennett's files said the nuke was in the barn under a tarp. The barn was the goal.

Raven whispered, "Ranger One in position."

"Ranger Two has the high ground," Callen Cord said.

Nothing from Abby.

"Ranger Three?"

"Wait one."

Raven turned his attention to the cottage. The place at least had electricity, wires extending from the roof to end somewhere in the trees surrounding the property. The electrical wires ran through the mountains and were properly maintained. It wouldn't take much to shoot the wire from the house to cut the power.

"Abby?" he said.

"In position near the barn," she said.

"What do you see?"

"It's dark inside. Two sentries near the front doors."

Excellent, Raven thought. *They wouldn't be there if there wasn't something to protect.* He said, "They got religion?"

"Say the word and I'll send 'em to their maker."

"Copy. Callen?"

"Word."

"Can you chop the wire coming out of the roof?"

"Easily."

Raven set down his SIG rifle and pulled from a holster on his left him a Heckler & Koch M320 grenade launcher. The breech-loaded weapon contained a high-explosive grenade. "On my mark, put out the lights. I'll put a hole in the front door. Abby, take the sentries."

"Copy," Abby said.

"Ready," Cord said.

Raven aimed the HK. "Three, two..."

ABBY FOX APPRECIATED the heavy brush because it provided some protection from the rough ground beneath. From her position on her belly, slightly above the top of the fence, she lined up the sights of the SG-553 on the sentry furthest from her. The man stood to the right of the barn door. If she killed his partner first, she'd miss him. He'd have time to run around the corner and out of her line of fire.

Her right index finger poised over the smooth trigger, she listened to Raven's countdown.

"One."

Cord's machine gun opened fire. The wire above the house split in two with a spark. The lights in the house snapped out. The sentries snapped to attention, weapons coming up, already shouting an alarm.

The meaning behind the belch of the HK grenade launcher might not mean anything to the average person, but she knew what it meant. Raven had fired a grenade. The front porch of the cottage exploded in bright orange flame.

Abby fired once. Her first target dropped with a single shot to the head. She shifted to the closer target as he reacted. He managed to start running, but he couldn't outrun the burst Abby fired through his spine. He tumbled to the ground and lay still.

"Sentries down," she announced.

CALLEN CORD HAD MADE many tough shots in his life, and blasting a thick wire in two didn't make him sweat.

His SG-553 hammered messengers of death on Raven's mark, and the wire snapped with a flash of sparks. As Raven's grenade blasted the porch, Cord examined the side of the cottage. A small patio with a short wall. Gunmen were running to the patio, clustering around the side door.

"They're coming out the side," Cord reported.

"Can't see them," Raven said. "Going over the fence."

Cord shifted his aim. He was on a small rise that provided a decent overview of the property. "You're covered," he said as he pulled the trigger again. The SG-553 spat flame in short bursts as he worked the trigger, sending a hell storm of fire at the patio doorway. The stock hammered into his shoulder, but he ignored the force of the recoil.

"Abby," Raven said over the com link, "with me."

"Up on your left," she said.

Cord fired some more, watching a gunner do down in the doorway, but others leaped over the body and the patio wall, firing back with automatic rifles of the Kalashnikov variety. None of the rounds came near Cord.

Yet.

Cord shifted his aim again and fired on the four gunners who'd escaped the cottage. One went down, but others fanned out.

"Three bad guys waiting for you, Raven," he said.

Raven didn't respond.

RAVEN PUT AWAY the HK grenade launcher, picked up his SIG rifle, and ran for the fence. The hammering of Cord's weapon provided minor comfort. It didn't hurt to know a guardian angel with a ton of firepower was watching over him.

He braced his left hand on the top of a vertical fence post, ignoring the horizonal planks which looked less than able to support his weight even for a brief moment. The post didn't collapse, and he swung his legs over the top, landing on the ground, tucking and rolling left.

Automatic weapons flashed ahead as the three gunners Cord warned about tried to beat back their attackers. Muzzles flashed from behind a broken-down tractor, another flashed from the middle of the open ground. Raven aimed for that gunner and fired, a scream signifying a hit.

The other two saw his muzzle flash and turned their fire on him. Slugs whistled overhead, smacking into the fence behind him, kicking up dirt. He couldn't move left. He'd run right into Abby's line of fire. He stayed on his belly and moved quickly to the right, staying near the fence line.

"Raven," Abby said, "I can't get to you."

"Keep your head down."

Abby's rifle crackled. The defenders continued firing, but Raven didn't hear any bullets buzzing close. He stopped near the truck of a chopped-down tree. The flame from the porch lit the area where the defenders had sought cover behind the tractor. Cord hosed the patio again, cutting down further resistance. Raven let off a burst of his own, rounds sparking against the vehicle before one found its mark. The gunner dropped.

The last shooter turned and fired in Raven's direction, but his plan to run was cut short by a string of fire from Cord. He fell beside the other shooter.

Raven waited while the echoes of battle faded. The cottage fire began to spread, thick smoke drifting across the property.

"We're gonna have us a nice forest fire," Cord said.

"Least of my worries," Raven said. "Abby?"

"I'm out in the open with the barn to my left."

"Coming to you," Raven said. "Cord?"

"Watch it," Cord said. "I think I see movement at the rear of the barn."

"How many?"

"Just shadows. Could be the wind."

"I admire your ability to give the benefit of the doubt," Raven said, "but there's no wind tonight."

"Then it's bad guys. Changing position for a better view."

"Copy." Raven reloaded his SG-553 and ran to Abby. "Stay on my left," he said.

"On your left," she confirmed.

Raven and Abby advanced at a slow trot, coming within feet of the barn when more hell broke loose.

Lights blared behind the closed doors, an engine surged, and a Land Rover crashed through. Bright halogen head-lamps spotlighted Raven and Abby in the open field.

A gunner leaning out the passenger window took full advantage. His auto rifle barked over the roar of the V8.

CORD JUMPED to his feet and ran. The ground rose and dipped a little as he circled the perimeter of the farm. He stopped short and braced against a tree when he heard the crash.

The Rover shed the two barn doors quickly, a gunner leaning out the passenger side. Cord opened fire, two quick bursts, but stopped as Raven and Abby rolled out of the way. The Rover surged onward. Cord aimed for the tires, firing, raising his aim to shoot at the driver. His rounds appeared to have no effect. He ran back the other way.

"Raven? Abby?"

"We're clear," Raven shouted.

Cord ran hard, the ground sloping. He ran into the open, the brush now waist-high, as the Rover plowed through the farm's exit and onto a dirt road. He raised his weapon, but trees blocked his shot.

"Where are you Cord?" Raven said.

"Watching that Rover get away."

"We found a Jeep. Stand by."

Cord grunted in reply and watched the rear lights off the Rover fade into the forest.

AT LEAST THE intel was correct. A tarp, hastily flung aside, with a heavy impression in the dirt below, suggested something heavy had been moved from a corner of the barn.

Like a crate containing a weapon of mass destruction.

Raven and Abby jumped into the front of a Jeep. The

engine fired with a single twist of the key, Abby steering the machine out of the barn and across the farm. She followed the ruts in the dirt left by the Rover, slowing at the exit. Cord jumped into the back. She floored the pedal and the Jeep lurched ahead.

Raven, in the passenger seat, held his SG-553 between his knees as he checked the breech of the HK grenade launcher, a high-explosive round nestled inside. He closed the breech and held the weapon in his right hand, finger off the trigger. The Jeep bounced along the dirt road, Abby fighting to keep the machine straight.

Cord shouted, "If they set up an ambush, we've had it!"

"Think positive!" Raven said.

Abby kept her eyes laser focused on the dirt road and the forest on either side. Running without lights, neither of the three commandos knew what to expect. They could very easily run off the road.

Raven strained his eyes to see through the dark and crowded road. "Anything?"

Cord, on his knees in the back seat, looking over the top of the Jeep's roll bar with his SG-553 braced in both hands, said, "Negative!"

The road curved left, then a sharp right, Abby taking the turns but the Jeep bouncing across ruts. Then the road straightened, and the Land Rover lay ahead. They could run without headlamps, but the brake lights still flared as the driver slowed for another turn.

Cord opened fire, single shots, the SIG popping over Raven's head as he leaned out to fire the HK grenade launcher. A tree with a branch hanging over the road rushed toward him instead and he pulled his arm back in quickly. The forest crowded the edge of the road, flashing by as the Jeep sped along, creating potential for injury if he wasn't careful.

Leaning out again, he aimed ahead of the Rover as it went into a left turn and pulled the trigger.

The grenade launcher thumped, Cord still firing, the high-explosive cartridge falling short and exploding near the Rover's left fender as it made the turn.

Raven cursed and opened the breech, shaking out the spent shell, loading another from his web vest. One left after this. He had to make the shots count. They needed the Rover disabled, not destroyed. They needed to recover the crate. He didn't want to accidentally set off the nuke, even if they were in the middle of nowhere. Population clusters were near enough that any such detonation would spell disaster for the region.

As the Rover completed the left turn, the unmistakable shadows of two figures leading from the passenger side into the growth off the road made Cord shout an alarm. He fired full-auto this time, raking the brush with a burst.

Muzzles flashes winked back as Abby approached the turn.

"Down!" Raven ducked his head under the dash, Cord dropping flat on the back seat, Abby ducking her head enough to still see the road as the rounds peppered the front of the Jeep and punched neat holes in the windshield.

Raven stayed low, leaned out, and fired the grenade launcher. The blast flung pieces of the two gunners into the forest, the force of the blast rocking the Jeep with a shock-wave, the flash of heat from the flames from the explosion touching his skin as Abby completed the turn.

Raven refilled the breech as the road straightened again. This last shot was it. If he didn't disable the Rover, there was no telling when the pursuit would end or what obstacle they'd face next.

The Rover pulled away again, the driver far more familiar with the road than Raven and his team. Abby floored the pedal and the Jeep surged, bouncing, throwing off Raven's aim as he tried to steady the HK. He couldn't aim in front of the vehicle, so he wanted the grenade blast to land alongside, enough to disable the Rover so they could finish the job with small arms.

"Hurry, Raven!" Abby shouted.

Raven used both hands to keep his arm from moving with the jolting Jeep.

Now!

He pulled the trigger.

The high-explosive shell belched from the launch tube and the blast lit the night alongside the road, shrapnel striking the Rover, shattering windows, but missing the tires. The Rover rocked a little and kept going.

Raven dropped the grenade launcher on the floor and, with his SG-553 under the dash at the bottom of the footwell, grabbed the handiest weapon available, the Nighthawk Custom .45 auto on his right hip. Raven wrapped his hands around the textured grips and pulled out the pistol.

"Tires, Cord!"

"Way ahead of you!"

Cord's rifle cracked overhead once again, Raven bracing his pistol in both hands, firing a string of shots at the back tires, Abby flinching as hot brass from Cord's gun landed on her, but then they received their reward.

The driver's side back tire popped, bits of rubber flying back to strike the Jeep.

"Got the bastard!" Cord shouted.

Raven fired some more, going for the second rear tire as the Rover began to drag. The Jeep closed the gap, and Raven scored.

As the Rover dug into the dirt and slowed, Abby stopped the Jeep. She and Cord jumped out with their rifles, Raven slapping a fresh magazine into the .45 as they ran to the struggling Rover. The driver finally quit, and the vehicle stopped entirely. He jumped from the side, bringing up a pistol. Abby fired twice. The driver's head snapped back as one bullet cored his forehead and the other punched through the center of his chest. He landed on the ground.

Raven, Abby, and Cord reached the Rover, and Raven opened the passenger door to climb inside and probe with the muzzle of the .45. He jumped out.

"Nobody else."

Abby, on the driver's side, pressed a button under the dash that popped the rear hatch. Cord raised the lid. The wooden crate from the barn sat securely in the rear.

"I suppose," Raven said, looking around at the thick forest surrounding them, "we have to drag this thing to the LZ."

"We'd better get started," she said.

Raven returned to the Jeep for his rifle first, then he and Cord set about pulling the crate from the Rover.

A LOOT AT BOOK ELEVEN: THE MURDER MIND

In the shadowy world of espionage thrillers, Sam Raven's racing against the clock to stop a catastrophic terror plot that threatens millions.

A failed sting in the Moroccan mountains leaves CIA operative Tracy Donahue the sole survivor of a deadly ambush. Just before her execution, Raven storms in. He saves Tracy—but the stolen nuclear components are already gone. Now, a volatile new terrorist threat is rising: a radicalized dropout with chaos in his soul and a shadowy sponsor bent on global blackmail.

As Raven and Donahue chase leads from Tangier to Berlin, Norway to Texas, they uncover a chilling truth: this isn't just about bombs or ideology—it's about power, manipulation, and a mastermind hiding in plain sight. The trail cuts through double agents, dead scientists, and dark money, dragging Raven into a world where trust kills and failure isn't an option.

The deeper he digs, the deadlier it gets. And with the clock ticking down, Raven faces a brutal question: What price will he pay to stop The Murder Mind?

AVAILABLE DECEMBER 2025

ABOUT THE AUTHOR

A twenty-five year veteran of radio and television broadcasting, Brian Drake has spent his career in San Francisco where he's filled writing, producing, and reporting duties with stations such as KPIX-TV, KCBS, KQED, among many others. Currently carrying out sports and traffic reporting duties for Bloomberg 960, Brian Drake spends time between reports and carefully guarded morning and evening hours cranking out action/adventure tales.

A love of reading when he was younger inspired him to create his own stories, and he sold his first short story, "The Desperate Minutes," to an obscure webzine when he was 25 (more years ago than he cares to remember, so don't ask).

Brian Drake lives in California with his wife and two cats, and when he's not writing he is usually blasting along the back roads in his Corvette with his wife telling him not to drive so fast, but the engine is so loud he usually can't hear her.

briandrakebooks.com

www.ingramcontent.com/pod-product-compliance
Lightning Source LLC
Chambersburg PA
CBHW010825250626
47169CB00010B/2955